HER
SECRET
PAST

KERRY WATTS

HER SECRET PAST

bookouture

Published by Bookouture in 2020

An imprint of Storyfire Ltd.
Carmelite House
50 Victoria Embankment
London EC4Y 0DZ

www.bookouture.com

ISBN: 978-1-78681-796-9
eBook ISBN: 978-1-78681-795-2

For Mark, Hannah and Flynn.
Thank you for your unwavering support.

PROLOGUE

Portree, Isle of Skye – Boxing Day 1990

Seeing her grandmother's wrists bound didn't fill Alice with the repulsion it should. Any normal fourteen-year-old girl from their small island community would be sickened by that scene of carnage. Or the tape fixed tight across the mouth of the only mother figure Alice had ever known. That sharp tongue would never scold Alice again. She would never again have to hear her grandmother's disappointment. Instead it excited and scared her in equal measure. She and David had talked about this day for so long. It hardly seemed real now that they were carrying out their plan. The plan that would free them. Free them from judgement.

Mary Connor whimpered. Her back was pressed hard against the range, which was still warm from Christmas lunch. The 75-year-old's body slumped forward against the leg of the long pine farmhouse table. Alice smiled, her grandfather's drying blood cracking on her cheek. She ran her fingers through her long, mousey hair peppered crimson from the cast-off spray each time the hammer had connected with Peter Connor's skull. Mary Connor stared up from the floor, her hands still bound behind her. Her jaw visibly broken and hanging. Her huge brown eyes begged David for mercy then stretched wide open before the hammer was struck for the last time with a blood-curdling crunch across her skull.

Then came the silence. The only sound, barely audible, was that of David's gasps as he began to catch his breath after the exertion of the attack. It had taken them just twenty minutes to achieve their goal. They would tell police they found them dead. Suggest it was a robbery gone wrong. The Connors were a wealthy couple. Make it look like burglars had been looking for something: jewellery, money, antiques. The place was full of expensive items. It wouldn't be difficult to convince people the Connors were a good target.

Alice stared at David, who at nineteen was five years older than her. He didn't appear fazed by what they had just done. He sniffed then wiped the back of his bloody hand across his cheek, smearing a cherry-red trail over his skin. Alice glanced from the corner of her eye to where her grandfather's lifeless body lay, his face spattered with his own blood. Her heart raced. Butterflies danced in her stomach – the way they did when David kissed her. She allowed her head to turn and stare, her eyes to drift beyond the motionless figure to the bloody footprints they had tracked all over her grandmother's immaculate wood floor. Mary Connor would not be pleased at the state of it. But it didn't have to come to this. Sure, David was a bit older than Alice but they were in love. He might be a bit rough around the edges but he truly cared for her. She'd pleaded when the couple tried to stop her from seeing him. They never understood and now they would never have to.

'Toss me that towel.' David's words pulled Alice out of her trance. She loved him.

'What? Yes, sure.' She reached out to retrieve the faded blue hand towel from the back of the kitchen door. The one laid aside for drying the family's three-year-old black cocker spaniel.

'Where's Daisy?' Alice tossed him the towel then panicked and spun around in a circle when she couldn't see her. She exhaled in relief when she eventually spotted the dog scratching at the back door to come inside. 'There you are.'

As soon as Alice opened the door Daisy shot inside and began barking.

'Shut her up!' David roared. 'The neighbours will hear her.'

Alice reached for her dog but Daisy's lips snapped back and she growled then sunk her teeth into David's shin.

'Daisy!' Alice tried to scold her.

'Argh, get off me you little...' He raised the hammer until Alice slammed her shoulder into him and got between them before he could smash it over the young dog's head.

'What are you doing? No!' Alice screamed. 'She's just trying to protect me.'

'Get her off me then,' David yelled again and tried to take her by the scruff of her neck until her face turned and her sharp dagger-like teeth pinched at his wrist. He snapped his hand back and held it close to his body. 'Get her out of here or I swear to God I'll—' He paused and clutched his stinging hand. 'We don't have much time to get this place sorted. We need to make it look like a break-in. Like we agreed.'

David wiped as much of the blood and fingerprints from each of the hammers as he could and ran back out to the couple's large double garage and hung them where Peter Connor kept them neatly lined up in order of size, next to the cabinet clearly labelled with screws, nuts and bolts. He spotted the trail of bloody footprints he'd tracked outside with him and cursed his own stupidity. He should have been more careful of where he stepped. From the other side of the neighbouring field he caught sight of his worst fear. They had heard that damn dog. He spun round on the gravel path and ran back inside to warn Alice. The unseasonably mild December day caused him to sweat despite wearing only a black vest top. Before he could find her, a police car could be seen coming up the long, chipped gravel driveway to the hundred-year-old farmhouse.

'Alice, where are you? We have to hide.' David's voice echoed through the kitchen. 'Shit, Alice, where the hell are you?' he spat through gritted teeth. Then he froze, horrified that he couldn't find her. This was slipping from his control. It wasn't like this in his head.

'Mr and Mrs Connor, is everything OK in here?' One of the local policemen had been sent to check on the elderly couple after reports that screaming had been heard coming from the property by a passing farmer. He pressed open the kitchen door with one finger. 'Mrs Connor—' The officer peered round the doorway then dropped to his knees as he radioed for help.

David Law held his breath, a bloody hand over his own mouth, from behind the utility-room door. A shooting pain flooded his temples. He watched through the crack as the officer made a futile search for signs of life in both Mary and Peter Connor. David could feel every pulse of blood speed through his veins, terrified to move an inch.

Unaware of the officer's arrival Alice returned from upstairs where she had gone to get blankets to cover her grandparents. A brief attack of guilt tugged at her, but they couldn't stop her happiness now. She was free to be with David. The least she could do was help retain some of their dignity.

Daisy the cocker spaniel bounded down the stairs ahead of her and burst into the kitchen, barking loudly.

'Daisy, get back here.' Alice stopped dead when she came face to face with the officer. Her body went cold and she wanted to run. This wasn't part of the plan. Where was David? What was she supposed to do now? David would know what to do.

The officer could see the blood covering her hair and face and stood to meet her. He was shocked by the sight of the teenager he'd known since she was a baby.

'Hello, Alice sweetheart, can you tell me what's happened here?' His arm trailed downwards to Mary Connor's body. His eyes glanced behind her before he pulled a dining chair out for her. He reached again for his radio. 'You come and sit down here.

Let's see if we can sort this out, shall we?' He patted the back of the chair. 'Are you OK? Are you hurt?'

Alice froze. She couldn't speak. She couldn't even swallow. She'd never felt so scared. Daisy shot through the half-open utility-room door and growled. David held his finger to his lips and tried to shoo the dog away. The officer moved closer. David held his breath until the door slid open.

'Come out here where I can see you.'

Alice dropped down onto a chair. It was over. Everything was gone.

CHAPTER ONE

2019

DC Dylan Logan nodded with a sombre face at DI Jessie Blake when he saw her Fiesta pull up outside the isolated Perthshire farmhouse. The strong winter sunshine glinted off her windscreen, an eerie contrast to the darkness inside the property. Jessie raised a hand to acknowledge him as she parked a little way back from the taped-off area. This wasn't how either of them had anticipated spending Boxing Day. She thanked the uniformed officer who handed her the blue plastic covers for her boots before heading over to meet Dylan.

'Merry Christmas,' Dylan whispered into her ear and nodded gently towards the front door of the farmhouse.

'Merry Christmas. I bet Shelly's not best pleased with you having to come out. Today of all days. Katie's first Christmas too,' Jessie commented. She wouldn't blame Dylan's wife for feeling peeved with him leaving her on Boxing Day with two small children to look after.

She pushed open the front door and moved through to the kitchen, taken aback to see a young, thin, pale lad of no more than twenty sitting eating a turkey sandwich at the table close to the recently deceased body of seventy-year-old Malcolm Angus who was face down in his bowl of porridge, a single gunshot wound in this temple. His grandfather. She turned and spotted Tommy Angus, the dead couple's son, smoking and trembling on the black leather sofa in the living room opposite. She asked Dylan to keep an eye on the young man at the table, seemingly indifferent to the horrific scene close to him. Dylan acknowledged her request and slowly closed the kitchen door once inside. Jessie crossed the short hallway, which was immaculate apart from the muddy footprints, incongruous in the beautifully kept hundred-year-old traditional farmhouse.

'Mr Angus, or can I call you Tommy?' Jessie held up her ID, her lips curling into a gentle smile. 'My name is Detective Inspector Jessie Blake. It was you that found your parents, is that right?'

Tommy Angus took a long draw on his cigarette, struggling to control his shaking hand before he flicked the ash into an empty mug on the clean pine coffee table and scratched at his head.

'Yes.' He coughed to find the words then swallowed back his nerves. 'I mean, yes, I did then I called the police.'

Tommy's black hair was greasy and in need of a good cut and it stuck out in several different directions. He carried more weight than he should and a faint whiff of stale sweat wafted in Jessie's direction. His bloodshot blue eyes conveyed the fact he didn't take care of himself. Even before this tragic turn of events. Then it hit Jessie. Tommy Angus. She'd gone to school with him. They weren't friends but he was in her year. He had not aged well. He might have kept the thick hair but he'd gained so much weight Jessie almost didn't recognise the former school athlete. Hundred-metre sprint champion, if her memory served her correctly. She didn't think he had recognised her either. Her eyes drifted around the well-kept room. Minimalist. Unusual for a farmhouse. Every surface free from dust and clutter. The only thing out of place was Tommy's mug, which he continued to flick ash into.

'Is it OK if I sit?' Jessie pushed her car keys into her pocket and pointed to the seat next him.

'What, yes of course.' He nodded and inhaled another huge draw on the cigarette. 'I've been trying to give up,' he scoffed.

'Today's not the day maybe,' Jessie mentioned as she lowered herself down opposite him.

'Aye, I expect not.' His head of thick hair dropped into his hands. 'Who would do this? My mum and dad wouldn't say boo to a goose, for goodness' sake.'

Tommy's anguish looked real enough but it was early days.

'When did you last speak to your parents?' Jessie asked, her eyes scanning the room for every detail.

Tommy lit another cigarette and took a long drag before answering. 'This morning.' He coughed and pulled his close-fitting Scotland rugby shirt further over his belly. 'I spoke to them at seven o'clock this morning.' He sniffed and wiped the tear that was gathering at the corner of his eye. 'I don't sleep well you see and I knew at least Mum would be up so I called to wish them Merry Christmas. I, er – I didn't quite manage it yesterday.' He blushed, causing Jessie's interest to pique. *Why not?* she thought. *Interesting.*

'How did she seem when you spoke to her? Did she seem worried? Was she anxious about anything?'

'That's what's weird. She was fine. Her usual cheery self. I can't get my head round this.' He glanced up at the clock above the stone mantelpiece which read eleven thirty. 'It's not even lunchtime...' His voice quivered then disappeared into barely audible whispers. 'She said she'd cooked us a roast because we'd missed the turkey yesterday.' He paused. 'Now they're both dead. This – it just can't be real, can it?'

Mm, interesting. Jessie's curiosity deepened.

She reached over to the box of tissues she spotted on the coffee table and handed one to Tommy. 'Here you go. Listen, the young lad through there, is he your son?' she murmured and allowed her eyes to wander around the immaculate room again. She stood up and walked over to the large bay window and looked out over the empty open field to the back of the property.

'Gordon, aye, he's my son.'

Jessie nodded, unsure what to make of Tommy's acceptance that his son seemed indifferent to the fact he was sitting next to a dead body, making no comment that he was eating next to his dead grandfather. She would leave that for now. Dylan was through there.

'Your mum and dad used to raise pedigree sheep, didn't they? I forget what breed,' she asked.

Tommy stared at Jessie; his eyes narrowed then immediately he widened them in recognition.

'I knew I knew your face.' He tried to smile through his tears and rubbed his wet puffy cheeks. 'Jessie Blake. You went to the Grammar, didn't you? Same year as me.'

Jessie smiled. 'Aye, I had that pleasure. Feels like a lifetime ago.'

Tommy's mouth fell into a warm grin. 'Dad loved his blackface ewes. Aye, but when his Parkinson's got diagnosed he and Mum both knew it would be wrong to keep them. Neither of them were fit enough to take proper care of them anymore.' He hesitated. 'Dad sold the paddock to her at the other side.' He stopped and stared at Jessie. 'Mum said on the phone she could see Rachel walking this way. She didn't know if she was coming here but she was walking in this direction. She said the horses were out in the field.'

Jessie grabbed her notebook and pen from her bag. 'Rachel is their closest neighbour? What's Rachel's surname?'

'Ferguson. She's married to that haulage firm guy. Kenny Ferguson. She trains a couple of racehorses over there. She wanted to turn the paddock into something for the stables – I don't know exactly what – but I think Mum and Dad objected to the planning application. They said it would be too close to the house or something. Mum was adamant she wasn't having her view ruined by a "racetrack", she called it. Rachel wasn't happy by all accounts. I believe she and Mum had words on the phone about it.'

Jessie tightened the lid back onto her pen just as she heard the pathologist's van coming up the gravel drive.

'And she definitely said it was Rachel who was on her way here?'

Tommy's eyes filled up again as he nodded. 'I'm sorry.'

Jessie dropped her hand onto Tommy's shoulder. 'Don't worry. We'll find out who did this.'

First stop would be the disgruntled neighbour. Jessie stood at the sound of the front door opening again.

'Excuse me, Tommy. I'll be back in soon.'

CHAPTER TWO

Jessie opened the front door to pathologist David Lyndhurst, dressed in his white forensic suit, and showed him into the kitchen.

'Merry Christmas,' David murmured as he moved through the long farmhouse hallway, careful to avoid as many of the muddy footprints on the wood floor as he could.

Jessie glanced again into the pitiful sight of Tommy slumped forward on the sofa wiping his face with tissues then met David's greeting with a smile. She felt anything but Christmassy. It had been a pleasant surprise not to get a card from her ex-husband Dan. She hoped he'd finally got the message their marriage was over at last. Jessie's years as Mrs Holland were a nightmare best left in the past.

As she walked into the kitchen behind David she noticed Tommy's son, Gordon, still sitting next to his grandfather's dead body. Her eyes moved from Malcolm Angus's slumped figure to his wife Jean's body, which had fallen forward and was resting precariously over the kitchen sink, dishcloth still in her hand, with a single gunshot wound to the back of her head. Her blood wound a trickling pattern of dark red streams through her short grey curls. Jessie fixed her eyes on Gordon Angus. He had finished his sandwich and was now playing a game on his phone, laughing inappropriately. Jessie was more than a little perplexed that he seemed completely detached from the horror around him.

'Gordon, my name is Detective Inspector Jessie Blake. I'm going to have to ask you to come with me so my colleague can examine your grandparents.' She waved her hand at him then pointed to the kitchen door.

'Have you got ID?' Gordon asked through his long, dyed-black fringe. He flicked his head quickly to one side to shift the hair that hung over his eyes. He fixed her with a steely glare, his eyes so pale they looked almost white. Jessie struggled to look away from his unusual appearance, which reminded her of a character from a gothic horror.

Jessie didn't answer. Instead she lifted her ID from her pocket and held it close to the young man's pale, anaemic face. He had piercings in his lips, nose and eyebrows. A moment later the chair he was sitting on scraped loudly on the floor and he wandered at his own pace, smirking at something on his phone, into the living room to join his father. Neither man spoke to each other; Tommy barely lifted his head to greet his son.

Jessie followed Gordon out of the kitchen and waved to one of the uniformed officers outside to come inside.

'Hi, yes, could you go and sit in with those two?' Jessie asked the young female officer. She kept her voice low, talking from behind her hand. She nodded towards the living room. 'Keep your ears and eyes open.'

'Sure, no problem.' The officer nodded before heading inside.

Jessie quietly pulled the living-room door closed after her and rejoined Dylan in the kitchen. Gordon Angus's behaviour was odd and unnerving. Downright bizarre if she was honest. Definitely suspicious.

'What can you tell me?' Jessie asked and leaned down to where David was examining Malcolm Angus's single gunshot wound.

'I can't see any signs of a struggle. At first glance, it looks to me like a straightforward gunshot as cause of death and it must have been damn quick because I can see no defence wounds. Poor man didn't even stand up. Mercifully quick, perhaps.' David shook his head. 'Shot where he sat.'

Jessie scanned the floor for shell casings then turned to look at Mrs Angus, still slumped over the sink. 'The same for his wife?'

David nodded. 'Most likely. Time of death can't be any more than two hours ago.'

Jessie whistled. 'Wow, their son almost caught the killer in the act then.' She glanced at Dylan, who had pulled on a pair of gloves and was looking through the drawers of the couple's pine Welsh dresser, which stood along the back wall of the long galley kitchen. 'If they were in here, their killer must have let themselves in. Any signs of forced entry?'

Dylan shook his head then lifted a sheet of paper out of the drawer. 'Not that anyone has seen.' He stopped to read the letter he'd just found. 'Look at this.'

He walked across and handed the letter to Jessie; it confirmed what Tommy had already told her about the planning application that the couple objected to, hinting at the ill feeling it had caused between the neighbours. She placed the letter into an evidence bag.

'Come on, Dylan. I think we need to pay the Fergusons a visit.'

But before they left Jessie ordered Tommy and Gordon's hands to be tested for gunshot residue. Right then nobody was above suspicion.

CHAPTER THREE

Kenny Ferguson poured himself a large nip of whisky from the bottle of Glenmorangie and swallowed it straight down before refilling his crystal glass. The sound of their three black Labradors barking alerted him to the arrival of unexpected visitors.

'Quiet,' he called outside to the luxury stone kennel block he kept his gundogs in. 'Rachel, there's someone at the door,' he continued to boom and poured himself another nip. When the doorbell rang out for a third time he sighed and muttered something inaudible under his breath. He was surprised to see two detectives on his doorstep holding their ID close to his face. 'Can I help you?'

'Mr Ferguson?' Jessie asked.

'Yes?' Kenny frowned and looked behind them to see his wife Rachel locking the stable door before heading around to the back of their five-bedroomed new-build bungalow.

'Could we come in and have a word, Mr Ferguson?' Jessie continued.

'What's this about? You do know it's Boxing Day, don't you?'

Jessie smiled. 'I'm well aware what day it is, sir. I'm afraid some of us don't have the luxury of office hours.'

Kenny Ferguson stared at the two detectives for a moment then opened the door wide for them and held out his hand. 'You better come in. I'll go and get my wife.'

'Thank you.' Dylan wiped his feet on the doormat and followed Jessie inside.

Jessie spotted immediately that the couple clearly weren't short of money. Expensive-looking works of art hung on the wall. Not that Jessie was any kind of art expert. The collection of heavy bronze horse ornaments displayed on the mahogany unit that lined the hallway couldn't have been cheap either. The Gucci shoebox under the table was also a clue to their wealth. Their haulage business must be doing well.

'Hello,' Rachel Ferguson greeted them, tying the belt of a pink fluffy dressing gown. The sound of a washing machine filling in the background echoed along the hallway before she closed the utility-room door behind her. 'Who are you?'

'These two detectives need to speak to us apparently,' Kenny told her and opened the living-room door for them. 'Please go through.'

'Oh.' Rachel blushed. 'I'll not be a minute. I'll just go and pop some clothes on.' She patted her hand over her chest. 'Just give me a minute.'

Jessie shook her head. 'This won't take long. There's no need to change on our account. I would appreciate it if you'd just come and answer a couple of questions for me.'

Rachel looked at her husband then back at Jessie. 'OK, sure,' she muttered.

Jessie smiled but sensed the atmosphere thicken. 'Thanks, I appreciate your cooperation.'

'What's this about?' Kenny boomed. 'What's so important my wife can't even put some more appropriate clothes on first?'

Rachel feared the detectives would see how she was trembling inside. Goosebumps trailed up her arms. A fog of cold air swarmed around her body.

'It's fine, Kenny,' Rachel tried to bluff her fear away.

Jessie spotted quickly that the couple didn't share the Anguses' minimalist taste. Cluttered wasn't the right word for their style. Chaotic perhaps was more appropriate. Half a dozen copies of a shooting magazine lay strewn across the small square coffee table that sat right in the centre of the room. Both detectives spotted the magazines at the same time and caught each other's gaze. A thick layer of dust was evident on the few bits of surface still visible, as well as the marks from hot drinks that had been laid down without the benefit of one of the pile of coasters that were gathering more dust at the edge of the table. What looked to Jessie like sticky, wet nose prints left a cloudy trail across the living-room window. The dogs clearly spent a lot of time in the house.

'I have some bad news,' Jessie began.

'What?' Rachel gasped. 'What is it?'

Jessie narrowed her eyes at her reaction and Dylan noticed Kenny reach for his bottle of malt.

'Your neighbours. Malcolm and Jean Angus.' She paused, searching their faces for signs they already knew what she was about to say. 'They were found dead at their home this morning.'

Rachel fell back onto the large blue leather recliner armchair that was right behind where she stood, her legs unable to support her any longer. She lifted both of her hands to cover her mouth. Her breathing quickened in line with her heart.

'Jesus, that's horrible.' Kenny sank his whisky then filled a second glass and handed it to Rachel who was now visibly shaking. 'Here, darling, drink this. For the shock.'

Jessie shot a glance at Dylan who tried to shrug without giving himself away.

'Thanks,' Rachel whispered then sank a huge gulp and winced from the bitterness, but held the glass out for more. 'What happened to them?'

Jessie dropped down onto the armchair opposite. 'They were shot.'

Rachel gasped again and sank more of the whisky then pressed her long, fine blonde hair close to her scalp. The mousey brown roots were beginning to show through. 'That's awful. Who would want to hurt such a nice old couple?'

'I have to ask,' Jessie began. 'Where were you both this morning between—' She paused when she spotted Kenny's demeanour change in an instant.

'You think we had something to do with this?' Kenny blasted and moved closer to where Jessie sat, standing over her. 'Are you kidding?'

'Mr Ferguson.' Dylan stepped forward, and being three inches taller made Kenny move backwards. 'You must realise we have to follow every line of enquiry.'

Kenny swallowed down more of the whisky, the nostrils of his red-veined nose flaring. 'Get out of my house. If you want to talk to me or my wife again I suggest you contact my solicitor.'

Jessie turned to face Rachel. 'Mrs Ferguson?'

'I already asked you to leave.' Kenny stormed into the hallway and snatched open the living-room door.

Jessie's eyes held Rachel's briefly until Rachel blinked first and stared down to the floor. There was no point in staying. That was clear. They would need a warrant to search their property.

'What now?' Dylan asked as the pair walked back across the bark-lined driveway to Jessie's Fiesta. The sound of barking from the back of the property as well as raised voices echoed through the unseasonably warm breeze. 'The letter we found doesn't threaten the Anguses at all. She just said how disappointed she was that they objected to her plans and could they talk, hinting she could offer them a substantial amount of money.'

'Time to do a little more digging I think,' Jessie replied.

'What did you make of the grandson?' Dylan probed. 'Creepy or what?'

Before Jessie could answer, the Fergusons' bungalow door opened with Rachel standing in the doorway. Jessie turned at the noise.

'DI Blake, there's something you need to know,' she called out to them. 'Something you'll find out very soon so I'd rather tell you myself.'

Kenny tried to grab hold of Rachel's arm to pull her back inside until she pushed her husband away.

'Rachel,' he said through gritted teeth. 'For goodness' sake. Think about what you're doing. This isn't a good idea. At least let me call our solicitor first.'

Rachel pulled away and shook her head before walking away from the front door.

Jessie looked at Dylan and clicked the car locked again before the two intrigued detectives followed the couple back inside.

CHAPTER FOUR

1990

Alice Connor's eyes snapped open. She gasped and sucked in as much air as she could take when she remembered what they'd done. She hoped the short, sharp puffs would be enough. She sat bolt upright and tugged the collar of the sweatshirt back from her skin. They'd taken her clothes and given her a pair of baggy jogging trousers and a sweatshirt that was far too big for her. A solicitor had told her last night that she would have to spend the night at the station and that she would be back to see her in the morning. She would explain what was to happen next then. Alice knew David had been taken to Dunvegan. She'd heard one of the policemen saying that and that he was to travel to Perth prison after that. She'd heard the words 'maximum security' as well as some swear words her grandmother would not approve of.

Alice was scared. David had assured her everything was going to be fine afterwards and she'd believed him. She always believed David. Meeting him was the best thing that had ever happened to her. He spoke to her like an equal, not a child. He told her she was pretty and that she should smile more. He liked it when Alice smiled. It wasn't hard to find reasons to smile around David. Alice thought this must be what love feels like. She couldn't get his face out of her mind. Being away from him made her heart hurt; tied her stomach in knots.

Her grandmother wanted to stop them being together. She said David was too old. She told her it wasn't appropriate for a man his age to be spending time with such a young teenage girl. He was sick. But her grandmother was wrong. What they had wasn't wrong. It wasn't sick; it was beautiful. David helped Alice see that. Their love felt right. This was the only way they could be together. The police would look at her grandparents' deaths as a robbery gone wrong then the couple would be free to be together, forever. David had promised he would always take care of her.

The sound of the cell door opening startled her into sitting up. She really needed to pee but she wasn't going to use that thing in the corner. The smiling face of the solicitor that had been allocated to Alice the previous night beamed in.

'Hello, again,' she greeted her.

Alice stared at her without smiling.

'I really need to pee.'

Her solicitor smiled. 'Come with me – I'll take you to the bathroom before your interview.'

Alice frowned. 'My interview?'

Alice was confused. They hadn't talked about any of this. Alice needed David more now than ever. He would know what to do.

CHAPTER FIVE

Rachel Ferguson sat close to her husband on the sofa, their fingers entwined. Kenny squeezed his wife's hand for support as his way of appreciating this wasn't easy for her. They had been in an intimate relationship for six months before she'd told him her secret. He could see the pained expression on her face now.

'I'm Alice Connor,' she began. 'When I was fourteen, along with my boyfriend, we murdered my grandparents in our farmhouse on Skye. We hit them with hammers until they were dead.' She said it rapidly as if ripping off a plaster quickly to get it over with, then sighed as if a weight had been lifted off her shoulders. 'The courts changed my name after I left the young offenders place.'

'Oh,' Jessie replied, stunned by her revelation. 'OK.'

'Please let me finish,' Rachel pleaded while Kenny squeezed her hand again. 'I'm not proud of what happened. I normally never speak about it. Very few people know who I am. Who I was,' she corrected herself. 'I'm telling you now because I don't want you to think I'm trying to hide away from it. I knew you would find out and then suspect me because of what David and I did all those years ago.'

Jessie tried to recall the name but it didn't sound familiar to her.

'I appreciate your honesty and you're right: if I'd found out later I would have come straight here, especially given the circumstances.'

Kenny allowed his fingers to fall away as he frowned. 'Circumstances? What circumstances?'

Jessie indicated to Dylan to retrieve the letter from his pocket and handed it to Kenny.

'I wanted to talk, that was all.' Rachel's tone sharpened. 'I wanted them to see that what I wanted to do wouldn't affect them or their property. I even offered them some compensation money.' She stood quickly and moved to her window to glance out over the paddock. 'They didn't even call me when they got the letter. I didn't even know they'd received it until now.'

'Where were you this morning?' Jessie probed and watched Rachel pace slowly back and forth. 'Tommy Angus said that his mum told him she could see you walking towards their property.'

Rachel turned and shot a panicked glance at her husband then looked straight at Jessie. 'I wasn't going to their house.' She shrugged then offered an explanation. 'I was out with the horses from half six. I like them to feel the fresh early-morning air on their backs. I rode out Dex for half an hour then Miss Molly. She might have seen me in the paddock but I wasn't on my way to see her.'

'The paddock we bought from them recently backs on to their driveway, Detectives,' Kenny added. 'Rachel must have been walking in the paddock when Jean saw her.'

Jessie turned at the sound of his voice. 'Where were you, Mr Ferguson?'

'Kenny was still in bed,' Rachel stated. 'Look, I was upset that they objected to my planning application, I admit that – and yes, I wrote to them asking to meet so we could talk but I did not kill my neighbours.' She pleaded: 'I'm not a mixed-up fourteen-year-old girl anymore.'

Either she was a very good liar or Rachel Ferguson was telling the truth, Jessie decided. Nothing about her body language gave the impression she was trying to conceal something or she was being deceptive. In fact, quite the opposite. She had shared a considerable amount of information. Jessie would still have the couple tested for gunshot residue, though.

'Well, thank you for your time. I know that must have been very difficult to tell us.' Jessie wanted her to know she realised the impact Rachel's revelation would have on her. 'Some of my colleagues will be over shortly to carry out a swab test for gunshot residue. I hope you understand that's just procedure.'

Rachel nodded without answering when Jessie stood. Dylan headed out to the car just in front of her with Kenny not far behind him. Kenny tried to protest until Rachel put her hand on his shoulder.

'No problem.' Rachel tried to smile. 'We understand, don't we?' She stared at Kenny, who sighed loudly before nodding.

Jessie had so many more questions but she would do her own research first. Her mind kept drifting back to the cold indifference shown by the dead couple's grandson. The bizarre sight of him enjoying a sandwich while he sat close to his dead grandfather's corpse was shocking. An image she wouldn't soon forget.

'What did you make of that then?' Dylan asked as they sat in her car.

'A bit of honesty for a change,' she answered while she pulled on her seatbelt and started the engine. 'Instead of having to drag it out of people.'

'That's your exhaust,' Dylan pointed out, hearing the low rumble. 'A huge hole by the sounds of it.'

Jessie sighed and indicated out of the Fergusons' drive. 'I know. MOT is coming up too. I'm thinking of getting a new car this time. Don't fancy spending loads of money patching this thing up again.'

Dylan smiled. 'Brilliant, what do you fancy?'

She laughed at his enthusiasm. 'I have no idea. I've had this for six, no going on for seven years.'

'I'll come with you if you like,' he suggested. 'To the showroom, I mean. I know my way round an engine a little.'

Jessie was touched. 'I might just take you up on that offer.'

As she pulled her car up outside the Anguses' cottage, they watched on in horror as Tommy Angus was loaded into the back of a police car, thrashing and shouting, struggling with officers who tried to contain him. Jessie quickly parked up and moved inside to see David Lyndhurst holding ice to his cheek.

'What the hell's going on?' Jessie exclaimed.

'All I said was that I was getting his parents ready to take to the mortuary with me and he flipped. He wasn't happy to have his hands swabbed as it was.' He pulled the ice away to show Jessie his face. 'Then he did this – he reeks of booze.'

Jessie was visibly shocked and turned to see Dylan walking towards her with a serious expression.

'Dylan, what is it?' she asked.

'Do either of you know where Tommy's son Gordon has gone?'

CHAPTER SIX

1990

Alice's solicitor had explained that she would be interviewed by two detectives but that she would be right there with her, along with a social worker. Alice watched two detectives join her in the cold interview room with the drab grey walls and a table and chairs in the centre. Just like in the cop shows on TV. One looked quite a bit younger than the other and better-looking with silk tie and tie pin.

'Alice, my name is Detective Crawford and this is my colleague Detective Harrison. Can we get you a glass of water or anything?' He shot a glance at the social worker who was sitting in on the interview. 'You have a copy of your rights. Is there anything you don't understand or that hasn't been explained to you properly?'

Alice shook her head and stared at the table. 'I'm fine,' she whispered.

'You'll have to speak up a little for me,' Detective Crawford explained.

'I'm fine,' Alice snapped her head up and repeated. She looked to see her solicitor smiling at her and scribbling on her notepad. The room suddenly felt small, like it was closing around her. Alice wanted to leave but she felt frozen to the chair.

'In your own time,' he asked, 'can you tell us what happened to your grandparents?'

The two detectives waited. Alice looked again at her solicitor and swallowed hard while she shuffled to get comfortable in her chair. It was getting hotter in that little room.

'It's OK – take your time,' Alice's solicitor explained.

'I think I do need a glass of water,' Alice replied.

Detective Crawford nodded and tapped the other detective's arm.

'I'll go and get you one,' he told her before he left the interview room.

Nobody spoke while they waited. Alice's solicitor wrote on her notepad and the social worker gave her a warm smile when she spotted the girl's nerves. Alice reciprocated as best she could, grateful when her drink soon arrived.

'Thank you,' she murmured then gulped half the glass quickly.

'Is that better?'

'Much better, thanks.'

'Do you feel up to telling me what happened last night?' the detective urged.

Alice thought her heart would explode at the speed it was beating. She became aware of a powerful pulsing sensation in her neck and felt a little light-headed. She finished the last of the water and pushed it away from her. Her mouth was still so dry. David hadn't told her about this. He hadn't told her what to say if this happened.

'I, erm, I'm not sure exactly.'

Alice knew she was talking but her voice didn't sound like her own. She was a stranger telling a story of something that happened to someone else.

'Take your time,' her solicitor reassured her.

Alice attempted a smile. She licked her drying lips, which she felt cracking at the edges. She scratched her arm with one hand and swept her fringe out of her eyes with the other before folding them tightly against her chest.

'We didn't—' Alice leaned her elbows on the table and lowered her head into her hands. 'It wasn't supposed to be like this.' She spoke quickly, mumbling the words.

'I'm sorry, I didn't quite catch that.' The detective leaned in closer.

'I said, erm, we, erm, I – it wasn't meant to end like this.' Alice looked up.

She watched the detective opposite her sit up, leaning back against the chair. He picked up his pen and pressed it against the table to expose the nib before lining up the sheet of paper in front of him. She could see the lines next to his eyes when he frowned at her.

'How was it supposed to end?' he asked her, then shrugged. 'If not like this, then how?'

'I don't know.' Alice's eyes dropped to the floor. 'David didn't tell me what to say if this happened.'

Alice daren't look up. She was scared she would cry and she didn't want to break down in front of everyone. David would want her to be strong. She listened to the sound of her own breath in sync with the detective's. She could hear the pen gliding across the paper. It made a scratching sound when it slid across the surface. It grew louder and louder in the silence. She gulped breath into her lungs and clasped her hands to her ears.

'Make it stop.' Alice struggled for breath and ran for the door, followed quickly by one of the detectives, who held her firmly in his arms. 'Let me go; you have to let me go. I can't stay here. I can't breathe.'

'You're OK; I've got you. Nice deep breaths.' His voice drifted through the fog in Alice's mind until her eyes closed and everything went black.

CHAPTER SEVEN

Jessie left Dylan at the Anguses' farmhouse to join the forensic search of the property and followed the patrol car with Tommy Angus in the back, still shouting by the looks of things. She'd been genuinely shocked to see him like that. He was naturally upset when she'd spoken to him but he'd said or done nothing to indicate he was about to do something like that – and Jessie hadn't smelled booze on him. Body odour sure, cigarettes too; he stank of them, but not booze. It was his son's behaviour that concerned Jessie the most. She knew grief affected people in different ways but he'd been weird and now he'd disappeared. Then she recalled the whisky both Rachel and Kenny Ferguson had knocked back in the short time she was with them. She wondered if the reason for Tommy's dishevelled state was a drink problem. A shame, because he'd been such a gifted athlete at school, he'd won every inter-school final, if Jessie recalled correctly.

Her phone buzzed and she pulled over to answer Dylan's call.

'What's up?' she said while she pulled on the handbrake and stared at her reflection in the rear-view mirror, annoyed that he hadn't pointed out she'd smudged her mascara. She listened to his information with interest. 'No way. You've found a will. That's interesting. Bag it and anything else you find. I'm on my way back to you now. Tommy can sober up in the cells for a bit.'

'Well,' she exclaimed aloud and tossed her phone onto the passenger seat, wincing at the horrible sound her exhaust was making. 'A will. Now there's a motive for murder.'

Before she could do anything else a loud crash followed by a scraping sound rang out and her car lurched to a stop, thankfully close to a petrol station.

'What the hell?' she announced and called Dylan right back to tell him she would be a bit later than she'd said. She slammed her palm on the steering wheel, annoyed with herself for allowing this to happen. It was Boxing Day. She doubted whether there would be anyone working at the petrol station. Jessie got out to take a look at what might have made that awful noise and gasped at the sight of a portion of her exhaust lying on the road under the back of her car. 'Oh my God, not today.'

Jessie flopped down onto the passenger seat and regretted that her RAC membership had recently expired. An older Vauxhall Astra pulled in behind her, with a man wearing large sunglasses in the passenger seat and a pretty blonde woman in the driver's seat. She watched in her mirror as the passenger got out and walked towards her stricken vehicle just as another call came in, this time from the station. Jessie couldn't hide her shock at the news.

'I'm on my way,' she answered, hoping that really was the case. 'I'll be there as soon as I can. Where was it used?'

A debit card belonging to Malcolm Angus had just been used at an ATM in Perth and the amount stolen was no loose change. Jessie now urgently had to get back to the station. She asked for a patrol car to come and collect her, relieved that there was one nearby that could be with her within a few minutes. She would have to abandon her car for now.

She tucked her phone back into her bag and looked up to see the Astra's passenger smiling at her.

'You look like you could do with some help?'

The familiar voice sent shivers down Jessie's spine – no, right through her entire body.

'No thank you.' She had to use every ounce of strength to maintain her composure.

'Are you sure? We can give you a lift; it's no trouble.' The man beamed. 'It's not like we're strangers.'

Jessie glanced over her shoulder at the driver in the car behind. Of all the cars to pass her it had to be his. The driver could only be in her late twenties at best and she was pretty, Jessie had to admit that. She was so relieved to see the police car come round the bend and pull up next to her.

'No thanks, Dan – my lift's here.'

Her ex-husband Dan Holland glanced at the driver of the patrol car and shrugged. 'No problem. Just thought you looked like you needed some help. It was my girlfriend Haley that suggested we stop.' Dan pointed towards her car and smiled. 'You would like her, Jess. She's lovely. You two have a lot in common actually.'

Dan put his sunglasses back on and he grinned when he walked away.

'You need a ride, DI Blake?' the approaching officer asked.

'Yes, please. Thanks for coming to get me so quickly.' Jessie felt her anxiety and the flush on her cheeks recede the further Dan moved away from her. 'Typical. What a day to break down, huh?'

'You won't be the only one that's happened to, I'm sure,' the chirpy officer told her.

Jessie abandoned her car and walked towards her waiting lift. She would have to arrange to pick it up later. Jessie didn't want to, but no matter how hard she tried to avoid it, her eyes were drawn by an irresistible force towards the young woman as she drove past. A sickening thud struck her stomach. She felt Dan's eyes burn into her too. She should have looked away but she couldn't. This woman's face was now etched in her brain. She couldn't pretend she hadn't seen it.

Jessie made a mental note of the registration number. It wouldn't hurt to just check who she was, would it? She wondered if this woman was living through the nightmare that had claimed the life of Jessie's son.

CHAPTER EIGHT

Jessie thanked the young officer who had been sent to rescue her from the broken-down wreck – as she had to admit her old Fiesta was – and headed back into the Anguses' farmhouse. Dylan waved her over as soon as he spotted her come in the front door.

'Where did you find it?' she asked.

Dylan held up a clear plastic evidence bag with a torn envelope inside it. 'It was stuffed between two big books on the Welsh dresser. It's unsigned and there's an appointment card in there too.'

Jessie thrust her hands into a pair of gloves and opened the bag to pull the envelope out. She thumbed the card.

'His solicitor was coming to the house on the third of next month. Interesting.'

'My thoughts exactly,' Dylan remarked. 'There's some pretty major changes to that will that I can't imagine would please Tommy Angus.'

Jessie read through the papers. She was shocked by the apparent brutality of Malcolm's wishes.

'So the entire estate was being put in Gordon's name after their deaths. Not Tommy's.'

Jessie pondered what would make a father do that until she read on. It became clear then just how big a problem Tommy Angus had with alcohol.

'Wow,' Jessie exclaimed. 'That's harsh.'

'Wow indeed,' Dylan replied. 'Gordon gets the lot and Tommy gets an allowance out of the estate to meet his needs. Malcolm must have thought Tommy was going to piss everything up against the wall.'

'Brutal,' Jessie added. 'Do you reckon Tommy knew? Or Gordon?'

Dylan shrugged. 'We won't know until we find Gordon and Tommy sobers up.'

'Aye, you're right there.' Her phone buzzed in her jacket pocket. 'Hang on.' She moved away to answer but the unknown caller ID made her heart sink. Of course Dan was going to call. Jessie pressed 'reject call' and pushed her phone deep into her pocket.

'Who was that?' Dylan was curious. He'd seen that look before. He'd seen her on edge many times over phone calls she'd received. He didn't want to pry but he was concerned. He'd heard about the incident with a man who'd said he was her husband in the cells a while back but didn't press her on it. 'Everything OK?'

Jessie looked up and wanted to scream, *No it's not! Help me. I don't know what to do. My abusive ex-husband has a new girlfriend and I'm scared for her.*

'It's nothing, don't worry. Wrong number, I imagine.' She smiled to hide her discomfort.

'Cool, OK,' Dylan replied then paused, searching for the right words. 'But if that changes to being not OK at any time…'

Jessie smiled again. This time it was genuine. She placed a hand on his arm.

'I know,' she whispered. 'Thanks, Dylan.'

Dylan shrugged. 'You're welcome. So what now?' He brought the conversation back to the case. 'Who's first then. Tommy or Gordon?'

'You haven't heard?' she asked.

'Heard what?'

'Malcolm Angus's bank card was used at an ATM in Perth a short time ago. I'm waiting on a call about the camera that's attached to that particular machine. It's the ATM at the Tesco on South Street.'

'Oh, the one that still—'

'Aye, the one that still gives you fivers,' Jessie interrupted him.

'You any idea how much was withdrawn?' Dylan probed.

'Yes, the full three hundred maximum. Whoever it was wanted as much as they could get, it would appear.'

Jessie's eyes scanned the kitchen for Jean Angus's handbag, which she quickly spotted hanging on the back of the utility-room door. She unhooked it and searched for the purse. Inside she found twenty pounds in cash but no bank cards. No cards at all.

'Can you see if you can locate Malcolm's wallet?'

'Sure, but I haven't seen one as yet,' Dylan replied.

Jessie moved the fruit bowl from the top of the fridge but found only a large bunch of keys.

'Bag these, will you?' She handed them to Dylan. 'That's a large bunch of keys for an elderly couple, don't you think? How many locked doors and cupboards do they have?'

'Clearly more than my granny and grandad had, that's for sure,' Dylan chirped.

'Did you check for a safe?' Jessie suggested. Her eyes scanned the kitchen, coming to rest on the top of the fridge, which was fitted tightly between the pine kitchen cabinets and the corner wall. Behind one box of cereal and a tin of loose porridge oats, tucked right at the back and almost hanging off the top of the fridge, was a locked red money tin. Jessie stood on her tiptoes to reach to the back and struggled to get hold of it.

Dylan moved over. 'Here, I might be able to reach it.' He pushed his hand up and grabbed the money tin with ease.

'Cheers.' Jessie shook the tin but there was no distinctive chink of coins inside.

Dylan began, 'I've seen folk at the farmers' market using them on their stalls. It's like a mini till with slots for different denominations of coins.'

Jessie shook the tin close to his ear. 'There's no coins in here.' She placed the tin down onto the table and tried the lid but, just as she expected, it was locked. 'Give me that bunch of keys, will you?'

She rummaged in the chaos of keys that must have been more than thirty strong and ruled out the larger ones immediately as being clearly way too big for the tiny lock. She tried every one that looked like it might fit but none of them would unlock it.

'Argh, typical,' she said. 'Bag the box. We'll take it with us.'

Dylan opened the cutlery drawer and retrieved a large knife. 'Couldn't we just jimmy it open with this?'

'Aye, good idea. Pass it here.' She held out her hand and took it from him but couldn't get the lid to budge.

'Give it here. Let me try.'

Dylan wiggled the tip of the knife under the lip of the lid and after a few jerks the lid popped open. 'Bingo.'

Jessie grinned at him. 'I'm not sure I like how impressed I am that you managed that, and I'm certainly not going to ask whether you've done that before.'

Dylan laughed. 'I wouldn't tell you anyway.'

The two detectives stared into the tin's contents then at each other, both stunned and sickened as the other. This was the last thing they'd expected to find.

CHAPTER NINE

January 1991

'They said you smashed your grandparents' heads with a hammer. Is that true?'

The overweight girl with the short, spiky hair and nose ring who sat on the table next to Alice scared her. Alice didn't think keeping her waiting for an answer was a good idea. She glanced behind the girl, who looked a lot older than her, and saw another two girls sitting nearby playing cards. Every girl in the young offenders place wore the same thing. A drab grey tracksuit. Very few bothered with make-up, she'd noticed, but neither did she anymore. She stared at the girl who had questioned her and straightened up in her chair at the dining table.

'I—' Alice found it hard to speak because of her anxiety. She feared another panic attack was always close. It made her throat feel dry and tight. This girl was twice her size, if not more. What if she didn't like Alice's answer? 'Yes, we did – I mean, it's not like it sounds,' she stuttered. She felt her cheeks flush pink and she looked down at the table. 'We just, just, I don't know…' she heard herself ramble but seemed unable to stop.

'Holy shit,' the other inmate replied and let out a laugh. 'Better not get on the wrong side of you.'

Alice glanced up into her grinning face, a little confused, and frowned, then couldn't stop the smile that grew on her own lips.

'Good to know,' the girl announced as she got up to walk away. 'If you need any help, with anything, just give me a shout.'

'Yes, sure, thanks,' Alice replied. 'My name is Alice.'

The girl smiled again. 'Oh, I know who you are. Everybody knows Alice Connor.'

Before Alice could respond an officer stood next to her.

'Come on, breakfast time's over. Get your plate and cutlery to the hatch. Alice, your solicitor is here. I've got to take you to see her.'

Alice hurriedly lifted her things and tidied them away at the serving hatch then followed the officer into a room with a table at the far end next to a window with a far-reaching view into the Grampian hills. It looked cold out there, snow resting on the peaks. The room was hot, with the central heating on full blast. The farmhouse Alice had been raised in was cold in the winter, apart from the kitchen, which was kept lovely and cosy by the range. A memory of sitting at the long dining table to do her homework while her grandmother laid out a plate of home-made shortbread next to a glass of milk crept into Alice's mind. She had to push it away. She couldn't think about things like that now.

Alice removed her sweatshirt because the small room was so hot.

'Hello, Alice.' A voice caused her to turn away from the window and she smiled at her solicitor, who was closing the door behind her. 'Come and sit down. We have a lot to get through before your court appearance.'

Alice's eyes widened.

The solicitor stopped rummaging in her briefcase. 'It's OK. I'm going to explain it all to you, don't worry.'

Alice pulled out a chair and slumped down opposite her, picking at her thumbnail as she stared at the floor under the table. She knew her solicitor was talking but Alice wasn't listening. Her mind drifted to thoughts of what David was going through. Alice missed him terribly. She missed the way his arms felt around her, enveloping her and making her feel less alone – because that's what she was before David. Alone. He was the first person who ever seemed to care what Alice thought. How she felt. Her opinion counted. For the first time in her life Alice had known what it meant to feel happy. David didn't care if she only got a B in a test and he certainly didn't flip out the way her grandmother did when she came home with a C for her history essay on the Second World War. She wondered if he was scared where he was. She'd been told he was being held on remand in Perth prison and was charged with two counts of murder and of sexually abusing Alice. David had never abused her. She vehemently denied he'd ever forced her to do anything she didn't want to do. She loved David and he loved her. This would never have happened if her grandparents had listened instead of trying to force them apart. But they wouldn't listen. They never listened.

'Alice, did you hear what I said?' her solicitor asked.

Alice sat bolt upright in her chair and blushed. 'What? Sorry, no, I was miles away.'

'I was explaining what was going to happen next.' Her solicitor was about to read from a piece of paper on the table when Alice grabbed her arm.

'How's David?'

Alice's solicitor ran her fingers through her curly brown hair as she looked into Alice's searching eyes. She'd been anxious when her boss asked her to take this on. It was such a huge case. The whole country was talking about the brutal slaying of an elderly couple in their own home, especially because one of the people accused of carrying out the crime was their fourteen-year-old granddaughter. She genuinely believed Alice when she told her that she loved David and he loved her. She believed that Alice truly believed that. It had to be something she thought was real to make a teenage girl create the sickening carnage she had witnessed on the crime-scene photos.

Her first interactions with Alice had been a shock. The girl sat cowering in a police cell did not look like the same girl that had smashed a hammer over her grandfather's head so hard that pieces of his brain became stuck to the wallpaper. Her face had been smeared red with his blood as she sat with her knees curled up to her chest, her eyes staring at the ground the whole time.

'David's doing fine,' the solicitor lied. She didn't need her client to be thinking about anything other than her own defence. Alice didn't need to know David was being kept away from other prisoners. For his own protection.

CHAPTER TEN

The low winter sun streamed in through Jessie's office window and she tilted the blinds to stop it dazzling her. She always felt bad about doing that. Her mum used to say she was shutting the sunlight out or tease her about hiding away in the dark. A small smile crossed Jessie's lips at the memory. She sipped the coffee that Dylan had left for her and stared at the red money tin on her desk. That she had not expected. Images of the sickening photographs and newspaper cuttings haunted her.

David Lyndhurst had no plans to take Tommy's assault any further. He didn't want the hassle and besides, he told her, he didn't think the man had even realised he'd hit him. He was so out of it. Jessie still needed to talk to Tommy, though. The revelations in the will and the upsetting contents of the box created several questions, but the text that she received distracted her briefly. Jessie had grown closer to Lyndhurst's former assistant in recent months and Benito's words made her smile. He made Jessie feel comfortable; safe.

Can't wait to see you

She replied to his suggestion that he travel from Edinburgh that night to see her. His reply made her blush and stuff her phone back into her pocket.

Jessie gulped the last of her coffee and stood up from her desk with the evidence bags tightly clutched in her hands. Dylan's voice called out from behind her just as she reached for the handle of the door to the interview room where Tommy was waiting for her.

'What's up?'

'There's been a sighting of Gordon Angus. You want me to check it out?' Dylan asked.

'Thanks, yes, that would be great.' Jessie dipped the handle then released it. She turned to call out after him. 'Dylan—'

He stopped and spun round. 'What?'

'Just be careful, will you?'

Dylan nodded and winked, then moved swiftly through the door towards the station exit.

Jessie meant what she'd said. Something about Gordon's response to the death of his grandparents made her shiver. Sitting there like that, so cold; indifferent at best. Certainly not grief-stricken like Tommy appeared to be. That wasn't normal. Was that red tin his perhaps? What significance did that array of sickening photos of dead and mutilated corpses have to the case?

'Hello again, Tommy.' Jessie pulled up a chair and joined him at the table in the small beige interview room.

Tommy lifted his head then dropped his gaze quickly back down. 'I'm sorry,' he muttered. 'About your colleague. I shouldn't have hit him. That doctor was just trying to do his job.'

Jessie nodded. 'I know you are. That's not what I'm here to talk to you about.'

Tommy's head snapped up to face her. 'No? Then what is it? Have you found the person who did that to Mum and Dad?' His voice quivered when he tried to control the emotions that bubbled in him. 'Who was it? Was it—' He hesitated. 'Rachel Ferguson?'

Jessie's eyes widened at that. She spotted the way Tommy's hands were shaking too. 'Why would you think Rachel had anything to do with your parents' death?'

Tommy arched his back and rubbed at his face with both palms. 'Och, I don't know. I don't really. It's just—' He sighed. 'Just, she was going there, wasn't she? Where's Gordon? I need to see that my son is all right.'

Jessie didn't want to acknowledge his theory for now. Neither did she want to tell Tommy nobody had seen Gordon since he'd left the scene of his grandparents' murder.

She placed the two pieces of evidence on the table between them. It was the will she slid closer to Tommy first.

'Do you recognise this?' she asked.

'What is it?' Tommy lifted the clear plastic bag and peered at the contents. 'I can't read this without my specs, not properly.' He handed it back to Jessie. 'You better tell me what it says.' He scratched at his head and sniffed.

'This is a copy of your parents' joint will, Tommy.'

Tommy rested his elbows on the table and clasped his hands together over his mouth. He inhaled a huge breath and exhaled slowly though his fingers.

'Aye, I figured that much already,' he admitted but avoided her eyes. 'But I don't know what it says.'

Jessie spotted that Tommy glanced to his side as he spoke. 'You've never seen this before?'

Tommy answered with a simple shake of his head and a sigh. If this was true Jessie figured that his reaction when she read the details to him should be interesting. She pulled the pile of papers from the bag.

'I'm going to read a small extract from it for you. Is that OK?'

Jessie glanced at Tommy's solicitor, who nodded and wrote something on his notepad. Tommy nodded too.

'OK,' she began. '*After our death the entire estate, including the Clachan farmhouse, is to be left to our grandson Gordon Angus.*'

She thought that was a good place to stop reading and waited for Tommy's reaction but instead he kept his eyes down and his

shoulders slumped. She allowed him another moment to say
something and started again when he continued not to speak.

'*Our son Tommy is to have a small allowance to meet his basic
needs on a weekly basis.*'

Jessie didn't bother going into the details of how it would work
or who would make the arrangements. Tommy held his head in
his hands. He seemed oddly unmoved. Emotionless.

'Tommy, do you have anything to say?' Jessie probed.

His answer came with another shake of his head.

'You don't seem very surprised,' Jessie suggested. 'It's a little
humiliating if you ask me. Your son gets everything, not you.'

Now Tommy's solicitor chose to speak up. 'I don't think that's
necessary. How my client feels is not in question here.'

Jessie held up her hand. 'I know; you're right. I'm sorry, Tommy.
I shouldn't have said that.'

Tommy shrugged. 'Why not? It's true, isn't it? My parents
were ashamed of me. Ashamed of the drunken waste of space
I've become.'

Tears bubbled up in his bloodshot eyes and Jessie noticed his
hands had started to tremble. Tommy shivered.

'God, it's cold in here,' he remarked.

'I think it might be a good idea to stop there, Detective,' his
solicitor interrupted. 'I think my client needs a break and to see
the doctor. Tommy, you're not looking too good.'

Tommy's trembling and agitation increased before he hammered
the table. 'I'm fine,' he roared then started to sob and clutch his
stomach. 'I just need a drink,' he ended in a whimper. 'I'll be fine
if I can just get a drink, one drink, just to take the edge off.'

Jessie tapped her thumb on the red box in the other evidence
bag. She was desperate to quiz Tommy about the contents but his
solicitor was right. Tommy needed help.

One last question couldn't hurt, though, could it? Jessie took a
chance and pushed the box towards him. 'Do you recognise this?'

'Detective,' Tommy's solicitor warned, growing increasingly frustrated by Jessie's persistence.

Tommy stared at her with a blank expression on his face. He winced from his abdominal cramps and held his stomach, then turned and vomited on the floor at the side of his chair. Jessie hoped Dylan was having better luck than her until a uniformed officer knocked on the interview-room door.

'DI Blake, can I have a word? It's important.'

CHAPTER ELEVEN

Gordon Angus paid the bus driver and headed to a seat at the back. He'd been surprised to find there were any buses running at all. He stuffed his wallet and keys into the bottom of the rucksack at his feet and pressed his earbuds in, then squeezed his bag closer to his legs and leaned his head on the window. The clouds overhead were black and looked heavy with rain. The branches of the trees that lined the winding country road bent and bowed in the strong winds that had increased in the past few hours. The song he was listening to stopped abruptly as a call came in on his phone. It was his mum. He knew rejecting her call would make her worry and that would result in her leaving loads of messages for him so it was easier to answer her.

'Hey, Mum.'

'Gordon, is everything OK – you didn't call me to wish me a happy Christmas.'

Gordon nibbled his fingernails and stared at the field of blackface sheep in the field. Just like Grandad's, he thought. He wondered if they were his grandad's sheep. His dad had explained that they'd had to sell them when Grandad became ill. He had asked why Tommy couldn't take over but his dad couldn't give him an answer. It wasn't worth pursuing the point.

'Sorry, I forgot…' he answered.

'You forgot,' his mum responded then paused. 'I've been trying to get hold of your dad. Is he there with you? Can I speak to him?'

Gordon Angus had lived with his dad since his parents' divorce a year ago. His mum wanted to move closer to her own parents in Crieff but Tommy wanted Gordon to stay with him so he could finish his course at Perth college first.

'No, Dad's not here.'

'Where are you? Are you outside somewhere? It sounds like you're on a bus,' she suggested. 'Are you on your way here? You should have said. I would have come and picked you up.'

'You don't have to do that. I can manage.'

He heard his mum sigh on the other end of the line. 'It would be nice to see you, son. It feels like ages since we've caught up and you can open your presents when you get here too. There's a few under the tree for you. Grandma and Grandpa miss you. It's been a long time since you visited them.'

The first huge raindrops began to hammer the roof of the bus as it slowed down at the set of traffic lights just outside the first village it would pass through. Gordon smiled when he remembered kissing a girl for the first time in the park there. More accurately, in the gazebo in the far corner of the playing field. He'd almost done a lot more for the first time in that hidden corner until a dog walker came close to catching him.

He realised he was hungry and reached down for the packet of crisps and can of Coke he'd grabbed from Grandad's kitchen. He wasn't going to need it, was he? Grandad shouldn't have been drinking that stuff anyway because of his high blood pressure.

'Gordon, are you still there?' his mum's voice drifted into his thoughts.

Gordon sat right up in the seat. 'Yes, I'm here.'

'When will I see you then?' she asked. 'I'll make the bed up for you, shall I?'

'Soon, I'll see you soon. I have to go.' Gordon abruptly ended the call.

The bus was almost at the far end of the village and Gordon rang the bell. He thrust his rucksack over his shoulder and pressed the end-call button on his phone as he stood to make his way to the front of the bus.

Dylan held his ID high enough up to show the woman who was sweeping up in the bus-station café. The middle-aged woman with tight brown curls, peppered grey, frowned at him.

'Hello, what can I do for you?' she asked.

Dylan held up a photo of Gordon Angus that he'd been given. 'Did this lad come through here recently?'

She took the photo from him and pulled a pair of glasses from her apron. 'Don't recognise him but if you ask in the office, maybe they've seen him.' She pressed the photo into Dylan's outstretched hand. 'What's he done?'

'Thanks for your help,' Dylan answered. He pushed open the office door, which squeaked loud enough to announce his arrival. He smiled at the dishevelled homeless man and his dog who were in there keeping dry from the torrential rain.

'What can I do for you?' a voice piped up from behind the counter. The man, who could be no more than five feet five, looked at Dylan's ID without expression.

Dylan produced Gordon's photo again. 'Have you seen him?'

The man took Gordon's photo then smiled and handed it back. 'Aye, I know Gordon.'

Dylan's eyes widened. This man knew his name. 'Great – has he been here today?'

The man shrugged. 'I couldn't tell you. I've just arrived myself.'

Dylan was confused. 'How do you know Gordon?'

A wry smile grew on the man's lips. 'That lad is here at least three or four times a week, sometimes more. He's a big traveller, Detective.'

Dylan frowned. 'What do you mean?'

The man behind the counter tapped his finger on his own temple and screwed up his face. 'The lad has some kind of bus obsession. He's got that, what do you call it? You know that thing they say bad kids have these days. Oh, I can't remember – but no, I haven't seen him today.'

'OK, thanks anyway.' Dylan turned to walk away when the man's voice echoed through the office.

'What's he done?'

Dylan didn't answer this time either and wondered why they'd both decided Gordon had done something rather than worrying he might need help. He was grateful to hear his phone ringing as he opened the door.

'Hey, Jess.'

He listened to Jessie's tale of her experience with Tommy and was about to disappoint her with his lack of progress when the homeless man tapped him on the shoulder.

'Hang on a minute, mate.' Dylan rummaged in his pocket for some change to give to him then handed him a two-pound coin. He smiled. 'Sorry, it's all the change I've got.'

The homeless man nodded and muttered 'thank you' and stuffed the change into the pocket of his ripped jeans. He tapped Dylan's shoulder again.

'Sorry, hang on, Jess.' He lifted his phone away from his mouth while the man's large cross-breed terrier jumped up at Dylan's waist. 'Look, I'm a bit busy, mate…'

'Don't you want to know where Gordon was going?' the man asked.

Dylan stared at him. 'Jess, I'll have to call you back.' He quickly ended the call and focused on the dishevelled man in front of him.

'He gave me a damn sight more money than you did, too.' The homeless man pressed his hand into his pocket and produced a wad of twenty-pound notes.

'Where was he when you saw him? When was it? And why did he give you that much money?' Dylan was shocked by the amount of cash he'd shown him.

This man was at least the same height as Dylan and looked bigger than the lean young man he'd seen up at the Anguses' farmhouse. He looked more than capable of robbing Gordon.

'I didn't ask him for it if that's what you're getting at and I certainly didn't steal it. I'm homeless. I'm not a thief.'

Dylan could see the look of indignation on his face and regretted that he'd offended his potential witness.

'Never mind the money. Do you have any idea where he is now? I need to speak to him urgently.'

The man shrugged. 'Don't know but he got on the bus that left that last stop up there half an hour ago.'

'Where do buses from that stop go?' Dylan urged. 'It's important.'

The man shrugged again. 'Don't know sorry. I didn't see the number on the bus but there's a timetable on the post over there.' He pointed to the far end of the station. 'That'll tell you probably.'

Dylan began to walk away while dialling Jessie's number. 'Thanks. You've been really helpful.'

The man's dog gave one loud, sharp bark as Dylan began to quicken his pace to a jog. He waited for Jessie to answer while he scanned the three timetables stuck to the post. Why would Gordon feel the need to leave town the same day his grandparents were killed? Dylan wondered.

CHAPTER TWELVE

Jessie hung up. Dylan's call had left her intrigued but optimistic, she had to admit. Between that and the forensics found at the scene, things looked promising. A hair and boot prints had been found in the soil outside the living-room window – the same boot prints left on the wooden floor inside. It wasn't often they were handed such simple, clean evidence this early in a case – or indeed even at all. It might have irked her to have the officer interrupt her chaotic interview with Tommy but it had been worth it.

Tommy had been examined immediately by the police doctor on duty who confirmed he was suffering withdrawal from alcohol and recommended detox treatment in hospital straight away. Not being able to question him about that damn red box irritated her but there was no choice. David Lyndhurst had also called to say he wanted to see her and Jessie was pleased to hear from him so soon. She was sure this wasn't the Christmas he had planned either. After a recent heart episode, David had led Jessie to believe he was about to retire but she had to admit she was pleased to still have him.

She grabbed her jacket from the back of her chair and lifted her keys before remembering her Fiesta was currently abandoned at the side of a road just outside Stanley. She searched her pocket for the car key and frowned when she thought she'd mislaid it. She would have to take a patrol car if she could get one. And she needed to let someone know about her stricken vehicle before it was reported by a member of the public.

She closed the door to her office and turned to see a female officer walking towards her with a bunch of flowers in her hand and a wry smile on her face.

'What's all this?' Jessie was surprised when the young officer handed her the freesias and the card that came with them.

How did Ben know I love freesias?

'They're lovely. You're a lucky lady. Wish my husband would send me flowers once in a while.'

Jessie thanked the woman and watched her retreat before opening the card. A wave of nausea rose in Jessie's stomach when she recognised the handwriting immediately. The flowers were not from Benito. They were from Dan.

'Wait,' she called out to the officer who'd brought them. 'Who delivered these?'

The woman shrugged with a grin. 'Not sure. A tall, good-looking guy in sunglasses was all I got told.'

Jessie had to steady herself on the desk in front of her. She inhaled a long, slow breath and exhaled to control the anxiety that had built inside her.

Why can't he just leave me alone?

Jessie tossed the flowers and the unopened card into the bin and walked away.

'You OK, Jessie? You look a bit peaky,' David Lyndhurst greeted her once she'd made her way to the mortuary, her mind reeling from her ex-husband's stunt. What the hell was he playing at? She couldn't dwell on it even if she wanted to. She didn't have time for Dan's nonsense today. Or any day for that matter.

'What? No, I'm fine,' she answered and painted a smile on her lips. 'You have a cause of death already.'

'Yes and no – I'm not sure.'

'What does that mean?' Jessie probed. 'I thought it was a simple gunshot wound that killed each of them.'

David nodded. 'It looks that way but I'll be happy to agree to that definitely after the toxicology results come back. Lack of defensive wounds mean it must have been hell of a quick attack.'

'Have you heard about the forensics we've found?'

David shook his head then winced from the pain in his hot fiery cheek.

Jessie felt bad for him. He'd been so kind to Tommy Angus about it but it looked really sore.

'We've got hair and a solid boot print.'

'My goodness, that's a lot.' But David gave the hint of a shrug. 'What?

'What do you mean "what"?'

'I know you too well, David Lyndhurst.'

David sighed and held his hands up. 'You got me. Don't you think a single hair and boot prints are a bit convenient?'

Jessie narrowed her eyes at him. 'Maybe their killer was careless.'

David shrugged. 'Maybe. It's your job to find out, isn't it?'

Jessie tried to ignore the nagging seed of doubt that David had sown. 'Have you got a definitive time of death for me?'

'Between nine and ten in the morning, I'd say.' He peeled off a pair of rubber gloves then pressed his size-fifteen boot on the flip-top bin's button and tossed them in. 'It would seem their son and grandson just missed them by such a short time. What time did he say he got there?'

'Half eleven.'

David sucked in a large breath though his teeth. 'Close, very close.'

CHAPTER THIRTEEN

Rachel Ferguson sat on the armchair that faced the large bay window in the conservatory and stared out over the paddock that had caused her neighbours such angst. Rachel considered whether it was worth reapplying for permission to create the gallops. Would that be inappropriate? She tried to flick through the *Racing Post* newspaper but her mind kept drifting back to what had happened to Malcolm and Jean. She glanced at her watch, which read just after 7 p.m. She and Kenny should be sitting back, enjoying a glass of wine or even a wee nip, but neither of them felt much like celebrating. Not after what happened. It didn't seem right. She would get in touch with Tommy in the coming days to ask if they needed anything. It was the least she could do.

'Rachel, I have to go out.'

Kenny's voice boomed towards her through the long hallway. Rachel had already seen the car pulling into their driveway. His PA Caroline Peters, a young woman who barely scraped five feet tall, waved to Rachel from her Mini. Rachel didn't bother to object, or ask questions anymore. It would start an argument and she didn't feel up to that tonight. She watched her husband's beaming smile greet his assistant, then looked away from them both.

She lifted her mug from the coffee table as the sound of Caroline's car disappeared. She wouldn't wait up. His meeting would perhaps go on all night again. He'd been working very hard recently.

She headed into her large galley kitchen and made a fuss of the three Labradors that hurtled from their beds to greet her, one of them buckling her knees under her and sending her crashing to the floor before licking her face with his slobbery wet tongue. Rachel laughed at the absurdity of anyone walking in and seeing her being pinned to the wood floor by three overenthusiastic chunky black dogs.

'You silly boys,' she said, giggling, and struggled to pull herself into a sitting position.

A strong gust of wind rattled the stable door behind the house and the heavy rain on the roof grew louder. Rachel stood up and ruffled the fur on one of the dogs before slipping her feet into a pair of boots at the back door and heading out to check on her horses. She tugged the hood of her green fleece tighter over her head against the frequent strong gusts that almost pushed her off balance.

'Shh, it's OK,' she called out to her horses because she knew how skittish they could be in strong winds. Rachel didn't blame them. She wasn't a fan of stormy weather herself. It often reminded her of her early years in her grandparents' farmhouse on the remote outskirts of Portree, where strong winds meant gusts of up to fifty miles an hour over open countryside, lifting the surface water from the lochs and forcing the spray onto land.

Rachel slid open the stable door and found her large chestnut stallion with three white socks scraping the floor with his hoof and violently thrashing his head up and down. If she couldn't get him calmed down he risked serious injury and she needed him for the race she'd entered him in at the next meeting at Perth. It would be great for her business as well as her bank balance if Dexter won; he was tipped favourite ante post because of his unbeaten record over two miles.

'Hey there, big man,' Rachel whispered but feared he couldn't hear her over the sound of the horrible wind and rain battering the roof. She held a hand up in front of her and unbolted the door to his stable. 'Hey, you.'

Within a couple of minutes his scraping and thrashing decreased until he moved closer and nuzzled his large head into her shoulder.

'There now.' She ran her fingers over his face and allowed that scent to envelop her. Rachel loved the distinctive smell of horses. There was nothing that could come close to the happy feeling it created in her. She'd been introduced to horses during her time in the young offenders centre. Her social worker thought she was perfect for the programme and she'd been right. Working with horses gave her structure and purpose when she felt she'd been cast adrift, not knowing where she belonged or who to trust. There were some dark days that she'd had to overcome. The confusion. The sense of betrayal, then the guilt.

A loud bang outside startled both Rachel and the horse, who reared and kicked out his front legs, almost colliding with Rachel. She lost her balance in her haste to avoid getting kicked and had to grab the stable doorframe to avoid falling onto the straw. She stood up and bolted his door after her then went to see what had happened. Whatever it was it sounded big.

Rachel turned the corner out of the stable and found the lid of one of the food buckets scraping across the yard in the wind. She smiled when she realised that was all it was and moved towards it. She picked the lid up and retraced her steps as the now torrential rain poured over her, soaking the fabric of her light hood quickly, until the raindrops dripped even from her eyelashes.

As she was removing her filthy boots outside the porch, she heard the house phone ring. She peeled her saturated fleece off and tossed it onto the floor next to them then jogged to answer the call, relieved to get back inside.

'Hello,' she said and waited for the caller's response but heard nothing. 'Hello, who's this?'

When she got no reply again she hung up, irritated that a cold caller would intrude on people tonight of all nights. She hated those silent calls. If you stayed on the line long enough you ended up talking to someone who began the conversation by hoping you were having a good day before trying to persuade you to buy something or do a survey.

Rachel had moved only three steps away from the hall table when the phone rang again. She sighed and turned back to answer it.

'Hello,' she said again. This time the silence irked her even more, and she shouted down the line, 'I don't want to buy anything. I haven't had an accident and I don't want to take your survey.'

As she removed the handset from her ear she heard a voice say her first name. She became fearful at the sinister tone. 'Hello, who is this?'

Her words were greeted with more silence. Rachel pressed the end-call button and tossed the phone onto the table, confused. Her heart raced when the phone rang again. She swallowed back her fear and slowly picked it up again.

'Hello,' she murmured. 'Who is this?'

There was no silence this time. 'I know what you've done.'

The anonymous caller had said what they needed to say and hung up.

Rachel dropped the phone and clasped her hands to her lips. She'd been so careful. Her head fizzed with all kinds of ideas until a loud knock hammered on the porch door. She froze.

The three dogs barked behind the utility-room door as the knock echoed along the hall again. She swallowed hard and opened the utility-room door to let the dogs through to join her. All three Labradors ran at the door and continued to bark in unison.

Rachel edged closer to the porch door. Her palms felt clammy when she reached for the handle.

She thrust the door open and all three dogs shot outside, barking and growling as they ran into the darkness. She peered out. There was nobody there. All she heard was the distant barking into the wind. She jumped with fright when her dogs came bounding back inside. This was a game to them.

She slammed the door shut and locked it behind her. Whoever had knocked on that door wasn't playing games.

CHAPTER FOURTEEN

Tommy Angus shivered in the driving rain that had intensified in the past five minutes. Rumbles of thunder echoed in the distance. He'd been transferred from the police station to hospital with just the clothes he stood up in and they weren't suitable for the conditions at all. Most of the journey had been a blur, his vision obscured through the alcohol. Voices came at him through the bubble of intoxication that enveloped him as he strode on, but he didn't stop. He heard laughter in the crowds he passed. The cramps had been so bad that the diazepam he'd been given had barely touched the surface. He'd lost count of the times he'd vomited. His whole body had ached for a drink. Tommy thought that death had to be better than this hell: there was nobody to bring his things to him. The nurse told him they couldn't get hold of Gordon and his parents were gone from his life forever. He'd disappointed his father. He'd broken his mother's heart. Now they were gone. He was so drunk that he struggled to focus on the road in front of him.

Tommy had had to get out of that hospital. He knew he had been there to get help but they didn't understand his desperation. Unless you've been through it it's impossible to understand the need. The beast inside that claws at your skin to escape. The agony that strips you of your dignity, forcing you, its victim, into acts of unthinkable degradation and horror.

Tommy couldn't take any of it back. The pain had been so bad it had been intolerable. He'd signed all the forms they'd asked him to. He'd said he understood the danger he was in without medical treatment but if he was honest, he didn't care anymore. Tommy had had to get a drink and had found the nearest off licence, downing half the bottle of cheap whisky he'd bought before he'd moved away from the shop doorway. It tasted terrible but that didn't matter. He wasn't buying it for the taste these days. Tommy needed it, craved it, to end the twisted agony in his body in the fastest way possible, and he didn't feel better until he'd drunk three quarters of the bottle.

He was onto at least two full bottles a day these days. Cheap supermarket own-brand whisky or vodka. He wasn't fussy. Tommy was past caring. Once the physical pain of withdrawal was gone the mental torture still remained; every second of every day, every heartbeat squeezed in its brutal grip.

Tommy staggered in a zig-zag line, his unbuttoned shirt open and flapping in the wind that whistled along the exposed tree-lined road that sliced a winding path through farmland on either side. The branches dipped against the breeze while the lights of the oncoming car lit up the path in front of him.

The driver of the Escort barely had time to brake when Tommy's outline came into view. The sickening thud came quickly after the long screech. Tommy's body was thrown over the bonnet before sliding back onto the rain-drenched, muddy, soaked ground. Snatches of light and images flashed into Tommy's mind. His mum's body, hunched over the sink. His dad, a bullet wound in his head. Gordon's face smiling. The argument. He felt the air grow cold around his body before the thud. Then nothing. Only black.

The driver of the car got out to check if Tommy was OK. She searched her trouser pocket for her phone before hurriedly dashing back to her car to find it in her bag. Her baby cried in his car seat on the passenger side.

'Oh God, no, no, no,' the woman pleaded then tried to console her sobbing child. 'It's OK, shh, Mummy will be back in a minute.'

The driver trembled as she returned to the man lying motionless in the road. So still against the treacherous conditions encircling them.

'Hello, I need an ambulance,' the panicked woman sobbed to the operator and gave them the details of the incident. 'He just came out of nowhere. Oh my God, I didn't see him.'

The trembling in her legs threatened to bring her to her knees. The rain became heavier in that instant, thrashing the ground in anger. She screwed up her eyes and hunched her shoulder against the force. 'Yes, we're on the back road between Luncarty and Stanley. He was just walking down the middle of the road. Please hurry. I'm so sorry,' she sobbed. 'I think he might be dead.'

CHAPTER FIFTEEN

1991

Alice Connor's heart thudded so fast she wondered if it was about to explode. The hot summer sun beat down on her neck and she wanted to swat away the flies that were buzzing around her face but she didn't want to spook the horse. She was too scared to move anyway.

The horse was beautiful, she had to admit that, but he was so big and he was getting close. She heard a voice behind her tell her to hold her hand out flat so he could nibble the carrot she had for him. His lips were soft and gentle. They tickled too. Alice smiled and pulled the other part of the carrot out of her pocket. She offered the large stallion more. He snuffled his face on her hand again. This time she immersed herself in the closeness. Alice lifted her hand and pressed her palm against his soft, smooth cheek. The horse didn't flinch. Neither did she. The moment was theirs. The gentle snickering sound soothed Alice's racing heart. She slid her hand around and moved it up and down his nose. The horse leaned closer. Alice leaned closer still. He closed his eyes. Alice's eyelids fell in time. There was a real connection. The connection that Alice was searching for.

Alice was stunned to learn that the big stallion that trusted her so quickly had been rescued from a farm where he had suffered a life of neglect. He'd never been struck but his care had been basic at best. He'd been alone for the first five years of his life, kept inside a stable with no access to other members of his herd. That was Alice; her grandparents tried to keep her hidden away. They just wouldn't listen.

Alice often wondered whether her mother would have treated her that way. But she would never know. Her grandparents told her that she had been very ill after Alice was born and died. It wasn't until Alice was twelve she learned that she'd committed suicide. Alice had been six months old.

'Alice,' a familiar voice called out from behind her.

She turned to see her solicitor walking towards the field.

'He's a handsome boy.' The smiling woman reached over to stroke the stallion, who thrust his face sideways, knocking her hand away. She grinned. 'Looks like you're his favourite person.'

Alice turned away from her and caught the stallion's eye once more. She rested her forehead on his cheek and wished the rest of the world would disappear.

'I'm here to give you some news; good news, hopefully.'

Alice wrapped her arms around the stallion's neck and held him tight.

'A date's been set for your appeal,' her solicitor began. 'I don't want you to go getting your hopes up but this is a very positive step.'

Alice turned on hearing that. 'What does that mean?'

Her solicitor smiled. 'It means you could be going home soon.'

'Where's home exactly?' Alice whispered.

Her solicitor hadn't finished yet. 'That's another thing I need to talk to you about.'

'Huh?'

'Well, it's been decided that perhaps it will be easier for you to have a normal life if you have a new identity.'

It took Alice a moment to process the news.

'I won't be Alice Connor anymore,' she whispered.

Her solicitor shook her head. 'The judge has approved the request, which doesn't happen very often, but he agreed, in the circumstances, it's what you need to be able to move on.'

Alice fell quiet. She nuzzled close to the stallion's neck, soothed by his warmth. His mane tickled her cheek.

'Do I have a choice?' she said without lifting her head.

Alice waited for the answer she knew was coming.

'No, you don't have a choice. I'm sorry.'

'Who will I be if I'm not Alice?'

'Well, we'll talk about all that. I'll explain everything to you, I promise.' Her solicitor reached out to stroke her arm.

'What happens to *Alice*?' she asked without meeting her eyes. 'Where does she go?'

Her solicitor sighed. 'I know this is confusing but Alice doesn't go anywhere. You just become Rachel.'

'Rachel?' Alice remarked. 'Don't I get a say in my new name?'

'Don't you like it?'

'It's not that – it's so overwhelming.'

'I know it's a lot to take in,' her solicitor added. 'I'm here to answer all your questions.'

Alice closed her eyes. She wrapped her arms around the horse's neck, her single tear dripping slowly down his chestnut skin. For a moment, she couldn't understand the black feeling in the pit of her stomach then it hit her. She lifted her face away and focused her attention on the woman who had the answer.

'How will David find me when he gets out if I'm not Alice anymore?' she asked.

CHAPTER SIXTEEN

Jessie stood in the doorway between her kitchen and living room with two fresh cups of coffee in her hand. She'd even wiped the dust off the top of the Tassimo machine that she'd bought in last year's January sale – which until recently had been used barely a handful of times. Benito was second-generation Italian. He knew good coffee when he tasted it and Jessie had to admit she wanted to impress him so she'd splashed out on the finest latte pods. She had even warmed the croissants she'd frozen last week. This might be another working day for Jessie but that didn't mean they couldn't share a nice breakfast. She watched him sleeping on her sofa, snuggled peacefully under her spare duvet. Benito stirred and exhaled deeply, still half asleep.

'How long have you been standing there?' he asked, his voice deep and husky from sleep.

'Long enough to see you drool all over my pillow,' Jessie teased and laid his cup on the coffee table.

Benito pulled himself into a sitting position and yawned. 'Is that croissants I can smell?'

'Yes, it is – help yourself. There's plenty of butter and jam in the fridge,' she said and sipped from her mug. 'Mm, this is delicious.'

Benito lifted his mug and sniffed. 'Smells like real coffee, Jessie Blake.'

Jessie smiled. 'Anyone would think I've started to like you or something.'

Their eyes met briefly until Jessie's phone buzzed in her cardigan pocket, startling her and causing her cheeks to blush pink.

'Hang on,' she whispered, pressing her hand down and pulling it out to open the text.

Part of her was desperate to click the message open. She'd asked a friend at the station to do a little research for her on a personal matter and he'd been as good as his word when he said he would email her whatever he found.

'Is everything OK?' Benito asked. 'You look like you've seen a ghost.'

'No, it's fine. It's just work.' Jessie stuffed her phone away. It would have to wait.

'Will you still be here when I get back?' she asked. 'You're more than welcome to stay.'

Benito nodded with a grin and placed his mug back onto the coffee table. He slid back down to drop his head onto the pillow and pull the duvet up around his chin.

'My only plan for today is to get another couple of hours of sleep.'

Jessie smiled as she watched him close his eyes. 'You can hop into my bed for a comfier snooze if you like.'

Benito's eyes snapped open. 'Whatever will the neighbours say?'

Jessie laughed and patted his arm playfully then glanced at the clock on the TV unit in the far corner. The sound of Dylan's car horn made her jump. 'I have to head off now.' She hesitated then leaned down to kiss his cheek, her heart thudding hard. 'See you later.'

Jessie stared back at her living-room window before getting into Dylan's car.

'Good morning,' Dylan greeted her. 'Good night last night?'

'Why do you ask that?' Jessie snapped.

Dylan frowned and indicated out of her street. 'No reason.'

Jessie quickly realised she'd been rude. She was still scared of anyone finding out about her relationship with Benito but that had been uncalled for.

'Sorry, Dylan. I didn't mean to bite your head off.'

Dylan shrugged. 'It's fine – I live with a tired wife and two toddlers; I'm used to it.' He pulled up to the roundabout close to the A9.

'Actually, before we go to Rachel's could we drop in at the station? I'd like to pick up the red box.'

'Sure, no problem. Do you think she'll know anything about it?'

'No, I want to ask Tommy again first. You heard about the accident?' she asked.

Dylan shook his head then stared at her. 'No – what accident? I thought he'd been taken to hospital for detox and rehab.'

'Me too but I got a call late last night to say he'd discharged himself and had been hit by a car just outside Stanley.'

'Was he at the house, do you think? I thought we'd locked it up securely,' Dylan remarked. 'I suppose he has a key?'

'Don't think he was there. I assigned a couple of uniforms to keep watch on the house.'

Dylan laughed. 'Who got that short straw? I bet that made their Christmas.'

Dylan pulled into the station car park. The low winter sun beamed into the windscreen as he lifted his sunglasses from the glove box.

'I won't be long. Hang on.'

Jessie shut the car door and headed inside to retrieve the red tin that had caused such repulsion and intrigue. She wasn't paying much attention to her surroundings while she considered the case and abruptly thanked the young man in the baseball cap who held the door open for her without paying attention to him. That email crept into her mind.

She walked past the ladies' bathroom on her way to her office then quickly turned and burst the bathroom door open, locking herself inside a cubicle. She grabbed her phone and clicked on the email. It had a link to Facebook and Instagram accounts for a pretty blonde woman. There she was: the driver of the car that had stopped to help Jessie. She opened Instagram first and instantly felt sick. Dan's grinning face stared back at her. He had his arms wrapped around a beaming young woman. They looked like any other happy couple. Jessie sighed and felt the knot in her stomach tighten when she remembered the pain Dan had caused her during their relationship. Emotional as well as physical.

'Haley McKenzie,' she whispered and browsed for more information.

Jessie frowned when she realised Haley worked in the same hospital as Benito. Not just that – in his department. She was a lab technician. How on earth did she know Dan? What could they have in common? A text gave Jessie a huge fright before she could learn more.

'Shit, Dylan, I'm just coming,' she muttered and pushed her phone deep into her pocket. She jogged to collect the tin and made her way back out to rejoin Dylan.

'DI Blake,' a voice shouted from behind her just as she got close to Dylan's car again.

Jessie turned to see a PC holding an envelope in his hand. Jessie moved back to meet him.

'What's this?'

The officer shrugged. 'He just said it was for you and to say he's sorry.'

Jessie clutched the A5 envelope in her hand and glanced back at Dylan – and gasped at the idea that shot through her mind.

'Is everything OK?' the officer asked.

'It's fine – thank you for bringing it to me.' Jessie smiled and nodded to him. 'I really appreciate it.'

Jessie got back into Dylan's car with the red tin in one hand and the envelope in the other.

'What's inside?' Dylan quizzed her.

Jessie didn't answer until she'd peeled it open and lifted out the contents. 'What the hell?' she muttered.

CHAPTER SEVENTEEN

Rachel could hear voices drift from the kitchen. Caroline Peters was clearly having a breakfast meeting with Kenny. Another one. Rachel snuggled her duvet further around her shoulders. She'd struggled to get much sleep after the phone calls. She wondered if she'd imagined the sound of hammering on the front door but the calls were real. All too real.

The sound of Caroline's laughter irked her. Why was she always so damn chirpy?

When the phone rang, memories of last night forced a rush of nausea through her. She might as well get up. She rubbed her cold arms then pulled on her dressing gown and headed into the kitchen.

'I didn't hear you come in last night.' Rachel kissed Kenny's cheek and switched on the kettle.

'Aye, I didn't want to disturb you, darling, so I crashed in the spare room. There's tea in the pot if you want some.'

Rachel exhaled loudly, tied the belt on her short pink dressing gown and grabbed the milk from the fridge. 'Thanks.'

'You look tired, Rachel. Is everything OK?' Caroline asked. 'Kenny told me about your neighbours. How awful.'

Rachel stirred a spoonful of sugar into her mug and stirred. 'Yep, awful.'

'I have a meeting in Dundee so I might be late—' Kenny started to say.

'Again?' Rachel expressed her dismay at his comment. 'What time will you be home?'

Rachel wasn't looking forward to being alone again but didn't want to tell him why in front of Caroline; the calls were none of Caroline's business. She was just an employee. Rachel didn't like the amount of time her husband spent with her, but she wasn't naïve enough to believe their relationship was just professional. Kenny's wandering eye went with the territory, but he knew her secret and had never let her down in the twenty years they'd been together. He provided for her and had helped her achieve her dream of becoming a racehorse trainer. She could forgive an affair or two as long as he didn't leave. She wouldn't ask questions and Kenny wouldn't have to lie.

'I'll get back as early as I can, I promise.' Kenny kissed Rachel's forehead and walked away. 'Just have to grab a couple of things from my office, Caroline. I won't be a minute.'

'Sure.' Caroline helped herself to a second cup of tea.

Rachel sipped from her mug and sat down at the dining table without speaking. She couldn't stop Caroline being there but she didn't have to like her. Rachel grabbed a copy of the *Racing Post* from the previous week and flicked through the pages in silence with Caroline standing behind her, hoping she would take the hint that Rachel didn't want conversation. She was sure she could feel her eyes burn into the back of her head. Rachel wondered what a pretty young woman like that saw in a middle-aged, balding, overweight man like her husband. He wasn't even good in bed. More of an undignified grunting style of lovemaking than a tender, passionate lover, though if Rachel was honest she was grateful Kenny didn't pester her to fill his needs these days. Caroline was welcome to that part of her husband.

'So how are you doing, Rachel?'

Rachel wished Caroline would get the hint she didn't want to chat. She turned and painted on a smile.

'Fine, Caroline, what about you? I hope my husband isn't working you too hard. Especially over Christmas like this. Your family must be missing you.'

Caroline shot her another smile. 'I live alone and both my parents are dead so…'

'Oh, I'm sorry I didn't realise.' Rachel felt terrible then wondered why that would be a reason to smile so widely.

'I don't mind working over Christmas really.' Caroline shrugged. 'It's not much of a celebration for me.'

'I'm sorry to hear that.' But in truth wasn't Rachel in exactly the same boat? She daren't tell Caroline that, though.

'I'm used to it now I suppose.'

Rachel couldn't stand the sickly-sweet niceness of the girl but could see exactly what Kenny saw in her. She would probably do sexual things for him that she could never do.

'Sorry about that, ladies.' Kenny came back into the kitchen and grabbed the keys for his Land Rover. He kissed Rachel's lips this time. 'See you tonight, darling. Don't wait up for me – just in case.'

'But you said—' Rachel stopped. What was the point? 'Have a good day then, you two.' She forced a smile.

'Goodbye.' Caroline beamed and followed Kenny outside, her high heels clip-clipping across the wood floor.

Rachel stood by the kitchen window and watched Kenny's Land Rover disappear out of the drive and onto the back road towards Perth. He would pick up the motorway to Dundee from there. She stared again at the empty paddock and imagined her horses thundering around the gallops she wanted to create. She could see the sand being kicked up behind their hooves and the sound of them on the ground drifted into her imagination. That was Rachel's favourite sound. It stirred a sense of excitement and calmness at the same time. If a noise could become your happy place then that was hers.

To the right of the paddock was the estate that had given the council permission to erect ten large wind turbines on their land. Rachel thought they were a blot on the open Perthshire countryside but Kenny told her how much they'd been paid for their trouble. She despaired that everything came down to that. Money. Before the turbines, she had hacked through the estate on the horses. Long summer evenings riding through the quiet country lanes were wonderful when the only sounds were your horses' hooves and the low hum of bumblebees. It was magical. She had considered asking the estate manager if she could rent some land for her gallops, then the chance to buy the Anguses' paddock had come up. Now that was tainted.

With her mind elsewhere, Rachel hadn't heard her visitor come into the house. She spun quickly when she became aware of footsteps. Recognising the face coming towards her, she asked, 'What are you doing here?'

CHAPTER EIGHTEEN

Jessie was still reeling from the fact she might well have just missed Gordon Angus by minutes or even seconds – if it was him who'd delivered the envelope with the bank cards in it. Returning them like that was strange, with a note too. Where the hell was he now? She hoped he would be at the hospital when she got there.

Jessie stared into the side room at the slim middle-aged woman sat on the chair at the side of Tommy Angus's bed, cradling his hand in hers. Jessie assumed she was his wife, but there was no sign of their son. Tommy had a mask over his mouth and an intravenous drip in each arm. It was then Jessie realised the accident was more serious than she'd first thought. Nobody had told her he was still unconscious.

'Go and grab us a couple of coffees.' She handed Dylan some change. 'I want to speak to her alone,' she whispered. 'She's probably the wife. Which makes her Gordon's mum.'

'Good idea.' Dylan took the money and walked away, leaving Jessie to go back to staring. For a divorced couple, she seemed genuinely concerned about Tommy. She held his hand – tight too by the looks of it, from where Jessie stood. Maybe she still loved him.

Jessie pressed on the handle and opened the side-room door as quietly as she could. The woman at Tommy's bedside turned. Her eyes looked red and sore from crying.

'I'm sorry to intrude. My name is Detective Inspector Jessie Blake. I'm in charge of the investigation into Tommy's parents' murder.' She showed her ID.

The shock on the woman's face abruptly informed Jessie that this woman hadn't been told that devastating news yet. The colour drained from Arlene Angus's cheeks and she dropped Tommy's hand from her grasp to clasp her own hand to her mouth.

'What? I don't understand,' she mumbled. 'What do you mean their murder? Tommy's parents can't be dead. Someone would have told me.'

Jessie pulled another plastic chair from under the window on the far side of the room and placed it next to her. She reached out and laid her hand softly on Arlene's arm.

'That must have been a terrible shock. I'm so sorry you had to find out like that. I had no idea you hadn't been told.'

'But I don't understand,' Arlene repeated. 'I only spoke to Jean yesterday morning. To wish them a happy Christmas.'

'What time did you talk to her?' Jessie grabbed her notebook from her pocket.

'It was, em, I think it was about nine-ish. What the hell? I don't understand. She sounded fine when I spoke to her.' She pulled her arm away from Jessie's grasp. 'When did they – I mean—' She couldn't finish her question as the foam of fizzy tears spewed from her eyes. 'I'm sorry, this is just such a shock. I mean, Gordon didn't mention anything when I spoke to him.'

'You've spoken to Gordon?'

'Yes, I called him when he didn't call to wish me a merry Christmas. Silly, I know.'

'Where was he when you spoke to him?'

Arlene narrowed her blue eyes. 'Why is that important?'

'Forgive me, I don't mean to imply anything. It would just be really good if we could find him and have a chat with him about a couple of things.'

'Find him? What do you mean "find him"?' She turned to look at Tommy. 'I can't believe this is happening. He's lying there close to death, Gordon's disappeared and his grandparents have been murdered. I knew there was something wrong. I knew it. I always know.' Arlene's tone sharpened. 'I hate this, being right, but I was then and I am now. Oh my God, what has he done?'

Jessie turned when Dylan knocked on the window of the side room. She shook her head and then nodded for him to leave them. She refocused her attention on Arlene.

'What does that mean? What has who done?' Jessie urged.

Arlene turned to face Jessie and raised a hand in the air. 'You have to understand something first.'

Jessie's curiosity deepened and she nodded. 'OK. I'm listening.'

Arlene closed her eyes and gave a sharp sigh. 'Gordon isn't like other young men his age. Sure he looks like any other 21-year-old.'

Jessie recalled the way Gordon Angus sat, coldly indifferent, close to his grandparents' still-warm dead bodies as he tucked into a sandwich. She wanted to shout out, *You're not wrong there*, but resisted.

'In what way do you mean he's different?' she asked instead.

'I said for years Gordon wasn't like the other kids in his class. I knew he was different. I just…' She paused. 'I knew. His behaviour was a struggle some days but he was my son, Detective, my son and I did love him. I *do* love him.'

Jessie was growing more curious by the minute and wished the woman would get to the point. She tried to hide her impatience with a sympathetic nod.

'We fought,' Arlene continued. 'No, that's not strictly true. *I* fought for Gordon to be assessed by a psychologist who just said he was immature, a little anxious perhaps, but he would grow out of it.'

Her emphasis on the 'I' told Jessie more than she needed to know. The couple clearly had differing views about their son. Perhaps disagreement about their son had been the cause of the breakdown of the marriage.

'Do you think Gordon is capable of doing something to hurt someone? His grandparents, even?' Jessie suggested cautiously.

But the boot print and the hair. Jessie's mind raced. Gordon's hair was jet black and the boot's size was just a four. It couldn't be Gordon, could it?

Arlene stood up and pressed the palm of her hand gently across her red, stinging eyes. She walked across to the small window that looked out onto the roof of the lower floors of the hospital. A large grey pipe billowed smoke from the middle of it.

'Gordon was such a sensitive little boy,' she declared. 'He didn't like the taste of certain foods and cleaning his teeth was a nightmare. Obsessive behaviour, too. Does that sound like autism to you?'

Jessie shrugged. 'I'm not a doctor. I couldn't possibly say but clearly you thought something was wrong. A mother's instinct, perhaps.'

'Exactly.' Arlene pointed her finger in Jessie's direction. 'But Tommy didn't listen. He thought we should just accept what they said and move on.' She shook her head. 'But I was right to worry, wasn't I?'

Arlene moved quickly back to Tommy's side and squeezed his arm. 'You should have listened to me, you stupid man.'

Jessie was alarmed at the darkness in her tone.

'Why don't you come and sit back down. I'm interested to hear more about Gordon.'

Arlene turned her attention back to Jessie.

'Jean, my mother-in-law, gave me the money, you know.'

Jessie was perplexed. 'The money?'

'For the private doctor – well, psychiatrist,' Arlene declared. 'It was the only way to prove I was right but I would give anything to be wrong. Anything.'

'You took Gordon to see a psychiatrist privately?' Jessie asked, wondering how much that had cost her mother-in-law. Private consultations were not cheap. Jean Angus must have been worried about her grandson too. 'Did you get the answers you were looking for?'

Arlene nodded. 'Part of me was relieved, you know.'

'I've heard people say that before,' Jessie replied. 'What did they tell you?'

Arlene's shoulders drooped and she stared at Tommy's motionless body next to her; listened to the gentle rhythm of the sounds of life coming from the monitors strapped to him. Then she stared at Jessie.

'Our son is on the autistic spectrum. Asperger's most likely, they said, just as I suspected all along.'

Jessie wondered if saying she was sorry to hear that was the right thing to do. Perhaps that would be wrong. It was the next part of the diagnosis that scared her.

'The doctor that assessed Gordon also suggested that he had a psychopathic personality.'

'Oh.' Jessie released an involuntary gasp at the same time.

'Yes, *oh*, indeed. So you see why I'm worried, Detective. My son is a psychopath and someone has just murdered his grandparents.' Arlene's gaze drifted to the floor. 'Gordon doesn't feel things like you and me. It's not his fault.'

Then Jessie remembered the contents of the red tin. She showed the tin to Arlene but before she could ask her about it Arlene was quick to explain.

'I know what's in there, Detective.' Arlene spoke with her eyes fixed on the floor. 'Gordon is obsessed with serial killers. Not them so much as their crimes. The violence fascinates him. How it feels to kill. He wants to go and talk to a serial killer. He's written to a couple too.' A hint of a laugh escaped to hide her discomfort. 'I've explained to him that people will find his interest strange and creepy but I'm in over my head. I don't know what else to do.'

Jessie didn't have to look at the pictures in the box again. The various newspaper clippings of grisly crime scenes connected to Ted Bundy and the Yorkshire Ripper to name a few still turned Jessie's stomach. She knew there was a fascination with serial killers these days. Some had even been romanticised by Hollywood.

'What I'm about to tell you has to be kept confidential, promise me. I don't even know if it's true but I don't want any of us getting into trouble for exposing someone.'

'I can't promise anything but please go on,' Jessie began.

Arlene stood and paced towards the side-room window. She stared out while she shook her head. Jessie could sense Arlene was about to tell her something shocking. She hoped it might help her get closer to uncovering what had happened to the elderly couple.

'Gordon has a—' Arlene paused to search for the right word. Jessie watched her nibble her top lip between her teeth and inhale a huge breath, before exhaling it slowly. 'He has a thing for Malcolm and Jean's neighbour. He thinks she's a serial killer or something, I don't know. Says he recognised her from a photo.'

Jessie frowned, unsure exactly what – if anything – Arlene knew for sure.

'Why would Gordon think something like that?' she responded, encouraging what Arlene knew out of her.

Arlene shook her head and sat back down opposite Jessie. 'He has it in his head she's really a woman called Alice Connor.' She shrugged. 'Have you heard of her?'

Jessie nodded. 'I've heard the name mentioned, yes.'

'She murdered her grandparents, Detective. Brutally by all accounts.'

Jessie had a fair idea where Arlene was going with this but didn't want to confirm or deny her suggestion. 'Did she?'

Arlene nodded. 'I looked the story up on the internet, you know, to be sure.' She sighed and drew her shoulders up towards her neck. 'It was horrible. He seems fixated though and I can't get through to him.'

Jessie pulled a card with her details on it and laid it on the bed next to Tommy's hand, then stood up and zipped her jacket right up.

'If you hear from Gordon please let me know right away, will you?'

Arlene picked up the card and nodded without meeting Jessie's gaze. 'I will,' she murmured then snapped her head up to meet Jessie's gaze. 'What will happen to him if—' She stopped herself before finishing her question. 'I'm sorry, ignore me, forget I said that.'

Jessie had a good idea exactly what Arlene was about to say and didn't blame her for feeling the need for answers – but it wasn't Jessie's job to reassure her. Her job was to find the person who shot and killed Malcolm and Jean Angus, and if that person happened to be related to them she couldn't allow that to get in the way of their conviction.

'I hope Tommy gets better soon,' Jessie commented before turning to walk out of the room. She took one last look at Arlene. Her defeated expression told Jessie she feared exactly the same thing as she did. Both women also had the same question in their minds.

Where the hell was Gordon Angus?

CHAPTER NINETEEN

'What do you want?' Rachel blasted despite the anxiety that gripped her chest. 'I didn't say you could come in. You can't just walk into someone's house uninvited.'

Rachel stared behind him and hoped the dogs were close, but then remembered that Kenny had probably closed them in the utility room to eat their breakfast. What did he want and why was he staring at her like that? She pulled her dressing gown tighter around her body. Her legs trembled and she wondered how to talk herself out of this situation. She swallowed back nausea that rose in her throat through fear. Sweat gathered on the back of Rachel's neck. She lifted her hand to dab it away then he moved forward.

'What is it you need. Is it money? I have money.' She knew she was rambling. She always did when she was nervous, and right then she was terrified. He must have been the one who'd called her last night. He must know her secret. 'I can pay. You name your price. Just please don't tell anyone. I'm not the same person.'

He moved closer but still didn't speak. He sat down on the armchair that looked directly out of the bay window and looked up at her.

'What about making us a cup of tea? I'd love a cup, wouldn't you? I have so many questions,' he said then pulled a dog-eared notebook from his hooded fleece pocket and leafed through the pages. 'I can't believe I've found you.'

Rachel couldn't move. She struggled to understand what was going on until he spoke again.

'Go on then, put the kettle on.' This time he smiled. 'If you've got any biscuits I'll take one of them too, chocolate preferably. Mm, have you got any Jaffa cakes?'

Rachel smiled at the absurdity of the situation. 'Em, yes, sure; I'll, em, just go and check.'

Before she turned she spotted an Audi moving along the driveway and saw that it was the two detectives coming back to speak to her. She'd figured they would. She was even prepared for the moment they asked her for her fingerprints and DNA. What she and David did to her grandparents all those years ago would never go away – and after such a horrific double murder so close to Rachel's own front door, of course they would look closely at her.

When she glanced back at the armchair, her guest had already disappeared through the back door.

CHAPTER TWENTY

1991

Rachel laid her bag down on the small bedroom floor. Her new name was growing on her, though she'd had no choice but to get used to it. She stared at the posters on the wall next to a single bed with a plain lilac duvet set. The pillow was covered in a variety of soft toys ranging from a small stuffed flamingo to a large brown teddy bear that almost covered the whole thing. On the bedside cabinet, there was a small red lamp and a glasses case next to a copy of a book she didn't recognise. Next to the book was a notebook. Rachel squinted to read some of the scribbles on the cover and could make out the words 'KEEP OUT' in bold blue writing as well as the name Ella but couldn't make out the rest of it – and there was a lot of it.

Rachel stared at the bed on the other side of the wall with the same lilac duvet set waiting to be put on it. The wall on this side was bare apart from the odd piece of Blu-Tack leftover from whoever last had this bed. Her solicitor explained that she was to live there with the foster family for now and they seemed nice. The foster parents knew who she really was but that was as far as the information had been shared. It was almost her fifteenth birthday and she was relieved not to be spending it in that place.

The pain that had grumbled in her stomach since earlier that day grew stronger. Just nerves, she told herself. She was always nervous of meeting new people, let alone moving in with them. Her stomach was bound to be upset.

Saying goodbye to the horses had been hard. Harder than anything Rachel had ever felt. With her stallion especially. He'd taught her to trust again. She'd been told so many times that David had abused her that eventually Rachel had tried to believe it. So many different people can't be wrong. But it still confused her that what they'd had felt so right.

'Hiya, whatcha doing?' The girl standing behind Rachel grinned at her, revealing her silver braces. 'I'm Ella. The only rule in this room is don't mess with my stuff and I won't mess with yours – got that?'

'Er yes, guess so.' Rachel was too overwhelmed to argue and it wasn't exactly a bad rule, she thought. 'You keep a diary?' she asked hesitantly, hoping to strike up a conversation with her new roommate. 'I think I should do that. A lot has happened to me recently.'

Ella held up one of her hands then opened the drawer in her bedside cabinet. Rachel took the chance to peer inside and saw it was as chaotic and untidy as Ella, who had short brown hair that stuck up in several different directions and wore her denim shirt half tucked in half out of her ripped blue denim jeans, which looked a little too big for her slight frame. Ella lifted a brand new notebook with flamingos on the cover then dipped her hand back in and produced a black pen.

'Here you go – consider it a "welcome to our room" gift.' She held the book and pen out to her.

'Thank you so much,' Rachel said. 'That's so kind of you.'

'As long as you don't mind flamingos,' Ella said with a laugh.

Rachel felt a little tear push from the back of her eye. She sniffed to stop its progress. The last thing she wanted was to embarrass herself in front of Ella.

'I quite like them actually. Flamingos, that is.' Rachel spoke quietly.

'They'll let you put up some posters if you want to.' Ella pointed to the drab bare wall. 'What are you into? What bands do you like listening to?'

'Not sure really. I quite like Bon Jovi.' Rachel nodded to the large picture of Jon Bon Jovi Ella had above her bed.

'Good taste.'

The two girls giggled as their foster mother called them down for dinner. Ella linked arms with Rachel and tugged her towards the bedroom door.

'Come on – we'd better go before the boys eat all the chicken.'

Was this what it was like to have a real friend? If it was then becoming Rachel had already increased her friends tally by a hundred per cent. Suddenly she wasn't sad in the slightest that Alice Connor was dead.

CHAPTER TWENTY-ONE

Gordon Angus didn't want to stop running until he felt he was far enough away to not be seen. It had been a mistake going there. He shouldn't have done that. He'd scared her. Gordon could see that. She was pretty in her dressing gown with her hair messy like that. His mum had told him about knocking and waiting for the door to be answered. He should have remembered that. But he had so much he wanted to ask her. Needed to ask her. Questions that had burned inside him since that day – the day his heart leaped at the idea he knew her.

Time had seemed to stop that day. It had been a day like every other until that point. He'd got up, had breakfast and left for the bus. Rain had threatened but hadn't arrived. The blonde girl with the beautiful skin was there as she was every day. The one that smiled at Gordon every time she got on the bus. He liked her – liked her a lot. She had started creeping into Gordon's thoughts at home.

Finding that article though had tossed his fantasy woman from the bus from his mind. There was nobody like the woman that stared back at him from his computer screen. The day he stumbled upon Alice Connor, she'd looked so small in the picture. Alice. So fragile yet so strong in his mind. He wanted to ask her how it had felt for her, in that moment – the moment death had arrived. Was it exhilarating for her? Did her heart race; feel like it might explode?

His phone rang in his pocket for the fifth time. He ignored the call again just as he had ignored his mum's other four calls.

At least the rain had stopped. He glanced back and couldn't see the house now from the other side of the wood. He startled a dog walker who quickened her pace when Gordon seemed to appear out of nowhere. He frowned at her just as his phone rang again.

'Mum, what is it?' He had no choice but to answer. He couldn't switch it off. That didn't feel right. He needed to be able to call for help at any given time. His gran had told him that. She fussed over Gordon and he liked that. Sometimes. Sometimes she irritated him. Sometimes a lot of people irritated Gordon. 'What do you mean Dad's in hospital?' he asked.

Gordon was confused. The last time he'd seen him he was fine. He couldn't be in hospital; his dad would have told him. He knew that Gordon didn't like surprises.

'I'm on my way, Mum.'

Gordon hung up the call from his mum and stuffed the phone deep into his jacket pocket, then he stopped walking and spun around slowly to get his bearings. He could see the top of the post office on the edge of Luncarty in the distance. He could probably be in Perth in an hour and a half, if he walked fast enough. He checked his watch. He thought he'd just missed the number 34 then he remembered because it was Christmas the buses were all different. These public holidays were hard for Gordon. Everything was different. Nothing was in the order he needed.

CHAPTER TWENTY-TWO

'What are you thinking?' Dylan quizzed her as his Audi twisted along the pot-holed driveway to Rachel's cottage, the ancient oaks that had long since shed their leaves lining the way.

Jessie pressed her head against the back of the passenger seat. She had so many thoughts spinning in her mind she didn't know where to begin. Gordon Angus and his obsession with serial killers. Was he a vulnerable, innocent autistic man or cunning double murderer? Did Gordon know about the will? Jessie couldn't decide. She hoped it wouldn't be long before she'd be able to ask him.

Then there was the evidence. She was still waiting to see if the DNA from the hair was on the database but the boot print was looking more like it came from a riding boot. Rachel Ferguson wore riding boots every day and she'd had a disagreement with the Anguses over their objection to her planning application. It was the boots and their disagreement that authorised the warrant to search Rachel's home. Her honesty had been refreshing but she must have known that Jessie would find out soon enough.

Jessie was tempted to believe her proclamation of innocence, though. She was convincing – Jessie had to admit that – but for the evidence. The bullets David found matched a gun commonly used in hunting, and Kenny Ferguson enjoyed shooting grouse on the moors. Jessie knew that much. Hunting was something Jessie could never understand; killing for sport didn't sit well with her.

'Jessie, you're miles away,' Dylan teased.

'No, I'm not,' Jessie said, smiling. 'I'm just thinking, that's all.'

It wasn't just the case that plagued her mind; she was struggling to get the image of Haley McKenzie's smiling face out of her head.

'About whether Rachel is really guilty?'

'Amongst other things,' she admitted. 'That and the envelope Gordon handed into the police station. Why give them to us and not just return them to the farmhouse?'

'Do you think he realised he'd done wrong?' Dylan suggested and stole a short glance in Jessie's direction. 'Had he figured out there would be police at the farmhouse and he wanted to avoid them?'

'I'm not sure I know anything about that lad,' Jessie conceded before sighing gently. 'I felt sorry for Arlene Angus, you know.'

'You did?'

'Aye, it couldn't have been easy seeing other folk's kids doing what she saw as normal stuff. You know what I mean?'

Dylan nodded and thought about his own son. He had so many hopes for his children and could relate to what Jessie had just suggested. He wasn't sure how he and his wife Shelly would cope.

'Jessie – look.' He lifted a finger up from the steering wheel to point to Rachel's front door.

Jessie looked over to see Rachel open the door for them before they stopped the car. She looked anxious. Like she'd seen a ghost, even. Jessie could see frown lines on her forehead even from that distance. Something she'd never noticed when they'd met last time.

'Interesting,' Dylan muttered.

'Mm, you could say that,' Jessie mumbled and smiled at Rachel as she approached the car. The sound of another vehicle approaching made Jessie turn to see Kenny's Land Rover speed towards the garage at the back of the property. Kenny shot a look of serious concern at them as he rushed past. Jessie spotted that Rachel was visibly relieved to see Kenny's car too.

'Is everything OK?' Jessie called out then frowned. Rachel looked like she was trembling, until Kenny scooped her into his arms and led her back inside.

Jessie heard him whisper to her that everything was OK now; he was here, while she and Dylan followed the couple inside to a cacophony of barking. Dylan threw a wide-eyed glance at Jessie as he closed the cottage door behind them all.

Jessie made her way through the chaos of dogs' bodies all fighting to get a share of her attention. She pressed her fingers against the search warrant in her black jacket pocket but left it there for now. She followed the couple into their long galley kitchen and watched Kenny attentively help his wife into a dining chair before pouring her a glass of water.

Kenny handed the glass into her trembling hands. 'Here you go, darling.'

'Has something happened?' Jessie asked, looking from Kenny to Rachel and back.

'I'll tell you what's happened.' Kenny dropped his hand onto his wife's shoulder and rubbed his thumb gently back and forth. 'That weird grandson of theirs was here. Scaring my wife half to death with his nonsense. Thank God I wasn't far away when she called and was able to turn back. I'm sorry that's happened to his grandparent's but—'

'Gordon was here?'

Rachel nodded.

'What are you lot going to do about him?' Kenny boomed. 'That lad's not right.' He tapped his temple with his finger.

Dylan moved forward and pulled out another dining chair from the eight that surrounded their large table.

'What did Gordon do?' Dylan scratched at his cropped brown hair and smiled at Rachel.

Rachel tried to smile back. 'He didn't exactly *do* anything. He just walked in and sat down.'

Dylan looked at Jessie. She had told him everything that Arlene Angus had confided in her on the drive back here. He wondered if Gordon realised he'd scared her like that because Rachel was clearly spooked by something.

'Did he say anything to you?' Jessie added.

Rachel shrugged and wiped a tear that had formed on the edge of her eye. 'He said he wanted some Jaffa cakes.'

'Jaffa cakes?' Jessie repeated.

'I asked him if he wanted a cup of tea, I think – or he asked for one. I can't remember.' She shook her head. 'It all happened so fast, to be honest.'

Jessie paused before commenting. Rachel was clearly flustered by his visit. She pursed her lips while she considered her words.

'He wanted a cup of tea and a biscuit?' she finally said.

Kenny grew impatient. 'It doesn't matter what the hell kind of biscuit that lunatic asked for. The point is he broke in here and intimidated my wife. I want him arrested, Detective.'

'Excuse me a minute.' Jessie moved into the hallway to make a call. She wanted to order more bodies on the search for Gordon Angus. It seemed his obsession with Rachel was escalating. Dylan overheard her call.

'What's she doing?' Rachel asked, her words a mere whisper.

'She's organising a search for Gordon,' Dylan answered just as Jessie walked back in.

'Right, that's—'

'We know – your colleague said you were arranging a search for Gordon.' Rachel's shoulders lowered as if she was relieved.

'I want police protection up here at the house,' Kenny boomed again.

Jessie stared at him then inhaled a large breath. Kenny was not going to like what she had to do.

'Mr and Mrs Ferguson,' she began while she pulled the search warrant from her pocket.

Rachel gasped when she spotted it. She knew exactly what it was and what it meant. She knew she was now a suspect.

'Kenny,' she cried out.

Her shriek focused his attention on Jessie. He held up his hand then grabbed his phone from his pocket. Jessie feared this would happen.

'I'm calling my solicitor. Do not move until I've spoken to them,' Kenny ordered.

Jessie lifted her shoulders and stood at her full five foot nine. She was glad to have Dylan's full height with her too. She handed the piece of paper into Rachel's trembling hand and walked away to the echo of Kenny's protests.

CHAPTER TWENTY-THREE

'Gordon, where have you been?' Arlene Angus rushed forward and took her son's hands in hers. She knew he wouldn't enjoy it but she pulled him close and hugged him to her chest. She didn't want to let him go. Her conversation with that detective had opened so many old wounds. Arlene wanted her baby back. The baby who loved her. Not the teenager he became; not the cold, indifferent man he'd become. Arlene wanted to hold him there forever. She was so relieved he was OK. When that Detective Blake said Gordon was missing, all kinds of horrific scenarios had rushed through her mind. Gordon didn't see the world the way other people did.

Gordon looked over his mum's shoulder at his dad lying on the hospital bed with wires coming out of his arms and an oxygen mask over his face. He pulled out of her embrace and moved forward, then stood next to the bed and touched Tommy's wrist with his fingers. His skin was warmer than he expected.

'Sit down, son.'

Arlene's voice carried from the doorway and Gordon followed her instruction automatically. He looked around to see her smiling at him.

'Talk to him. The nurse says he can probably hear us. Tell him you're there.'

Arlene's words faded into another round of sobs. Gordon frowned at her then turned his focus back to his dad.

'Dad,' Gordon said and patted Tommy's arm. He looked up and down his dad's motionless body then lifted his arm and shook it. 'Dad,' he shouted.

Arlene laid her hand on Gordon's shoulder. 'Not quite so loud.'

Gordon looked up into her eyes, his own pale ones narrowed. 'But he didn't hear me when I said it quietly.'

Arlene sighed then whispered. 'I know, I know. It's OK, Gordon, just hold his hand.'

She dropped her body into the empty chair next to him and reached for Gordon's hand to place it on top of Tommy's. She rested her own on top of both of them. The family sat in silence while the beeping continued to show that Tommy still had life left to fight for.

Arlene watched her son look at his father and thought about what that detective had told her about Malcolm and Jean's murder. She thought about the will. If Tommy knew about the changes Malcolm had wanted to make he would have been so humiliated. It was maybe good that it wasn't signed off before he died, despite the fact she knew Tommy would drink it all away within months. Now it was unclear whether Tommy would ever do anything again, let alone have another drink.

'Dad.'

Arlene looked up to see Tommy's eyes flicker then burst open before they narrowed sharply.

'What's happening?' Tommy tried to sit up but fell back onto the pillow with each attempt.

'Shh, it's OK – just relax. You've been involved in an accident,' Arlene told him. 'You've been unconscious for twenty-four hours.'

Tommy tried to focus. 'Arlene? What are you doing here?' His fingers tugged at the oxygen mask.

Arlene leaned over him. 'Leave that. You need that just now.'

Tommy pressed his fingers on the IV cannulae in his hands. 'I don't understand. What's happened to me? Why am I here?' He scrunched up his eyes against the searing pain that grew in his head. 'Argh, my head really hurts.'

'Gordon, go and get one of the nurses,' Arlene instructed.

'OK.' Gordon stood up without question. 'What do I say to her?'

Arlene sighed. 'Just tell her your dad needs help.'

Gordon nodded and walked out of the side room.

Tommy held his head in his hands and tried to control his breathing. He'd never felt pain like it.

'You were hit by a car. Do you remember anything about that?' Arlene informed him.

Tommy shook his head at her question. 'No.' He lay back on the pillow and squeezed his eyes shut. 'Close the blinds. That light is hurting my eyes.'

Arlene leaped up and tilted the blinds to block out the sun that was streaming into the room.

'Is that any better?' she asked.

'A little,' Tommy murmured and reached for the glass of water next to his bed.

'Here, let me.' Arlene smiled and lifted the glass. She pressed the straw to his lips.

Tommy enjoyed the cool drink. His mouth was so dry. He felt his lips crack at the edges and wondered how he'd got there. He had no memory of any accident. He was struggling to remember much of anything at all. He wasn't even sure what day it was.

Arlene helped him back and pulled his blanket further over him.

'You don't have to be here,' Tommy pointed out.

'I want to be here.' She smiled and reached down to kiss his forehead, allowing the erupting tear to form and trail down over her cheek before pressing her thumb across her damp skin. 'I was so worried when the hospital called. You still have me as your next of kin.'

Tommy tried to laugh and held his hand to his head when the pain tugged on him more intensely. 'Mum will love that. Have you seen her?'

Another tear formed in the corner of Arlene's eye when she realised she would have to tell him the worst news imaginable.

CHAPTER TWENTY-FOUR

Gordon sliced through the chaos of different members of staff, unsure which nurse his mum wanted him to tell. He looked at each of their uniforms and tried to figure out which one he should approach. The woman in lilac looked like she was carrying a bin bag so it probably wasn't her he wanted. A cleaner wouldn't be much help. Not with this. The two younger girls in pale blue tunic and trousers had 'Student Nurse' written on their badges. Probably not them either. He watched the elderly man shuffle slowly past, irritated at having to move around him.

Gordon chewed his thumbnail until a tall, bearded man in a dark navy uniform came out of the lift at the entrance to the intensive care ward. This could be the one he needed.

'Excuse me,' Gordon called out. 'Mum says Dad needs a nurse.'

'Sure, no problem. Who's your dad?'

Gordon had to glance up at the man, who stood a good three inches taller than him. He looked him once in the eye then slid his gaze to the side. That was enough time to make eye contact, Gordon thought. That was more than he was really comfortable with.

'Tommy Angus – he was hit by a car.'

'Ah yes, I know him.' The nurse smiled. 'Come on then, let's see what's happening.'

Gordon followed the middle-aged man to the side-room door, unsure why the man was smiling after Gordon told him what had happened to his dad. He looked inside at his dad writhing in agony and clutching his head. He looked worse than he had only moments before. He was making loud whining noises and Gordon didn't like that. Gordon frowned. That didn't look right.

'Mr Angus, can you hear me?' the nurse called out over the sound of Tommy's anguished cries.

'Do something!' Arlene insisted while she paced the side-room floor.

'Tommy, where does it hurt?' The look on the nurse's face grew from concern to alarm when Tommy's pain seemed to be intensifying.

Gordon looked on from the doorway, unsure what exactly was going on. He'd never seen his dad look so bad – he'd seen him in some states in the past few months but this seemed different. That nurse looked quite worried now after smiling like that. He was pressing a loud buzzer and a flurry of activity erupted around his dad's bed. His mum was leaning over his dad and didn't notice Gordon turn and walk away.

He pulled his notebook from his pocket and pressed the button for the lift, narrowing his eyes at the greying woman with tears in her eyes who got in with him. She sniffed and wiped her nose with a tissue she retrieved from the cuff of the grey cardigan that matched her hair, Gordon noticed. He wondered if that was deliberate. She smelled like apples, he noticed too. He knew that meant she hadn't eaten for a long time. Ketosis, he remembered it was called.

He shifted his eyes to the floor when she spotted him staring.

The woman sniffed again and blew her nose. Gordon tried to ignore her. He opened the notebook to the first page and looked at the list of questions that remained unanswered. He planned to write a book – an idea that had burned in him for a few months. It wouldn't be fiction; it would be a true-crime bestseller about the brutal murder of an elderly couple.

The sound of Gordon's ringtone startled the other passenger in the lift, making her cry out in fright slightly before blushing. His mum had told him to turn the tone down several times, particularly because it was a thrash metal tune. Gordon's favourite. His lips curled into a smile at her response.

'Hello,' he answered but got no response before the call ended with the screen showing no signal. 'Shit,' he exclaimed.

'My phone doesn't work in here either,' the woman informed him just as the lift stopped on the ground floor. She smiled awkwardly at Gordon before walking out ahead of him.

Gordon dialled the number, disappointed to be put through to voicemail right away. He hammered the end-call button without leaving a message. He'd recognised the number right away and was surprised to have heard from him so soon, if at all even. The thought of their meeting made Gordon's heart race. Seeing pictures of their crime scene stirred Gordon in ways he'd never experienced. Ways he couldn't explain. He was so close he could taste it.

Gordon dialled the number one more time and paced back and forth outside the hospital entrance while he waited. One more ring meant voicemail again but this time he wasn't disappointed.

'Hello,' the deep, gravelly voice came down the line.

'Is it really you?' Gordon asked. 'When can we meet? I have so many questions.'

'Not so fast,' the man interrupted. 'Did you get the money? The amount we agreed.'

Gordon confirmed the details immediately and checked his watch. He headed to the bus station hoping he'd catch the next bus to Dundee. Everything was falling into place. Gordon would finally meet his hero.

CHAPTER TWENTY-FIVE

Rachel poured another nip of whisky while she listened to drawers being opened in her bedroom and Detective Logan moving things around in the utility room. She sank the burning liquid in one mouthful. Kenny was still shouting down the phone at their solicitor. She winced at the bitter taste but poured another straight away.

A memory of her grandfather sipping whisky from a small crystal glass on New Year's Eve burst into her head. The only time Peter Connor ever drank alcohol was on Christmas Day and at Hogmanay. He said it was important to mark the start of a new year. But she and David had stopped him from reaching that final new year. What they did had returned to haunt her. She could hear the young male detective moving something in the utility room. The dogs barked and he spoke softly to them. He liked dogs, she mused, and sank the last of her nip. She turned to see Kenny stride back into the living room.

'What did he say?' Rachel asked and poured him a nip.

She stared out of the bay window at the wind turbines in the distance. The sun was low in the grey winter sky. It looked like more rain would deluge the village any time soon. She heard the horses kicking up a fuss in the stable. They must be able to feel the heavy atmosphere. Rachel wouldn't be surprised if it thundered later that night. Her horses hated thunder.

She reached up and opened the top part of the window to smell the air. Yes, a storm was definitely brewing. Outside of the cottage as well as inside.

'Just sit tight was all he advised. Let him know if we need him.'
Kenny took the glass out of her hand and sank his whisky in one
gulp then refilled it. 'Can you believe that? What the hell am I
paying him for?'

Rachel looked back out of the window at the darkening clouds.

'I'm sorry,' she murmured. 'If it wasn't for my past they wouldn't
be here tearing our home apart.'

Kenny pulled Rachel into his arms and tightened his embrace.
'Now that's enough. I don't want to hear any more of that. None
of this is your fault.' He pulled her back and looked into her eyes,
which had filled with frightened tears. A single one erupted and slid
slowly down her cheek until Kenny wiped his thumb over her skin.

'This is not your fault,' he repeated and kissed the top of her
head before he held her close to his chest again.

Jessie crouched down and opened the drawer in Rachel's bedside
unit. It looked expensive. Solid pine, she thought. It was heavier
than the one she had at home. She flicked through a pile of old
photographs. Rachel looked about fifteen, maybe sixteen. She was
standing next to a girl with a shock of auburn hair and freckles.
The two girls were smiling widely. It had been taken by a river that
looked like it rushed past noisily. The white of the current looked
angry. A memory of an old case crashed into her mind, making
Jessie shiver. Next to the girls there was a tartan picnic blanket
with an older woman eating a sandwich on it, a large blue flask
in her hand. Jessie returned the pictures and closed the drawer.

She moved to the fitted wardrobe and slid open the door. Inside
she found a unit of drawers and she opened the top one. Rachel
had expensive taste in underwear, she noticed.

Jessie rummaged through each of the four drawers but found
nothing but designer clothes. A jewellery box sat on top of the unit.
She heard herself audibly gasp at the array of very expensive pieces

inside. She lifted the top compartment of the box and found more photographs. Two this time. Both of a newborn baby. The person holding the infant looked very much like Rachel but she wasn't smiling in these ones. Her eyes looked red and sore. From crying perhaps. She turned over a photo to see the date – 14 July 1991.

Jessie pursed her lips while she considered whether these were relevant. She tapped them a couple of times on her chin then studied the sadness in the girl's eyes again.

Jessie laid the photos back into the box and replaced the lid before putting it back where she found it. They didn't seem important but Jessie made a mental note of their existence.

'Why have you got my boots in a bag?' Rachel surged forward to take them from Dylan but Kenny grabbed her arm. She turned to face him and frowned. 'Kenny? What are they doing?'

Rachel didn't wait to hear his answer. She pushed past Dylan, who was thrown by the force when she thudded into him. Jessie took off after Rachel, who was now outside the front door and running towards the stable. She left the front door swinging open behind her.

CHAPTER TWENTY-SIX

'Rachel, stop,' Jessie roared over the strengthening gusts of wind. She screwed up her eyes against the huge raindrops that splashed onto her face.

Rachel ignored Jessie's pleas and carried on into the stable. She thrust the door shut before Jessie could catch up. Jessie heard the bolt slam over from inside. She hammered the palm of her hand on the thick wood. Then her phone rang out in her pocket, the ringtone barely audible over the howling winds that blew dust and debris around the yard.

Dylan stood next to Kenny and both men peered out into the torrential downpour without speaking. Dylan dialled Jessie's number again. This time he could see her lift her phone from her jacket pocket.

'Dylan, Kenny Ferguson does not leave that house, do you understand?' she roared down the line.

Dylan hung up and stuffed his phone away as he turned.

'DI Blake wants us to wait here, Mr Ferguson.'

'But I can't just stand here and wait…' Kenny began while he tried to move past Dylan in pursuit of his wife.

Dylan reached out and caught hold of Kenny's arm.

'No, it's better that we wait here.' He paused and recalled the times he'd seen Jessie handle these tense, electrically charged situations before. 'Jessie can handle it.'

'You don't understand, Detective; my wife is extremely vulnerable.'

'She'll be OK, I promise. My colleague knows what she's doing.'

Dylan felt Kenny's arm soften against his grip and fall to his side. Kenny walked back into the kitchen and flopped down into one of the dining chairs, his head low in his hands. Dylan hoped he was right about Jessie's abilities.

Jessie hammered her fist hard on the stable door and winced from the pain of her bruised knuckles.

'Rachel, open the door. We need to talk,' she shouted above the violent, stormy wind. She heard Rachel's voice; it sounded like she was talking to someone. Jessie feared she was now trapped inside there with someone. 'Rachel!' Jessie screamed.

The moments that passed felt like hours as Jessie banged her palm against the timber frame. Then silence. Even the wind seemed to die down and the horses became quiet. No more voices. She heard footsteps walking towards the door. The bolt slid across again and the door opened. Jessie watched Rachel walk away from the open door without talking.

'Please stop,' she called out again. 'What's going on?'

Rachel did stop this time and moved to the corner where there were several bales of hay lined up. She slumped down onto one of them and dropped her phone down beside her.

'I can't do this,' Rachel murmured and pressed her face into her hands. 'I can't let you lock me up again. I just can't.'

CHAPTER TWENTY-SEVEN

1991

She ran and didn't look back. She could hear them snarling and growling behind her. They were gaining on her – she was sure of it. The trees grew thicker the deeper she moved into the woods. The path had disappeared long since and she was now scrambling through gnarled, overgrown trunks and shrubs. She whimpered as she tripped over a protruding branch and crashed to the dirt. She couldn't stop. They would smell her.

She stood and rubbed the blood from her knee and fled. The growling grew closer. She could smell them now. They must be so close. Up ahead a cottage came into view. She could hide in there. Her lungs burned from running. It felt like days since she'd been able to rest. They'd hunted her ever since that night.

She grabbed for the handle. The hounds were close and baying for her blood. They wanted to tear her apart and devour her heart. She tugged and pulled but it wouldn't budge.

There they were; they were right behind her now. She had nowhere left to run. They stalked closer, their shoulders hunkered low, moving carefully, their teeth bared. She watched blood-streaked saliva drip from the edges of their jaws. She closed her eyes and listened to her heart race. Fear gripped her. She leaned back and felt the cold air hit her cheek when the first bite came at her. She smelled their rancid breath. She squealed and tried to be brave.

Just as she thought the final killer bite was coming, the door behind her gave way and she fell inside. She gathered up all of her strength and slammed the door shut, the sound of howling and snarling and scratching coming from outside. She tried to swallow. Her throat stung and her mouth was so dry. The pain grew inside her head. The room spun. She had to grab hold of the carpet to stop herself from being thrown around. It got faster and faster until she felt her body being pulled downwards into a black hole that had opened up in the floor. Thunder roared outside. The midnight sky lit up with lightning; the smell of sulphur filled the air.

He'd come for her. The devil had come for her just like her grand-mother had said he would. Heat hit her feet and the flames licked up her calves until they reached her knees. She grabbed hold of the edge of the abyss and tried to climb back out to save herself. She didn't want to go. She was sorry. She didn't mean it.

She heard the voice grow louder and louder.

Rachel's eyes snapped open and she sat bolt upright in her bed. Her foster mother sat on the edge of her bed, a look of serious concern on her face.

'You've had a bad dream, that's all.'

Rachel ran her fingers through her sweat-soaked hair and glanced across at her roommate, who yawned and turned over, then tugged her duvet over her face. She gasped to gain control of her breath.

Rachel reached for the plastic tumbler of orange squash on the table between the two beds in the small room they shared. She sank the full amount in one. She'd had that dream three times now. Every time she woke before he could get her.

CHAPTER TWENTY-EIGHT

Arlene wanted to be anywhere in the world than there with Tommy. His eyes searched hers for the answer to his simple question. She could lie. Perhaps she should lie until Tommy felt stronger. He'd been through a horrific experience, and he was lucky to be alive. He wasn't strong enough to hear that his parents had been murdered.

The doctor who'd examined him increased his observations of Tommy to every fifteen minutes.

'Is Gordon with you?' Tommy coughed once and held his ribs. 'I can't remember much from today.'

Arlene watched him look around the room then back into her eyes.

'Gordon is here somewhere. I think he might have popped out to grab a coffee for me,' Arlene lied. Gordon hadn't been back for more than half an hour. Not since she'd sent him to find the nurse. She knew that detective was looking for him too and hoped she would find her son before the police did.

'Since when do you drink coffee?' Tommy tried to smile despite the headache that was building in intensity again.

Arlene laughed to cover her anxiety. 'There are a lot of things you don't know about me, Tommy Angus.'

'Yes.' Tommy grabbed his temple again and sucked air in through his teeth at the pain. 'L-like what?' he stammered.

'Do you need me to get the nurse, Tommy?'

Then Arlene shrieked and rushed to the nurses' station, leaving the side-room door wide open. 'Help me, somebody, please. My husband. There's something wrong.'

When Arlene returned she was horrified to see Tommy slumped, unconscious on his bed. She stood back and watched the chaos of nurses and doctors surround him again. They muttered amongst themselves, saying things Arlene didn't like the sound of.

She felt helpless as Tommy's bed was wheeled past her at speed. The words 'bleed' and 'brain' rushed over her in the fog of panic.

A young student nurse offered to make Arlene a cup of tea. At least that was what Arlene thought she said. It all happened so fast. She grabbed her phone and pressed on Gordon's number.

'Come on, come on; pick up, son.' Arlene listened to her call go straight to his voicemail. She tried again; she knew he would pick up eventually. He always did. Why had he run off like that? She wondered if he'd struggled to process seeing his dad like that.

Arlene had never felt so alone. Sure, she and Tommy were divorced and they'd had their problems over the years, but the thought of life without him in it in some form or another was too awful to contemplate. How would Gordon cope? How was he processing the death of his grandparents?

A horrifying thought struck her. Nausea gripped her stomach and she prayed Gordon wasn't in some way involved.

CHAPTER TWENTY-NINE

'Nobody is saying they're going to lock you up, Rachel.' Jessie edged closer and pointed to the hay bale next to her. 'Can I sit?'

'Sure,' Rachel answered with her head down, her eyes fixed on her bare feet.

'I wouldn't be doing my job if I didn't go where the evidence takes me – you must know that.'

Rachel shrugged. 'But what evidence? I've been nowhere near the Anguses' place since I bought the paddock.' She scoffed before shaking her head. 'All I wanted was to create a gallops for my horses. That's not a crime, is it?'

'There's a size-four boot print and a hair.'

'I suppose you've decided it's my boot and hair then?' Rachel's voice oozed defeat.

Jessie could see how frustrated Rachel felt but it wasn't a lie. She had to go where the physical evidence led her.

'I'm going to need a DNA swab from both you and Kenny.'

'Kenny is a suspect too then? Doesn't the gunshot-residue test prove our innocence?' Rachel snapped. 'Why the hell would he want to kill them?'

Jessie didn't have an answer for her. There was no reason to suspect him, not really.

'Shall we go back to the house?' Jessie stood up and wiped loose hay from her clothes.

Rachel sighed, resigned to her fate almost. 'Can I have five minutes with the horses?'

Jessie was reluctant to oblige but the look in Rachel's eyes won her over. She hoped showing a measure of trust wasn't a mistake.

'Five minutes,' Jessie whispered and moved away just far enough to allow her a little privacy.

'What the hell are they doing out there?' Kenny paced back and forth.

Dylan felt dizzy just watching him.

'Jessie knows what she's doing, don't worry.'

Kenny scoffed. 'Rachel is more vulnerable than either of you know.'

'I understand,' Dylan started to say.

'Do you, Detective? Do you really?'

Dylan had read up on the Alice Connor case after they'd discovered Rachel's real identity. Manipulated and groomed at the age of fourteen. Coerced by a young man into murdering the only parents she'd ever known was the defence at the time. She'd given birth to David's baby the summer that followed, and the child had been put up for adoption within a couple of days. The best thing for Rachel and the baby, he agreed. Now with the death of Malcolm and Jean Angus, he wanted to keep an open mind on the level of manipulation involved. The crime scenes couldn't be more different, though. The photos from the Connors crime scene had turned Dylan's stomach when he'd viewed them. So much blood. At least the Anguses hadn't suffered that same horror.

'I do try, Mr Ferguson, but no, I can't understand fully what she's been through. How can I?'

Kenny glanced behind him when he saw Rachel walk back towards the front door and rushed out to greet her.

'Rachel,' he called out and wrapped his arms around her.

Dylan followed him and looked to see what expression Jessie wore in a bid to find out what had happened out there.

'I'm fine. I just want to get this over with.' Rachel spoke softly. 'They want DNA from both of us.'

'What?' Kenny began to protest until Rachel squeezed his hand and shook her head.

Her eyes pleaded with him. 'Let's just do it so that they can leave us alone, yes?'

Kenny closed his eyes with a long sigh and kissed the top of her head, then led his wife back inside.

'Have you got the swab kits on you?' Jessie asked and held out a hand.

'Sure.' Dylan took two kits from his inside pocket and handed her a pair of gloves.

Nobody spoke while the samples were taken but the atmosphere was electric. Jessie placed the second swab into the container and sealed the bag.

'When will we know?' Rachel asked and dabbed her thumb over the saliva on the edge of her mouth. 'I just want to get on with my life.'

'When I'm officially able to rule you out, I promise I will let you know as soon as possible.'

'Thank you,' Rachel whispered. 'I'm sorry about running away. I just panicked. This and the phone calls. I just had to get out of here. I couldn't breathe all of a sudden.'

Dylan shot a wide-eyed stare at Jessie.

'Phone calls?' Jessie probed.

'What phone calls? You didn't tell me about any calls,' Kenny interrupted.

Rachel remembered the fear she'd felt when the mysterious caller had spoken to her. *I know what you've done.* That's what he'd said. What did he mean? Did he mean what she'd done as a teenager or did he think it was her that killed the Anguses?

She felt her heart rate increase again. There were too many people crowding her in that small hallway. That detective was standing right in front of the door, obstructing her escape. She tried to inhale a huge gasp of breath but it was like she was unable to force enough oxygen inside. The room became so hot. Her chest tightened and she thought she was about to die. Rachel stared at Kenny. Then there was nothing but darkness.

CHAPTER THIRTY

'Get her a glass of water,' Jessie told Dylan.

Kenny looked on as his wife slowly sat up from the floor, where she'd fallen after she passed out, knocking her head on the hall table as she went down. He crouched low next to her.

'Are you OK, sweetheart?' Kenny reached for the cut on the top of Rachel's forehead.

She pushed him away and blushed. 'Don't fuss. I'm fine. It's nothing.'

Dylan handed her a tall glass of cold water and smiled. 'Here you go. Take it easy with that.'

'Thanks,' she muttered and sank half the chilled water straight away.

'That was quite a clatter your head took. I think maybe you should get a doctor to have a wee look at that.' Dylan added.

'You're very kind.' She drank the remainder of the water and handed him back the glass. 'I'll be fine, honestly. I just got a little light-headed, that's all.' Rachel got to her knees and began to stand up again. Jessie offered her hand to her and a sympathetic smile.

'Thanks,' Rachel murmured.

'Dylan's right. It wouldn't hurt to have that checked out,' Jessie agreed.

Kenny wrapped an arm around his wife's shoulder and led her back into the living room. 'She says she's fine so could you please just do whatever it is you came here to do and get out of my house?'

Before Jessie could respond the living-room door was shut firmly in her face.

'What do you make of that?' Dylan asked.

Before she could tell him what she thought, Jessie had to answer her phone, which was buzzing inside her pocket. She lifted a finger to her lips to motion Dylan to be quiet then frowned. Dylan did as he was told and turned away. He moved into the Fergusons' kitchen to wait for Jessie to end her call.

'Sorry, Dylan, that was forensics. No gunshot residue on any of them.'

'Shit. What now?' he commented.

'Come on, let's get back to the station,' Jessie conceded. 'Grab the boots.'

Once they were outside, Dylan nodded towards an outbuilding tucked at the back of the cottage, close to the kennel block.

'What about searching in there?' Dylan pointed to the timber structure with a flick of his head. 'What about his guns? Where does he keep them?'

Jessie turned to face him and pursed her lips. 'Do you reckon he keeps any at home. Rather than Stanley gun club, I mean?'

Dylan shrugged as Jessie hammered on the Fergusons' door again. She was about to knock again until the door swung open to reveal a red-faced Rachel. It was clear she had been crying.

'Kenny's guns. Where does he keep them?'

Rachel frowned. 'He keeps them at the club usually...' Her words drifted away.

'Usually?' Jessie probed.

'Yes, he's got one here just now.' Rachel snatched a set of keys from the hall table. 'There's one in the shed. Locked in a cabinet, though.'

Dylan's eyes widened as he caught Jessie's gaze.

'Could you show me please?' Jessie requested.

'Sure, follow me.'

Rachel led the two detectives into the back of the large outbuilding Dylan had pointed to moments before. She battled with the padlock for several minutes, giving Jessie ample time to scan the state of what appeared to be Kenny's office. Sheets of paper strewn everywhere on his desk and other surfaces gave the impression he was a very disorganised man, though the success of his haulage company seemed at odds with that chaos. Ferguson Haulage was an award-winning company, scoring accolades for environmental and business programmes.

'Shall I have a go?' Dylan suggested while he watched Rachel struggle.

Rachel shook her head. 'No, I think I've got it.' The lock opened with one final push. 'There, look for yourselves.' The cabinet door swung open with a loud creaking sound. 'Not exactly an easy weapon to access, is it—'

Rachel's audible gasp filled the room. 'I don't understand.' She pointed to the empty space inside the cabinet. 'It was here.' She hesitated. 'I'm sure it was here.'

CHAPTER THIRTY-ONE

Caroline Peters grinned and stood to greet her friend who'd arrived for coffee. Julia Dean had been working for the Fergusons for six months and the two women had hit it off immediately. Julia was keen to hear more from Caroline about the rumours concerning the deaths of her employers' neighbours. The police had even questioned them, she'd heard.

'Hey.' Julia hugged her then removed her navy leather jacket and slung it over the back of the coffee-shop chair. 'Any more news?' she asked.

'Not as far as I know,' Caroline answered. 'I've ordered you an Americano, by the way – hope that's OK – and a fruit scone.'

'You know me so well.' Julia grinned and rubbed her fingers through her cropped brown hair.

'Rachel wasn't pleased with them. Did you know that?' Caroline beamed without attempting to keep her voice down. 'They objected to her plans or something. Got her application rejected.' Pride at knowing this information oozed from her features.

'That doesn't mean she'd bump them off.' Julia disagreed with her friend's theory. 'That's a bit of a leap, don't you think?'

'I'm just telling you what I've heard.'

'I can't believe that Rachel could be capable of something like that,' Julia insisted. 'So what do you think happened? She took a gun and blasted her neighbours dead because they messed up her plans? I just don't see it. Come on – don't be daft!'

Caroline shrugged and poured milk into her cup. 'Stranger things have happened, I can assure you.'

Julia shook her head as Caroline's phone rang inside her handbag.

'Hang on – sorry, I better get this.'

Julia sipped and frowned as the look on Caroline's face changed. She watched her hang up quickly and gather her things.

'I have to go; I'm really sorry,' Caroline blurted out.

'What's happened? Is there something wrong?'

'It's, erm—' Caroline stammered. 'It's Rachel; she's been taken to the police station to answer questions.'

Julia gasped. 'No!'

'Do you still believe your boss is innocent?' Caroline chirped as she grabbed her coat and hurried out of the café after tossing a ten-pound note down onto the table.

Julia's heart thundered so fast she worried she was having a heart attack. This couldn't be happening. Not now. Not when she was so close.

CHAPTER THIRTY-TWO

Opening the cupboard and finding the gun missing, Jessie explained that she felt she had enough to take Rachel in for questioning. A call to the gun club confirmed that Kenny's gun was logged as being off the premises at the moment. So where was it? Neither Kenny nor Rachel could answer that question. Given that the missing weapon matched the calibre of the bullets that had killed the Anguses, Jessie had no choice but to pursue that line of enquiry.

Rachel tried to keep calm. The last thing she wanted was a panic attack in the back of this Audi, in handcuffs. She closed her eyes and focused on her breathing, then stared out of the back window of Dylan's car at the stunned face of her husband, who held his phone next to his ear. He'd pressed the number for their solicitor almost as soon as the detective had said Rachel was to be questioned.

Jessie twisted round to see Rachel leaning her head on the window with her eyes tight shut. It looked like she was carrying out some kind of meditation. No bad thing maybe. Jessie didn't fancy dealing with another of Rachel's fainting episodes en route to the station and hoped Dylan would get there as soon as the speed limits would allow. A quick phone call to the station arranged a further search of the Fergusons' property, using a bigger team with a firearms canine too. Kenny was adamant his gun should be in the cupboard. So where was it? she'd asked and Rachel's face told Jessie she knew exactly what was coming next. Once she had a DNA match, Rachel would be charged without question.

'I feel sick. Can I have some air?' Rachel called out and gasped for breath.

The sign for Luncarty was up ahead, which meant another couple of miles and they would be back at the station.

'Open the window,' Jessie whispered to Dylan, who pressed the window button until fresh air smacked Rachel in the face.

The strong wind that blew in as they travelled at fifty-five miles an hour was a shock, and Rachel screwed up her eyes against the cold blast. Dylan peered into his rear-view mirror and made the window go up a little just to reduce the blast.

'I need air,' Rachel screamed and panted now to catch her breath. 'My chest feels so tight. You have to stop the car!' she roared and kicked the back of Jessie's seat. The car was almost at the entrance to the dual carriageway and if they didn't stop now they would be committed to their destination and unable to stop until they got back to Perth.

'Pull over,' Jessie ordered.

'Here?' Dylan questioned.

'Yes, here!' she repeated.

Dylan indicated and stopped his Audi at the entrance to the slip road onto the A9 towards Perth. He glanced in his rear-view mirror, relieved the road was quiet behind him, then switched on his hazard lights.

'Help me; I can't breathe,' Rachel shouted and snatched at her handcuffs. 'Get these off me.'

Jessie leaped from the passenger seat and ran round to the back door and tugged it open. She helped Rachel out of her seat and moved her away from the slip road and back towards the main road through the village. When the two women were out of his car Dylan spun the vehicle around, illegally, and drove it the small distance back into Luncarty.

Rachel continued to pant. Her lips started to tingle then her nose and cheeks. If she didn't regain control she was going to pass out.

'Rachel, look at me. Focus on my voice.' Jessie was out of her depth. She'd only seen this done once before on a training exercise. She had to get Rachel to focus her attention on one spot then work on her breathing. 'Focus your eyes on my eyes. Come on – look at me. Copy me.' Jessie inhaled a huge breath and held it.

Rachel was aware that the detective was saying something but all she wanted to do was escape. Her chest was tight and she feared she was now having a heart attack.

'Look at me.' Jessie had a hold of her arm in one hand and tugged Rachel's face towards her with the other. The contact made Rachel gasp and push her away. Jessie stumbled and lost her grip. This was Rachel's chance. She shot back into the centre of the village, down the steep hill onto Scarth Road.

'Get her!' Jessie roared.

Dylan didn't need to be told twice. He leaped from the car and bolted after her in a heartbeat, catching up with her within seconds. He took firm hold of her wrist and pulled her towards him.

'Hey, come on.'

Dylan's voice was deep and soothing. He held her close to him and Rachel felt protected. She couldn't explain it. Then it hit her. He reminded her of David. Part of her was horrified by the way his touch made her feel but another part had been searching for it for the past thirty years. She broke down and sobbed into Dylan's chest as his arms enveloped her. He kept tight hold of her and guided her back up the hill towards his car. Jessie nodded a simple thank you to Dylan as they passed.

'I'm sorry,' Rachel whispered while Jessie helped her back into the back seat.

Jessie crouched low next to her. 'We'll be in Perth in five minutes tops. I'll ask the doctor to have a chat with you when we get there.'

Rachel nodded. 'Thanks, I just panicked. I suffer with anxiety but you've probably already figured that one out for yourself.' She tried to laugh to hide her embarrassment.

'Do you usually take any medication for it?'

'Not anymore, but I used to.' Rachel sighed. 'It's been a long time since it's been this bad.'

Jessie closed the back door and spied another clutch of black clouds circling overhead. She feared it was an omen for the night ahead.

CHAPTER THIRTY-THREE

Gordon stood in the doorway and watched his mum in silence. She didn't seem to notice he was there yet. He could turn and leave. Maybe he should. This was inconvenient. Then Arlene's head snapped round.

'Gordon,' she called out to him and surged from her chair. She pulled him close to her and nestled her head into his chest. Gordon pushed her back. She knew he didn't like that. Physical contact irritated him.

'Where's Dad?' Gordon asked then frowned at the empty bed where his dad had been earlier.

Arlene's eyes filled with tears until she pressed her thumbs across them. 'He's in surgery. They've found a small bleed in his brain. It probably happened when he was hit by the car.'

'When will he be back?'

'The doctor said she would come and get me when your dad is in recovery.' Arlene sniffed and grabbed a tissue from her cardigan sleeve and blew her nose. 'Where did you go, son?'

Emotional people were tiresome to Gordon Angus. Their need to unnecessarily complicate decisions with feelings irritated him. He'd always known he was different but it was his mum's reaction to the death of their family dog when he was six that had highlighted it to him the most clearly. Kaiser was a golden Labrador and was often labelled as Gordon's best friend. Mainly by his mum, it had to be said. It had been his mum's breakdown when Gordon asked when they were getting another dog – the same day Kaiser was put down – that began his questions. She had been so emotional that day.

Sure, Gordon had liked Kaiser. He was great company and his fur was soft and warm to snuggle into. The dog had also seemed to know when Gordon was stressed and there had been some pretty difficult times in his younger years. People thought the bullying didn't bother Gordon but it did, though that psychiatrist had been surprised when Gordon told him that. The bullying was horrible because what they said wasn't true – Gordon wasn't weird or a monster. Those boys were stupid. They were just jealous that they weren't as intelligent as him.

Straight As were the norm for Gordon Angus. He couldn't understand how people found exams so difficult. Working with a partner was the hard part for Gordon. It didn't matter who he'd get paired with because they were all always equally stupid and often didn't like Gordon pointing that out to them. He had no time for anyone whose IQ didn't match his – which didn't leave very many people for Gordon to get along with. His mum had always told Gordon to tell the truth, but when he did – and he regularly did – people seemed to object…

Gordon watched his mum's face. It was pink and she looked hot and flushed. Like she'd been running.

'Your face is all red.'

Arlene wiped her nose and smiled. Gordon's trademark rudeness was strangely comforting. She reached out and rubbed his arm. 'Thanks, son,' she whispered.

'Mrs Angus?' The voice from the doorway startled her.

'Yes, that's me.' Arlene surged forward to greet the young, slim doctor who looked like she should still be at school to Arlene. 'This is my son, Gordon.'

The doctor smiled at Gordon, who frowned back.

'Is Tommy OK? Can we see him?' Arlene instinctively reached for Gordon's hand and clung to it then realised what she'd done and pulled away. He wouldn't like that.

'Your husband is sleeping but the operation went very well.' The doctor split her gaze between the two of them. 'He's in recovery and of course you can see him for a few moments.'

'You hear that, Gordon?' Arlene was so happy. 'Your dad's OK.' She slammed her hand over her face and burst into tears again.

Gordon stared at her. He frowned then looked at the doctor, who leaned forward and squeezed Arlene's hand.

'Your husband is a lucky man,' she began.

'He's my mum's ex-husband. They got divorced last year,' Gordon chirped. 'But they're still friends.'

Arlene blushed but she should be used to this now. 'It's OK, son; she doesn't need to know everything.'

'I know but she called him your husband.'

The young doctor smiled at Arlene. 'Come with me and I'll take you through to see him.'

Arlene and Gordon followed behind in silence until they came to a room with four beds in it. Each bed had someone with their life being assisted by tubes and wires. All four faces wore an oxygen mask and the whistling of the oxygen echoed in the air along with the regular beeps from pulse monitors. The bed in the far corner was occupied by an elderly woman whose tight grey curls were barely visible behind everything that was fighting to keep her alive.

Arlene scanned the room with frightened eyes then inhaled a huge breath when she spotted Tommy, his head wrapped in a bandage almost covering his left eye.

'There's your dad,' she whispered and gently nudged Gordon forward.

'You can have five minutes,' the doctor informed them. 'He needs to rest more than anything else now. We removed a small area of bleeding and the operation was relatively simple.'

'Thank you so much,' Arlene murmured as the young woman walked back out to the small recovery unit.

Gordon stared at his motionless father, his eyes scanning the numerous wires that stuck out in several directions. He looked down to see urine draining into a bag that was attached to the side of the bed. If it wasn't for all the beeping, he would have thought his dad was dead. He looked grey. Just like his grandad had. Grey and still.

CHAPTER THIRTY-FOUR

Jessie flopped down onto the chair at her desk and sipped from the mug of hot, sweet coffee Dylan had brought her before he'd headed home for the night. She'd told him he should get back to his two little ones. Dylan was a really great dad and a lovely husband to Shelly. More than once Jessie had been forced to squash down a pang of jealousy. Not that it was Dylan Jessie wanted. She longed for the relationship he had with Shelly, that was all. Growing up, Jessie had experienced nothing but violence and dysfunction and so began to think that was normal. Meeting and marrying Dan had done nothing but continue that cycle.

The sound of footsteps approaching in her empty office made her lift her head.

'Hello, what's up?' Jessie stood to greet the uniformed officer and was confused when she recognised the key that he had in his hand.

'A man handed this in a wee while ago with this note addressed to you.'

'Thanks.' Jessie took the envelope and recognised the handwriting on it immediately. 'Did you see who handed this in?'

The officer shook his head as he turned to leave. 'No, sorry.'

'OK, thanks.' She fell back down into the chair, frozen with the fear of what might be inside the envelope. She turned it over and smelled it instinctively, then quickly pulled it away from her face.

'Come on – stop being stupid,' she whispered and ripped it open.

Hi Jess,

Not sure if you realised but you left your car key in the ignition so I arranged for your Fiesta to be picked up and repaired. I'm working now so it wasn't a problem. It's not much but it pays the bills. I've got a little flat now too. It's not much either but it does me.

There's no need to pay me back. I was more than happy to help.

You had lost a clasp from your exhaust and you also had a small hole in your centre silencer. You must have been getting a real noise from it but it's all fixed now anyway. I've parked it round the back of the station and given your key to the bloke on reception, but you probably figured that out already.

Seeing you again brought back a lot of feelings for me, Jess. You looked great. Just like the girl I married all those years ago. I know I don't deserve anything from you but I've suffered too. I've grieved for him too. I would love to catch up and have a coffee sometime. I haven't had a drink for a few months. I'm trying to be a better man, I promise. I'll be in touch. I still miss you.

Dan x

Jessie thought she was going to be sick. The rush of nausea those simple words caused was so powerful. She ripped up the note and tossed it into her bin then stuffed her car key into her bag. The sound of her phone buzzing made her jump. It was Benito.

'Hello, Ben. I'm sorry, I know I said I wouldn't be late back but—'

Jessie listened to him tell her not to worry so much. He would wait for her. He was just checking in, making sure she was OK.

She hung up her call with him, so grateful he'd called exactly when he did. Like divine intervention perhaps – if Jessie believed in such things that was.

She grabbed her bag and made her way down to check on Rachel Ferguson.

CHAPTER THIRTY-FIVE

'Hello, Mrs Ferguson. I'm the doctor on duty.' He smiled as he sat in the chair opposite her, his leather bag at his feet. 'How are you feeling now?'

'Better, thanks. It was just a panic attack. I know that.'

'You've experienced this kind of feeling before?' He reached for her wrist to check her pulse.

Rachel nodded. 'Yes, but not for a while.' She hesitated and searched his face for signs that he knew who she was. She wondered if that detective was allowed to tell him about her past. Was she bound by some kind of confidentiality clause? Rachel hoped so. Having to talk about it with another stranger would probably bring on a further panic attack.

'Look straight ahead.' He shone his torch in each of Rachel's eyes then asked her to follow his finger with only her eyes. 'That's fine.'

He tucked his stethoscope into his ears and listened to her chest. 'Big deep breath for me.' He paused. 'And out.'

Rachel did as she was asked, relieved she couldn't talk while he listened to her heart and lungs.

'OK, your pulse is a little faster than I would like but under the circumstances it's normal.'

He produced a cuff and tightened it around her arm. Rachel waited, expecting to be told her blood pressure was high. Of course it would be high. It was bound to be.

'That's fine. Not too bad. Certainly nothing to worry about – and you feel better, you said?'

His smile seemed warm and genuine. 'Honestly, I'm OK now. I feel silly, that's all.' Rachel felt the heat rise from her neck to her cheeks. What must they think of her? She supposed that detective thought she was trying to escape.

After the doctor left he was replaced within minutes by that detective again. But not before muffled voices could be heard outside the room.

'Hello,' Jessie greeted her as she shut the door. 'Doctor says you're fit and healthy.'

Rachel shrugged then sipped from her cup of water. 'I'm not sure about that exactly but I do feel better now and I'm sorry about before.'

'Don't worry about that now.' Jessie pulled out a chair and sat opposite her. 'Your solicitor will be joining us soon.'

Rachel nodded before the silence descended over them. Jessie didn't want to be told anything until Rachel had legal representation present. She even considered walking back out of the room until her solicitor arrived. Thankfully they didn't have long to wait. Rachel turned and smiled at the middle-aged, balding man. He held out his hand to shake Jessie's before he sat next to his client.

'My client has been read her rights, I assume,' he asked while he removed papers from his bag and put his glasses on.

'Yes, I have, thank you,' Rachel muttered. 'I've been examined by the doctor too.'

'Good, that's good.' The solicitor peered over the top of his glasses. 'I think we can get started then, Detective.'

Jessie smiled at them both. She had news Rachel wasn't going to like. Since arriving at the station, the DNA results had come back positive – it was Rachel's hair. She had motive, opportunity and the evidence conclusively proved a link to her. Not to mention Rachel's history.

'Thank you,' Jessie answered then looked at Rachel. 'I have to inform you, Rachel Ferguson, that it is my intention to charge you with the murders of Jean and Malcolm Angus. Your DNA has been matched to the scene and your boots are a match to the prints found in the mud outside of their living-room window.'

Rachel's solicitor ripped off his glasses immediately. 'Detective, I should have been informed of this. My client is under the impression she is here to answer questions, that's all.'

Jessie shrugged and watched the panic grow on Rachel's face again, then sighed.

'No!' Rachel called out. 'It's not true. I haven't done anything. I wouldn't hurt them. I wouldn't – I couldn't – hurt anyone.'

She stood up, abruptly knocking her chair behind her before grabbing her solicitor's shoulder. 'You have to do something. How can my DNA be there?' Her voice grew louder the more desperate she got. 'I was nowhere near that house – that day or any other.'

'Rachel!' Jessie shouted. 'Sit down.'

Rachel released her grip on her solicitor and stared, red-faced, at Jessie before starting to pace around the small interview room. Jessie felt uncomfortable, suddenly threatened by Rachel's proximity to the back of her chair. It was clear this seemingly mild-mannered woman had two sides to her personality.

'Do as the detective says,' the solicitor advised. 'Come on, sit back down.'

'No, I won't sit down,' Rachel snapped. 'I haven't done this.'

Jessie had seen enough. 'Sit down or I'll have no choice but to restrain you.'

Rachel's eyes burst open wider with that threat.

'Thank you,' Jessie commented as she watched Rachel pick the chair back up and place it next to the table. She lowered herself gently opposite her. 'Let's start again, shall we?'

CHAPTER THIRTY-SIX

Kenny Ferguson tossed the ball for his dogs and watched the three of them bolt off in pursuit. Rachel had asked him not to follow her to the station. She would call or get her solicitor to if she wasn't allowed. He'd tried to protest but agreed. He didn't want to add to Rachel's stress.

He opened the gate into the paddock his wife wanted for training her horses. All that old couple had to do was agree. He couldn't understand what their problem was, though Kenny did fear that it was Malcolm's dislike of him. Kenny knew when someone didn't like him. He didn't let it stop him getting where he was today but he knew. Bullied mercilessly as a boy, Kenny was determined to succeed despite it all. His father had never wrapped him up in cotton wool, that was for sure.

Kenny turned at the sound of his name being called from the driveway. He waved and smiled when he saw her.

'Hello, Caroline. I'm so glad you came.'

Kenny unlocked the front door and held out his hand to allow her to go in first.

'Of course I was going to come. Why have the police taken Rachel in for questioning? It doesn't make any sense,' Caroline remarked.

'The police have—' He stopped to catch the lump that had appeared in his throat.

Caroline gasped. 'The police have *what*? Tell me.'

Kenny could only shake his head then turn away to hide his tears. 'I-I can't,' he stuttered.

Caroline lifted her hand to his face and lightly brushed her fingers over his cheek. 'You can tell me anything,' she whispered.

'The police have got evidence. DNA for one thing. I don't know what else exactly.' His voice trembled.

'But why – I mean, how? I know about your neighbours objecting to the planning application,' Caroline heard herself ramble.

'They were here, the police, searching the place,' Kenny struggled to continue.

Caroline gasped once again. 'Oh, Kenny, I'm so sorry. But they can't seriously think Rachel has done anything, can they?'

Kenny shrugged and squeezed his eyes shut. 'One of my guns is—' He stopped and bit back the words. He just couldn't say them.

'No!' Caroline looked appalled at what he was saying.

Kenny swallowed hard and stared at the look of horror on her face. Then he nodded. 'One of my guns is missing.'

The house phone rang before Kenny could say anything else.

'Hello,' Kenny answered, irritated by the silence that greeted his response. 'I said, hello.'

He was about to hang up when he heard the voice that was barely audible. He listened to what she had to say in horror and stared at Caroline, his eyes wide and his heart racing. Kenny couldn't speak. His face was white with shock as he dropped the phone.

CHAPTER THIRTY-SEVEN

1991

Rachel clutched her stomach and let out a guttural roar of agony. Then the flood of warm liquid trickled down her leg.

'What?' she whimpered and reached down to touch it just as a stronger gush of water rushed out of her and splashed onto the floor at her feet. 'Help! Help me!' she called out just as another wave of pain ripped into her stomach.

Her roommate Ella dried herself and slipped into her pyjamas then switched off the bathroom light. With the light off, the fan stopped whirring and she ran towards the cries she heard coming from her room.

'Rachel!' she shouted then dropped to her knees next to her. Rachel was now on all fours between the two beds in their small room.

'Help me!' Rachel cried out.

Ella leaped back up and fled.

'Don't leave me,' Rachel called after her as another wave of agony tore into her. 'Argh, God, please help me. Somebody help me. Come back!'

She felt her stomach tighten and nausea clawed her throat before she threw up on the floor at her side. She wiped her mouth on the edge of her duvet and was grateful when the pain began to subside. She fell back and propped herself up against the bed, then she heard footsteps running towards the room and the door burst open, thumping the bottom of the bed she rested on and jolting her back.

'Oh my goodness,' their foster mother cried out and clasped her fingers over her mouth. She stared at the puddle of water all over the carpet. 'Ella, go and phone for an ambulance, sweetheart.'

'What's happening to her?' Ella sobbed, fearing for her friend – the girl she'd come to think of as a sister.

'Just do it,' their foster mother snapped and grabbed hold of Rachel's hand. She stared into the teenager's frightened eyes and knew exactly what was happening.

'Help me!' Rachel screamed and grabbed her stomach as the pain returned.

'I need you to listen very carefully to me.'

Rachel's wide eyes hung on her every word as she battled against the agony.

'Do you understand what's happening, darling?'

Rachel burst into floods of tears and screamed. 'Yes, yes I know. I'm sorry; I should have told you.'

Her foster mother squeezed her hand. 'That doesn't matter now. I want you to concentrate on your breathing. The ambulance is coming and you're not alone.'

'I'm so scared,' Rachel murmured between pants. 'David should be with me.'

More warm liquid trickled out; this time rather than being clear it had a light brown tinge to it. Her foster mother tried not to show her fear. The sound of the ambulance sirens was the best sound she'd ever heard. Ella's heavy footsteps returned.

'That's the ambulance,' Ella announced. 'Don't worry, Rachel – help's arrived. You're going to be fine.'

Rachel stared up at her friend. Apart from David the only other friend she had ever had. Then it happened.

'Something's happening!' Rachel screamed. 'Ow, make it stop.' She reached down between her legs. 'There's something there.'

'OK, OK, shh, calm down. It's your baby's head. This is what's supposed to happen. Don't worry.'

'Don't worry?' Rachel grabbed hold of her foster mother's arm and dug her short nails into her flesh. '*Don't worry!* How can I *not* worry?' she screamed, droplets of spit escaping at speed and hitting her foster mother's cheek.

More footsteps thumped up the stairs and two paramedics burst into the small bedroom.

'Come on, Ella – we need to give them some space.' Their foster mother tried to pull Ella away, but Ella couldn't move. She watched in awe at the little head enter the world, followed by the bloody shoulders then the whole perfect tiny human that lay on the floor between her best friend's legs.

Rachel stared down, unable to comprehend what she saw. The paramedic wrapped her baby daughter in a towel and placed the tiny bundle into her arms.

'She's beautiful,' Rachel whispered.

Ella wiped away the tears that streamed down her freckled cheeks.

'What will you call her?' she asked.

Their foster mother was horrified to think of the conversation she would soon be having with Rachel about this baby's future.

CHAPTER THIRTY-EIGHT

Julia Dean tossed her bag onto the kitchen table as she lifted her feet out of her trainers. She ran her hand over the back of her neck. She needed to shower. Going for a run had helped a little. Running in bad weather made it feel like more of a workout – Julia's thinking time. Let's face it, there had been a lot to think about these past few months.

She tugged her earphones out and threw her phone onto the worktop. There was no message from Caroline. She didn't want to text her again – that would look too desperate. She would have to wait.

Julia opened the fridge and lifted out the carton of orange juice, disappointed to find it was almost empty. She scribbled the letters 'OJ' on her whiteboard above the fridge.

The buzzing on the worktop made her grab the phone in anticipation. She sighed when it was her mum's picture that came up on the caller ID.

'Hi, Mum,' she answered it. 'How are you?'

Julia balanced her iPhone between her ear and shoulder as she retrieved the butter and cheese from the fridge then laid them on the surface in front of her. 'Hang on, I'll have to put you on speaker. I'm making dinner.'

Julia listened to her mum's list of questions. The same list she asked every time she called. How was work? Are you eating enough fruit? Getting enough sleep? Have you met anyone?

The usual – fine, yes, yes and no seemed to be enough once again.

'How are you feeling, Mum?' Julia added.

'Oh, you know me. I'm just getting on with things. Nothing else for it, is there?' Her quiet voice filled the kitchen.

That always caught Julia off guard no matter how many times she heard it. Her mum's cancer treatment wasn't having the desired effect and her surgeon's optimism was diminishing.

'I thought I might come by this weekend. Let you feed me.' Julia grinned as she rubbed away the tear that had dripped onto her cheek. She listened to her mum's laughter followed by a long bout of coughing. 'Mum, you still there? You go and get some water. I'll call back later.'

Julia would go over for dinner this Sunday because there might not be many Sunday dinners left for them to enjoy. The fact that the two women were still mourning the loss of her dad made the cancer all the more cruel.

She poured water into her mug and stirred the teabag round briefly before tossing it into the bin. Julia was gasping for a good cup of tea. So much had happened in the past few hours.

She took her sandwich to the kitchen table and sat down to open her laptop. Her mouse hovered over the link to the newspaper article. She pulled her finger back and sipped from her mug, then rested her elbows on the edge of the table and dropped her chin onto her hands. Julia wanted to read it again. She really did. No matter how horrific it was.

She inhaled a huge breath and exhaled through her fingers before clicking the link. Julia struggled to comprehend the horror on the pages of the article. It didn't seem real, not for such a dark thing to happen in such a beautiful place.

Julia slammed down the lid of her laptop and sat back in her chair, swallowing down the repulsion that rose every time. She'd kept her secret for so long she thought she would burst.

CHAPTER THIRTY-NINE

Kenny hung up the phone in disbelief. The look of shock on his face alarmed Caroline.

'You're scaring me now,' she urged. 'Who was that?'

A single hot, stinging tear filled Kenny's eye. He rubbed it away with the back of his hand and pushed past her.

'I have to go; I have so much to organise.'

'Kenny.' Caroline rushed after him and grabbed hold of his arm. 'Tell me.'

Kenny stopped dead and turned to face her. 'That was Rachel.'

'What did she say?' Caroline asked. 'When is she coming home?'

Kenny frowned. 'Why would you ask that?'

Caroline blushed. 'I'm sorry, I didn't think – I don't know how these things work.'

'Forget it. I'll call you. I have to go and pick her up.'

Caroline followed him, tugging his shirt sleeve. 'Don't be silly – you're in no fit state to drive. I'll take you,' she suggested. 'Then I'll bring you both home.'

'No, I can't expect you to do that.'

Caroline ran her thumb over his wrist and smiled. 'I'll take you,' she whispered.

Kenny took firm hold of both of her hands and kissed one of them, his voice shaking with emotion as he said, 'Thank you.'

'I'm happy to help. You've both been so good to me.' She paused to wipe away her own tear. 'You must be relieved she's not being charged.'

Kenny shook his head. 'Rachel *has* been charged. She's been granted bail pending further investigations.' Kenny exhaled sharply between his fingers. 'Her mental health would suffer if she remained in custody, the doctor said. Thank God he spoke up for her! I could barely understand her on the phone she was sobbing so much.'

Caroline wrapped her arms around Kenny's wide shoulders and held on to him tight.

'It's OK, don't worry,' she attempted to reassure him. 'Let's just go and get her and bring her home.'

Kenny held on to her. She meant well, he knew that, but this wasn't looking good.

Caroline watched Kenny support Rachel's body with his as they walked back towards his Land Rover. They would have all been comfortable in her Mini so he suggested she could drive his car. Caroline loved driving it. It wasn't the first time he'd allowed her behind the wheel of one of his luxury vehicles but this Land Rover was by far Caroline's favourite. The personal number plate added that extra touch of class to the experience.

She hadn't been lying when she said they'd both been good to her. Caroline avoided talking about her life when she could but she had confided in Kenny once, mistakenly, that her childhood wasn't something she ever wanted to remember, which was the reason she no longer spoke to her adopted parents – preferring instead to tell people they were dead like she wished they were. Caroline had told him that he and Rachel were more like family to her than her own apart from her brother. She missed him dreadfully.

Rachel spotted Caroline in the driver's seat of Kenny's Land Rover and knew she should hate it. But she just didn't have the energy to hate Caroline Peters today. What she'd experienced in that interview was so much worse than the first time round. Back then she was a vulnerable teenager and they took pity on her, but that detective, Jessie Blake, had made it plain that she believed Rachel was guilty. She'd even looked disappointed when it was recommended that Rachel go home to be with Kenny rather than be held in custody. Rachel was so grateful to both her solicitor and that lovely doctor who'd spoken up for her.

She waved back at Caroline, who smiled in her direction. It was sweet of her to help them. She didn't have to; this certainly wasn't part of her job description. Maybe Rachel had underestimated the girl.

Caroline got out and opened the back-passenger door for Rachel.

'Hey,' she greeted her. 'Are you OK?' Caroline leaned forward and hugged her.

Rachel didn't have the strength to object.

'I'm fine, Caroline, thank you, and thank you for this. For driving Kenny to collect me.'

Caroline smiled and gave a slight shrug. 'He wasn't in a fit state to drive himself anywhere. The two of you need to get home and have a large nip of something. Come on – hop in.'

Rachel nodded and slid onto the back seat and tugged on the seatbelt. She was exhausted. All those questions. All the evidence they said they had against her, but she kept telling that detective she wasn't there so it *couldn't* be her hair or her footprints inside or outside the house. She didn't know where Kenny's gun was. She didn't want the Anguses dead. It wasn't worth killing them for a bit of land, was it? But that detective wasn't having any of it.

Kenny turned round see Rachel dozing on the back seat with her head resting against the window. Caroline glanced in the rear-view mirror to see what he was staring at.

'She must be exhausted,' Caroline whispered. 'A hot bath and an early night, I think.'

'That sounds perfect,' Rachel piped up and made Caroline blush.

'I'm sorry, I thought you were asleep.'

Caroline indicated onto the short farm track towards the house and could see the smoke rise from a distance.

'What the hell?' Kenny yelled and grabbed for his phone. 'Phone the fire brigade – *hurry!*'

Rachel listened to her husband's frantic call for help, unable to take her eyes off the flames that now rose into the sky. All she could think about was the horses.

'Hurry up!' Rachel screamed at Caroline. 'I have to get to the stables.'

Caroline accelerated until she came to a skidding halt close to the bungalow's drive. Rachel raced from the vehicle with her sleeve over her face to stop the smoke entering her lungs. She could hear the dogs barking furiously from the kennel block and Kenny ran past her to retrieve them.

Rachel could hear the horses kicking at their stable doors from outside the main door. They would be able to smell the smoke and they'd be scared. She had to get inside.

A loud bang came from the burning bungalow and she heard Caroline scream. Rachel opened the bolt on the stable door and rushed inside. She was quickly able to lead both of her precious racehorses outside and locked them in their paddock, away from the smoking ruin of her home. They were more important to Rachel than any building.

She walked backwards and allowed her weight to fall onto an upturned feed bucket and watched the flames lick and dance through her house. The sound and smell was terrifying.

Kenny struggled to contain the three terrified Labradors who strained against their leads in a bid to escape the chaos. Sirens blared over the sound of the crackling flames. Kenny stood silently next to his wife and Rachel reached up for his hand. A horrible thought slammed into her mind. The photograph. The only one she had of her daughter was gone forever. Lost in the flames. The designer clothes could be replaced but that precious photograph could not. Hot tears bubbled behind her eyes. Kenny's gaze met hers.

'I have to ask the two of you to move back,' the first firefighter called out to the dazed couple.

Rachel stood first and held tightly onto Kenny's hand. 'Come on. Let's get out of their way.'

Rachel took one of the dog's leads from him and began to move towards the paddock. Kenny followed behind in silence before the couple flopped down onto the grass and watched them tackle the blaze. Neither spoke. Instead they sat close together and held hands. First her arrest, now this. Surely her day couldn't get any worse? Forty-eight hours ago all Rachel had to worry about was getting Dexter ready for his upcoming race.

Kenny's eyes snapped wide open when he saw what the firefighter held in his hand as he walked out of the front door of the bungalow. The shock propelled him to his feet and he surged forward. It was scorched but unmistakable.

'Where did you find that?' he shouted.

'It was under the bed in the master bedroom, sir.'

Kenny turned back to see Rachel avoid his expression, her head now dropped into her hands as she shook it.

CHAPTER FORTY

Jessie poured a tall glass of Chardonnay for herself and one for Benito.

'What did you get up to today then?' she quizzed him. 'While I was hard at work.' She ended that teasing statement with a wide grin.

Benito laughed. 'I'll have you know I've been busy tidying up your kitchen. When did you last wash any dishes?'

Jessie laughed too. 'Can't remember to be honest but it's usually just me and the cat so not really a top priority.'

Jessie loved that Benito felt so at home in her place. His flat in Edinburgh was lovely but she still felt a little awkward in someone else's home. She always had. Jessie needed to be around her own things. Her stuff. On the rare occasions she visited her sister Freya, Jessie couldn't wait to get home. Hearing Benito talk about his sisters made her wish she and Freya were closer, but they weren't so she had to forget about it, didn't she? Benito and his sisters hadn't been raised like Jessie and Freya, though.

'Well, you have a cupboard full of clean plates now.'

'Thank you.'

For a split-second Jessie entertained the idea of reaching up and pulling him close to kiss him passionately on the lips – but only for a second. She lifted her wine glass to her lips instead and swallowed a large gulp before she did something she knew she would regret. Her mind was still trying to comprehend what

Dan had done for her. She knew that he never acted without a reason – there always had to be something in it for him.

Jessie's attention and her gratitude were much sought after by her ex-husband, she knew that. She had once been happy with Dan – before the control and manipulation, which evolved into violence. She should have seen it coming, really. What Jessie saw her mum live through – what they had all lived through – should have made her run a mile after Dan first raised his voice, let alone his fist. Haley McKenzie's smiling face kept popping into her head too. Jessie wondered how far into her journey Haley was. Perhaps he was still Mr Nice Guy with her.

Benito's words snapped Jessie out of her thoughts.

'Did you hear what I said?' Ben sipped his wine and grinned. 'You were miles away. Is everything OK?'

'What? No, I mean, yes, I'm sorry, I'm just—' she rambled and sipped from her glass. 'What was it you said?'

'How's the case going? I know it's a double murder,' Ben said.

Jessie could tell Ben wanted details. She supposed, like David Lyndhurst, Ben was never off duty.

'I've charged their neighbour with two counts of murder,' Jessie informed him.

Benito's eyes widened and he whistled through his teeth. 'Wow, that was quick.'

'Not you too.'

'Me too what?' Benito's gentle laughed filled the air between them.

'David Lyndhurst already suggested the evidence seems too convenient.'

'What do you think?' Ben asked. 'You're the detective.'

Jessie didn't hesitate. 'DNA, motive, opportunity and history of violence.'

'Murder weapon?'

'Still working on that one.' Jessie lifted her glass and walked away but not before she grabbed the bottle.

Later, as the two of them sat close together on Jessie's sofa, she realised it felt good. No, it was better than that – it felt right. The urge to kiss him rose again and if it wasn't for the buzz from her phone she thought she would really have gone through with it that time.

CHAPTER FORTY-ONE

1991

The pretty blonde midwife handed Rachel's baby back to her and smiled.

'She looks like you. She has her mum's big green eyes.'

Rachel thought she might still be in shock. That's what her foster mum had suggested earlier. Rachel suspected she was pregnant but hadn't told a soul. Not even Ella and she trusted her more than anyone.

She looked down at her daughter's yawning face and couldn't stop the smile that grew on her lips. She was beautiful. The midwife said she looked like Rachel but she didn't; she was the spitting image of her dad. Rachel wished she could speak to David. To tell him he was a father.

She turned at the sound of her room door opening.

'Hello, you two.' Rachel's foster mum walked in with another woman Rachel didn't recognise. Both women looked very serious. She didn't like the feeling she got from this other woman. She had a large bag with her. Bigger than any handbag Rachel had ever seen.

The midwife came when she was called and suggested she could take the baby to the nursery so the three of them could talk. Rachel didn't want to talk. She didn't think she wanted to listen either. The other woman was introduced as a social worker. Rachel hated social workers and something about this one didn't fill her with confidence. She was aware of the words 'it's for the best' and 'for both of you', but little else. They asked if she had any questions. Rachel couldn't think of any that made any sense. She shook her head. The woman placed a piece of paper on the table over her bed and pointed to two spots marked with a cross. Rachel lifted the pen. She must have signed it because the papers were swept away. The social worker left her room without saying another word. Rachel searched her foster mum's face for comfort.

'What's happening to my baby?' she murmured and felt hot tears erupt from her eyes. She heard her baby cry. Rachel's breasts leaked the milk her daughter was crying for. Again, the door opened and her baby was laid close to her breast to feed. The midwife helped the infant to latch on. The sensation filled Rachel's heart with pure love.

Her daughter glanced up into her eyes and gripped Rachel's finger while she suckled. Her foster mum took a photo for Rachel to keep. This wasn't the first time one of her girls had gone through this. She knew this photo would be important to them later.

CHAPTER FORTY-TWO

Jessie waved to Dylan as he pulled his Audi up outside her block of flats and glanced back at Benito waving to her from her window. She smiled back at him, a reflex she couldn't help. He made her feel the happiness that triggered it. Dylan was surprised to see the figure in the window and looked away before Jessie caught him staring. *Interesting,* he thought.

'I was hoping I wouldn't have to look at your ugly mug again until morning,' Jessie joked and pulled on her seatbelt.

'Oh, ha ha,' Dylan replied as he indicated out of her drive. He nodded at her Fiesta parked at the far end. 'You got that fixed quick. When did you get time to sort it out?'

Jessie was irked by his question. More so because she didn't want to admit how it had happened than his curiosity.

'You know me, I'm good at multi-tasking – like most women. Ask Shelly; she'll explain how it's done.' Jessie avoided eye contact while she said it and hoped he would leave it at that.

'Aye, watch me. I wouldn't dare ask her anything right now.'

Dylan's answer concerned Jessie. She found the timing of this investigation irritating because she wanted to spend time with Ben but for Shelly this must be harder. Christmas at home alone with two toddlers. Neither of them had any family that could help out either.

'Like that, is it?' she suggested. 'I can arrange for you to take some personal time if you need it. Family comes first, Dylan.'

She saw Dylan's shoulders droop.

'Thanks, Jessie. I appreciate that. I really do but forget I said anything. We're fine. It's just that Katie doesn't sleep well, that's all. Jack was so easy compared to his sister.'

'Well, if you change your mind, you know I'm always here,' Jessie told him right before they turned onto the A9 to head out to see the Fergusons'.

A text broke into the silence that had descended on the two detectives. Jessie reached down for her bag and rummaged for it.

'Everything but the kitchen sink in there, is it?' Dylan teased.

'Not quite,' she replied with a smile as she opened the text. She knew who the unknown number belonged to now so she should really delete it without reading it.

> *I wondered if you were free for coffee tomorrow. It's my day off. D*

Jessie shuddered. Ending his message with just the single letter 'D'. What did he think their relationship was? 'D' indicated intimacy to her. Benito ends his texts with 'B'. Jessie and Dan weren't friends; they never would be. And she still had to get to the bottom of who'd given him her number in the first place.

'Everything OK?' Dylan interrupted her musing.

'What? No, it's fine. It's not important.'

Jessie deleted Dan's message and stuffed her phone into her jacket pocket. The acrid smell of smoke hung in the air as they made their way up the drive to the Fergusons' destroyed bungalow.

'Jeez,' Dylan exclaimed. 'What a mess.'

Jessie sighed. He was right. The fire must have taken hold quickly but it wasn't the fire she was interested in. Rachel and Kenny had already been taken to a safe house. Even Jessie hadn't been given the location yet. Until the reason for the fire had been established it was safer for Rachel to be kept where she could be protected. Jessie argued that a cell was the best place for her but she'd been overruled on that again. She was pleased to see forensics had arrived and were already hard at work.

'Where was it?' she asked one of the forensic team who handed the bagged gun to her to look at.

'Under the bed.'

'Rachel's bed, I assume?'

He nodded as she handed it back to him. Jessie shook her head and exhaled loudly. It must have been put there after she'd searched the room because she would have seen it, wouldn't she? Sure, she'd been a bit distracted by finding out Haley's identity but still, Jessie wouldn't miss that – which begged the question: who'd put it there and why? Was it the same person who'd set fire to the property?

'What a mess,' Dylan commented and coughed to combat the smoke smell that hung in the air. 'Do you reckon it was the same person who made the threatening phone calls?'

'A bit of a coincidence if it wasn't, eh?'

'Aye, right enough but why?'

Jessie didn't answer. Instead she scanned the scene by turning a complete 360 degrees. The full moon sitting high above the property illuminated the scene to its maximum, in stark contrast to the black smoke that still billowed above them. Why try to burn it to the ground? What did that achieve?

CHAPTER FORTY-THREE

Arlene checked her watch before she got in her car. She wondered where Gordon was at this time of night. She found it weird being back in what was once their family home. She still had her key but only used it when she couldn't get an answer when she knocked. *Her family*. Tommy and Gordon were her family. It hadn't been all bad when she and Tommy were married, until his drinking spiralled out of control. But it wasn't just the drinking; it was the lies that hurt the most. Arlene began to distrust everything that came out of Tommy's mouth in the end. Then there was Gordon. Tommy had never backed Arlene up over her suspicions about Gordon's issues. Tommy preferred to bury his head in the sand or the nearest bottle of whatever alcohol he could get his hands on. The day she found out the extent of their debt had been the last straw.

Arlene waved and flashed a warm smile to her old neighbour who tugged her dressing gown tighter around her ample waist and nodded in Arlene's direction.

She checked her phone again and sighed when she saw there was no message from Gordon.

'Where are you, son?' She feared something had happened to him. Her son was vulnerable and he didn't have his dad to keep him in line. Every time she thought of Tommy lying there with tubes and wires sticking out everywhere a lump choked her throat. His body was already battered from the booze. He wasn't strong enough to fight this. Then there was Malcolm and Jean's funeral to organise. Arlene would have to take care of that, wouldn't she? There was nobody else. Gordon certainly couldn't do it.

It was no use; Arlene wouldn't be able to sleep if she went home. She got out and locked up her car and headed back inside the house to wait for her son. Once inside she spotted Gordon's laptop sitting on the coffee table.

'Gordon, are you here?' she called out into the empty house and frowned. Gordon never left his laptop out, not even in his room. She grabbed it and flipped open the lid. She was desperate. His privacy wasn't as important to her as finding him. Her mind went blank. No possible passwords sprung to mind. She wondered if she even knew her son at all.

Arlene had only closed her eyes for a minute. The last time she remembered checking the clock on the fireplace was 1 a.m.; Gordon still wasn't home. She rubbed sleep from her eyes. The clock now read 5.30 a.m.

Arlene sat up and yawned. She stared at the laptop again. If only she could access it. The answers must be in there. She grabbed her phone – still no messages. She got up and headed straight up to Gordon's room. The door was wide open but his bed had not been slept in and the curtains were still open from yesterday. She hit Gordon's number and listened to it ring his trademark six times before going to voicemail.

'Come on – pick up,' she urged.

Arlene hung up, thudded down the stairs and pressed the kettle on. She looked in the cupboard for the coffee. Typical, she thought. Tommy was out of it as usual. She checked the tea caddy and found one solitary tea bag stuck to the bottom of the tin. She needed a cuppa so she prised the precious bag out and rinsed a mug from the draining board to use – she couldn't guarantee how well it had been washed or indeed if any soap had been involved.

Arlene added the last thimbleful of milk from the fridge into her mug and sipped the hot, soothing liquid. Definitely supermarket own brand but drinkable. She would go and get a few bits in for them later. Tommy would be in no fit state to go shopping for a while. She decided then that moving back in was probably for the best too. Her boys needed her. At least she knew where Tommy was even if it was horrible to think of him there.

A text made her jump and she scrambled to check her phone.

'Shit,' she muttered and threw it onto the worktop. Damn Vodafone. 'I don't want to bloody upgrade. I want to know where my son is.'

CHAPTER FORTY-FOUR

When Jessie got home the previous night she had questioned exactly what she and Dylan had achieved by going to see the Fergusons' burnt-out property. They hadn't learned anything new but they now had the suspected murder weapon. She hoped forensics would come back to her with a match to the murder weapon quickly. If Rachel could be persuaded to confess that would make everything much simpler. On the phone late last night, Kenny had made it clear to Jessie that he wanted no stone left unturned in her pursuit of the person who had set fire to his home. He reminded her that they were victims. She assured him she understood perfectly.

'Detective Inspector, this lady says she needs to speak to you urgently.'

Jessie turned her head from the crime-scene photos of Jean and Malcolm Angus on the whiteboard to see an anxious Arlene Angus being directed towards her. She quickly closed a folder on the desk and stood up to open her office door wide.

'Hello, Arlene. What can I do for you?' The look on Arlene's face troubled her. 'Is it Tommy?'

Arlene shook her head. 'No, Tommy's OK – well, as OK as he can be for now.' She tried to smile. 'No, it's Gordon. He didn't come home last night.'

'OK, come on in and have a wee seat. When did you last speak to your son?'

Arlene pulled a tissue from her bag to wipe her nose. 'I'm sorry, I just can't seem to stop crying. Tommy used to complain I was overemotional.'

'Don't worry,' Jessie told her. 'Can I get you a cup of tea or coffee maybe?'

Arlene nodded. 'Coffee would be great.'

Jessie was about to leave her office and put the kettle on until she intercepted Dylan who had just arrived.

'Morning, Jess,' he said, beaming.

'Good morning, Dylan. Listen, could you make me a coffee and get one for Arlene Angus while you're there?'

'Arlene Angus,' he whispered.

Jessie answered with a simple nod and made her way back.

'Dylan is going to bring our coffees in,' Jessie told her.

'He's well trained.' Arlene tried to smile.

Jessie knew she shouldn't grin but couldn't help it. 'Aye, something like that, Arlene.'

After bringing in a tray of mugs and the packet of custard creams he'd found at the back of the cupboard, Dylan left and Arlene was free to express her fears to Jessie.

'Gordon is a vulnerable adult, Detective. You must agree with me on that surely.'

Jessie wasn't exactly sure how vulnerable he was. He'd managed to get hold of plenty of his grandparents' money no problem. He was clearly extremely intelligent. But his mum was worried and she knew Gordon better than anyone else.

'When did you last see or speak to him?'

'Last night at the hospital. He said he was going straight home. I wanted to spend a little bit more time with Tommy, you know, alone.' She swallowed back the tears that threatened to erupt again.

'How is Tommy?'

'He's getting there. There was a small bleed they had to drain but the operation went well, they said, so it's just a waiting game now, I suppose.' Arlene sniffed and wiped her face again. 'We won't know until they bring him out of the induced coma.'

Jessie sipped her coffee and allowed Arlene to continue. The woman looked like she had the weight of the world on her shoulders.

'I've left five messages for Gordon. It's not like him to ignore them. He doesn't like his phone to clog up with them.' Arlene gave a small wry chuckle. 'It's part of his condition. He needs things neat and tidy.' She sank half of her cup of coffee in two gulps. 'I'm sorry; I really needed that. Tommy was out, as usual.'

'I can get you another one if you need it.'

'No, no, don't worry. You've more important things to do than look after me.'

Jessie felt sorry for the woman who was now sobbing on the chair across from her.

'Look at the state of me. You must think I'm pathetic,' Arlene said, wiping tears from her eyes.

'Don't be daft; you're not pathetic at all and don't worry. I'll get a search under way for Gordon.' Jessie didn't add that she suspected Gordon of setting a fire.

'You'll need a recent photo.' Arlene scrolled through the pictures on her phone.

'No, it's OK – we have a photo of Gordon.'

Arlene's head snapped up. 'Why do you have a photo of my son?'

'OK, please calm down, Mrs Angus and I'll explain.'

Arlene interrupted before Jessie could go any further.

'I think the fact that the police have a photo of my son is a good excuse to be anything but calm, don't you, Detective?'

Jessie sensed the anger rise in Arlene's tone.

'Arlene, there's no need to get worked up—'

'*Worked up?* Oh, you've no idea what worked up is! Do you have kids, Detective?'

Jessie hated this question more than any other. What she really wanted to do was scream, 'Yes, I had a son but he was killed!' Instead she chose the easy answer every time.

Jessie shook her head. 'No, I don't.'

'Well, you have no right to lecture me about anything.'

Jessie raised her hands. 'You're right, but if you'll just let me explain—'

Jessie watched Arlene's anger wither as quickly as it had developed. The woman clearly had a temper.

'Gordon's behaviour up at the farmhouse was…' Jessie searched for a word that would cause the least offence.

'Odd?' Arlene suggested. 'Weird, mental, freaky. I've heard them all.'

'I was about to say it gave me cause for concern.' Jessie was pleased she'd found such a diplomatic answer. 'Then he walked out and disappeared just as Tommy lashed out at our forensic pathologist.'

Arlene was visibly shocked and covered her cheeks with both hands. 'I'm so sorry. Is he OK?'

'Yes, it was just a scratch,' Jessie reassured her.

'But you thought Gordon might have done it. Murdered his grandparents, I mean.'

Jessie chose her next words very carefully.

'His behaviour was suspicious, I have to admit.'

'What was he doing?'

Jessie tried to discourage her. 'I'm not sure that's really relevant.'

'Please tell me,' Arlene pleaded.

Jessie looked into Arlene's eyes – the eyes of a desperate mother who was scared to death that something had happened to her son. Her flesh and blood. Arlene had already seen her husband close to death. She was clinging to anything Jessie offered her.

'He was eating a sandwich. Right next to Malcolm's body. And his demeanour was almost happy – as if he was distanced emotionally from what had happened to his grandparents.' Jessie hated saying that. It sounded so horrible and cold. Arlene didn't look surprised.

'Thank you,' she whispered. 'I appreciate your honesty – without recoiling in horror, that is. I've had that so many times over the years.'

'You're welcome.'

The two women sat in silence until Arlene's phone rang, startling them both.

'Gordon, where have you *been*?'

Jessie's eyes widened as she listened.

'Slow down; I can't understand what you're saying,' Arlene shouted down the phone. 'Gordon, are you still there? Gordon?'

Jessie's alarm increased the more urgent Arlene's voice became.

'Gordon,' she cried out again. 'Gordon, are you still there?'

Arlene pulled the phone away from her ear.

'Where is he?' Jessie urged.

'I don't know.'

'Did he say anything?'

Arlene clasped her hand over her mouth and paced back and forth. 'Oh God, oh God, what if he's hurt?'

Dylan became aware of the raised voices and rushed to Jessie's office.

'Is everything all right in here?' he shouted.

Jessie could only shrug. She had no idea what had upset Arlene like that, but she wasn't about to find out any time soon as Arlene grabbed her bag and sprinted away from them.

'You want me to go after her?' Dylan asked.

Jessie leaned her head back and peered out of her window to see which car Arlene got in. She scribbled down her registration number then handed the paper to him. 'No, leave her. Give that to the boys in traffic. Tell them to see where she's gone but not to approach for now. I just want to see what she's up to.'

CHAPTER FORTY-FIVE

'Gordon, what have you done?' Arlene's shock was plain to see, despite how hard she tried to hide it from him. 'Come here, son.' She leaned forward to pull him into her arms. It was a reflex action she couldn't stop.

Gordon stepped back – his reflex action. Gordon's retreat was a gentle reminder of the emotional distance that would always be between them. Instead Arlene peeled her arms out of her jacket and draped it loosely around Gordon's shoulders to stop his shivering. He looked like he'd seen a ghost, his eyes wide and staring.

Arlene held out her hand and Gordon walked on ahead of her towards her car. Mother and son drove in silence. Arlene was forced to swallow down the screams that were stalking her throat. They built from the heart of her stomach. It was obvious what he'd done – she could smell it on him. She thought he'd stopped starting fires long ago.

The blue light of the police car behind her was joined by the short blink of the siren. The road wasn't busy. He would be able to pass easily but Arlene pulled in anyway. They couldn't possibly suspect her of anything.

Arlene's attempt at a confident smile failed miserably and she prayed the young officer couldn't see her legs trembling.

'Hello, Officer,' she said. 'What's the problem? I don't think I was speeding, was I?'

The tall, blonde traffic officer bent down and glanced past Arlene and her heart sank. *That detective had them follow me.* The realisation slammed into Arlene and it hurt. She felt guilty that she'd effectively led the police to her son.

'Would you mind stepping out of the car and following me, madam?' He looked back across at Gordon, whose pale piercing eyes peered out from under his long black fringe.

'Why?' Gordon asked.

'Could you just please switch off your engine and step out of the vehicle?'

Arlene gripped the steering wheel until she saw the whites of her knuckles stare up at her.

No, you're not taking my son.

She glanced at Gordon now playing on his phone then slammed her car into reverse and left the young officer standing at the side of the road, desperately calling for help into his radio.

What the hell have I done? She feared she'd just made the biggest mistake of her life. Her heart raced but Gordon remained emotionless in the passenger seat checking his Facebook account. Arlene's heart couldn't beat any faster if it tried, she feared. She felt sick to her stomach. What the hell had she just done?

CHAPTER FORTY-SIX

Kenny Ferguson handed his wife a cup of strong tea. He knew she hadn't slept much at all last night. Neither had he. He'd heard her get up a couple of times. He'd heard her crying too. Kenny had a meeting today that he couldn't put off, but he hadn't plucked up the courage to tell Rachel yet. The little place the police had put them up in wasn't too bad but it wasn't home.

'Thank you,' Rachel said, her eyes almost glued shut. She yawned.

'Why don't you have another forty winks, sweetheart? You look exhausted.'

'Thanks.' Rachel tried to smile. 'You don't look that brilliant yourself.'

Kenny perched his hefty frame on the edge of the double bed, which felt more like a single compared to his extra king size back at home. The one he used to own that was. It was probably just ashes now. The flames must have taken hold quickly to have caused such devastation in that relatively short time. He reached out and pressed Rachel's fringe out of her eyes. She'd looked so scared when she'd walked out of that police station. Thank God she wasn't remanded in custody. Kenny was terrified of what that would do to her.

Rachel allowed his fingers to stroke her forehead. She closed her eyes again. It felt good, good to have human contact. They lived such separate lives these days and until now that had suited Rachel fine. But she needed Kenny. She was scared – terrified they would find her guilty and lock her up. For good this time.

'Listen, I have to pop out for a bit this morning.'

Rachel sat bolt upright on hearing his comment.

'What do you mean you have to pop out? We have so much to sort out. The insurance and the—'

Kenny grabbed hold of her hands.

'We can't do anything about the insurance until the investigation is complete. It was probably arson, sweetheart.'

Rachel had tried to put that thought out of her head. It was a simple accident, she'd tried to convince herself.

'But where do you have to be that's so important? What about me?' Rachel cried.

Kenny stood and started to walk away. Rachel attempted to grab hold of his wrist but missed and fell forward onto the bed.

'Kenny,' she called after him. 'Answer me.'

Kenny Ferguson closed the bathroom door on his wife's pleas, then closed his eyes and leaned his head back on the bathroom door. He inhaled a huge breath as he listened to her continue to call out for him then exhaled slowly through the hand that was covering his mouth to stifle the scream that wanted to erupt violently from his lips.

CHAPTER FORTY-SEVEN

1991

Rachel ignored her calls for the fourth time. There was no way she was getting up out of this bed, let alone dressing and getting on that school bus. No way in hell that was happening. She had only been back at school for a week before she'd decided enough was enough. School had nothing to offer her. Not after what she'd been through. She struggled to get her daughter's beautiful face out of her mind. The way she smelled; her soft skin and sweet baby breath. She'd called her daughter Angela, after her own mum. She wondered what her mum would say about being a grandmother. Rachel had been informed by social services that her new family would probably want to call her something else but she would always be Angela to her.

'Rachel, I'm not going to tell you again,' the voice boomed at her from the bottom of the stairs. 'Hurry up or you'll miss the bus.'

'Good,' Rachel muttered and pulled the duvet back over her head. Then the footsteps banged up the stairs before the room door burst open and the duvet was abruptly pulled back.

'I asked you to get up,' her foster mum pleaded. 'Now I'm telling you – come on.'

Rachel tugged her nightshirt over her legs and turned to face the wall. 'I'm not feeling well.'

'What's up, pet?'

'My stomach hurts. Ladies' trouble.'

Her foster mother sighed. Rachel wasn't for shifting. She'd give the counsellor a call. See if she could fit her in today. She gently covered her back with the duvet. Rachel grabbed it and enveloped herself back in its warmth then smiled.

'I'll go and give the school a call. I'll bring you up some toast and orange juice in a bit.'

'Thanks,' Rachel answered from deep inside her duvet cocoon. A little guilt bubbled in her stomach where she'd told her the pain was.

Rachel was glad to hear the footsteps retreat but before she could doze off she heard a voice down the hall, the words echoing up to her room. *Great*, she sighed. *Another talking session.*

Rachel said nothing the whole ride to the office. These appointments were pointless. She leaned her head against the passenger-side window as the ten-year-old Ford Escort rumbled up the steep hill towards the psychiatric hospital and parked in the grounds of the Children's and Adolescents' Mental Health Service building. The apple trees outside the front door were heavy with fruit this time of year, some branches bowed with the weight. They'd said Rachel could help herself last time, which she did. She stuffed half a dozen in her bag for her and Ella to scoff later too.

'Right, come on then.' Her foster mum smiled, the crow's feet around her soft blue eyes crinkling as she spoke.

Rachel sulked as she got out of the car and pulled her Bon Jovi T-shirt further down to cover her bum, which she felt was way too big now.

Her foster mother gave her name to the slim, pretty blonde receptionist who looked to Rachel like that supermodel Linda Evangelista with her big eyes and skinny frame.

'Take a seat, Dr Carr will be with you in a minute.'

Rachel forced a smile before she sat down next to the huge bucket of Lego bricks and table full of *Beano* and *Dandy* magazines.

Classical music piped from a speaker mounted high in the corner of the room, which was once a drawing room in the Victorian-era building. The ceilings were so high Rachel wondered where they kept the ladder they needed for changing the CD every time.

'Hello.' The doctor beamed as she approached. 'Come on through.'

Rachel sighed and walked with her shoulders drooping into the psychologist's bright, airy consulting room. The walls of the room were painted a pale blue with light pink butterflies stencilled over it. Even the lampshade had butterflies on it. Rachel knew Ella would love this décor. She loved pastels and pinks. But flamingos were her favourite. Rachel painted on that smile again as she flopped down on the pink-and-white polka-dot beanbag.

'It's been a couple of weeks since I last spoke to you,' Dr Carr began. 'How are things?'

'Don't know,' Rachel said and shrugged without looking up from picking at her leather bracelet.

'How's school?' Dr Carr persisted. 'I hear you've not been feeling up to going lately. Has something happened?'

Has something happened? Rachel wanted to scream. *Apart from my baby being stolen from me, not much.*

Instead she shrugged. 'Just not been feeling great.'

'Do you feel like telling me how you feel? Can you describe it?'

Rachel picked at the frayed edge of the bracelet while she tried to think of a way to describe her feelings. She could hear the music from the waiting room drift into the room. She sighed then answered without looking at the doctor.

'Empty,' she said. 'I feel empty.'

'What does empty feel like?'

Rachel finally stared at Dr Carr and shrugged at her response. 'I dunno. You tell me.'

Dr Carr smiled a little. 'I can't tell you how you feel. Only you know that.'

So many flipping questions. Rachel stood up from the beanbag and clutched the dull ache that was growing in her stomach. *Period – great.* She moved closer to the window behind Dr Carr's chair.

'The trees look lovely when they're so heavy with fruit, don't they?' the doctor commented as she joined Rachel.

'But they'll soon be empty too, won't they?'

CHAPTER FORTY-EIGHT

Rachel opened the door to find the officer standing on the doorstep next to a welcome familiar face. One of Kenny's drivers – the first female driver in the company's history.

'It's fine, Officer, but thank you.'

Rachel ushered Julia Dean inside the flat; she'd been informed an unauthorised person had tried to get access to her, and while she'd been a little taken aback when she'd been told who it was, she was pleased to see her anyway.

'I'm sorry to just turn up like this but when Caroline told me what happened and where you were I wanted to see if there was anything I could do.'

Rachel wasn't surprised to hear either that Caroline had told her or that Julia wanted to help.

'No, I'm delighted to see you, to be honest.' Rachel tidied away the dinner dishes. 'Excuse the mess.'

Julia looked at the few plates lining the worktop and smiled. 'Listen, I hope you won't be offended but I've taken the liberty of putting a few bits together for you since your things are—' She stopped. 'Well, you know, I just thought you might need some bits.' She held out the carrier bag for Rachel. 'It's not much.'

Rachel took the bag and glanced inside. 'That was so thoughtful of you. Thank you.' She turned to switch the kettle on. 'You'll stay for coffee? Decaf, I promise.'

Julia wanted nothing more than to stay but couldn't tell Rachel that.

She nodded as she sat down on one of the kitchen chairs. Her eyes narrowed at the papers in front of her before Rachel quickly tidied them away. 'Sure, that would be nice.'

Julia blushed at the text that buzzed. She couldn't answer his message while she was here. The irony of that wasn't lost on her.

'Is everything OK?' Rachel asked as she laid a cup of coffee in front of her guest then pulled the milk from the fridge. 'Do you like milk and sugar?'

'Just milk, thanks.' Julia stuffed her phone deep into the pocket of her khaki cargo trousers and crossed her legs. 'This is a nice little flat,' she commented in order to change the subject.

Rachel laid the milk carton down on the table then sat down. 'It could be worse.' She sighed.

Julia sipped the coffee then licked her lips. 'Have you got any idea about how the fire started?'

Rachel shook her head. 'The horses and the dogs were fine, though. That's the most important thing.'

Rachel seemed very calm for a woman accused of a double murder, Julia decided. Julia's ringtone sounded from her pocket and she watched a warm smile spread across Rachel's lips.

'He's persistent,' Rachel commented. She obviously thought it was a boyfriend.

Her comment made Julia smile in response. 'You could say that,' she admitted and retrieved the phone and switched it to silent.

'Have you known him long?'

'Erm.' Julia avoided Rachel's emerald-green eyes this time. 'Kind of, I guess.'

Rachel grinned. 'That's nice. I'm happy for you.'

Julia shook her head. 'It's not like that. We're— It's not what you think.'

Rachel lifted up her hand to wave away her protest. 'Don't be embarrassed.'

'Really, it's not what you think,' Julia insisted. 'He's not a boyfriend.'

The room started to feel very small to Julia suddenly. She feared she would say something or give something away. The time wasn't right – not yet.

'I'm sorry, it's none of my business,' Rachel replied and stood to pour water from the kettle into her mug. 'It was just nice to talk about something other than—' She stopped herself before the tears erupted.

Julia watched her tug a tissue from her sleeve to wipe her nose and wanted to hug her and tell her it was going to be fine, but the truth was she couldn't, could she? Julia didn't know. She couldn't see into the future.

'I'm sorry; I didn't mean to upset you,' Julia commented. That was the only thing she felt able to say. 'I'll leave you in peace; you must have things to organise.' She stood up from the table and handed Rachel her mug. 'Thanks for the drink.'

Rachel reached out and took the half-drunk cup of coffee from her. 'You're welcome.'

Julia grabbed her jacket from the back of the chair and scratched at her cropped brown hair. She could have kicked herself for being unable to find something more useful to say. She'd rehearsed the words so much on the way over there.

She waved to Rachel and stood briefly to see the door close after her. She nodded to the police officer in his patrol car and lifted her helmet from the motorbike she'd parked not far from him. Her phone vibrated in her pocket. She pulled it out to look at the caller ID and smiled. Rachel was right. He was persistent and she didn't blame him.

CHAPTER FORTY-NINE

Jessie had literally just opened the front door and called out to Ben when her phone rang. She kicked off her boots, switched on the hall light and grabbed the short note Ben had left on her hall table as Smokey curled his body around her legs. She was disappointed but understood completely. Murder doesn't stop in Edinburgh either just because it's Christmas. He didn't go into details but being a forensic pathologist meant Ben was needed elsewhere. She got the impression it was a big one, though. She picked her phone out from deep in her coat pocket and frowned. She'd just left the station fifteen minutes ago.

'DI Blake,' she answered and listened in horror. 'You are kidding me? Yes, thanks for letting me know.'

It didn't surprise her to hear of the officer's description of the smell that filled Arlene's car as he'd leaned in. The stench of petrol was thick, he explained. *Of course it was Gordon. But why?*

Jessie considered slipping her feet right back into her boots and heading straight back to the station. She'd sent Dylan home for the night. He should be with his kids. She put down her phone, pressed the switch on the kettle down and walked through to her bedroom.

'What is it, Smokey?' She reached down for the cat, the hair on his neck standing on end and his back arched. 'You silly thing, what are you doing?' She lifted him into her arms and held him close so he could nuzzle his face into her cheek. When he started purring she gave him one simple kiss on his forehead and allowed him to leap from her arms, landing on her bed before jumping down and running from her room. She was about to open her wardrobe for a clean shirt when her phone buzzed again from the hall table.

It was no use. She might as well be back at the station. She wouldn't sleep now. Not with all this going on. This investigation was consuming her thoughts twenty-four hours a day but Jessie didn't mind, not really. Malcolm and Jean Angus deserved nothing less than her one hundred per cent attention.

Jessie slipped her feet back into her boots and grabbed for her keys then rushed back down to her car.

Dan finally allowed himself to breathe after having to abort his mission so quickly. That was close. He hadn't expected Jessie home so soon. He was sure she was busy at the station when he'd arrived at her flat. Getting in through the back-bedroom window was so much easier than he'd anticipated. That had been a pleasant surprise. All he wanted was to get to know her better: this new Jessie. This confident woman she'd become. He liked her. All he was going to do was look. He wouldn't have taken anything. That wouldn't have been right.

CHAPTER FIFTY

'Dylan, what are you doing here?' Jessie asked as she slung her coat and scarf onto the back of her chair.

'Och, I thought you needed me here.'

His answer might have been one sentence but Jessie got the feeling there was more to it.

'Everything OK?'

'What? Yes, sure, of course. Everything's fine. What makes you say that?'

Dylan's defensive posture troubled her but it was none of her concern. She didn't want him in her business so she should stay well out of his.

'Arlene and Gordon are, or at least were, in the wind albeit briefly. The traffic officer who stopped her car said there was a strong smell of petrol coming from one or both of the occupants. Now, Arlene was with me for a period of time but that doesn't rule her out completely as the person who started the fire at the Ferguson property.'

'Why, though, boss? What did she have to gain?'

'I don't know and sure, Gordon looks more like our arsonist to me.'

Dylan nodded at Jessie's suggestion. 'Absolutely. Psychopath behaviour, isn't it? Do you think he's done it before – started fires, I mean?'

Jessie could only shrug. She didn't have any evidence of that but there was so much she didn't know about Gordon Angus. Sure, the evidence all pointed to Rachel Ferguson having murdered her neighbours but Jessie's conversation with Arlene Angus had contained far more than mere words. Both detectives stared at each other.

'Is he capable of murder?' Dylan suggested.

Jessie wanted to scream, 'Hell yes,' but resisted. They need evidence to convict a killer and right then the evidence conveniently pointed in Rachel Ferguson's direction.

Jessie opened the text that buzzed into her phone.

'Arlene's car has been located abandoned close to Kinnoull Hill.'

'Christ,' Dylan said. 'You reckon they're going to jump?'

'I wish I knew. There's a team heading up there. Nothing obvious. We don't want to spook them into doing something daft.'

'Gordon's clever, Jessie. He'll know that car being there will send you after them.'

Jessie listened intently. 'Go on.'

'I think they've parked up there to put us off the scent of their real location. I think they're headed back to Perth.'

'The hospital!' Jessie exclaimed.

CHAPTER FIFTY-ONE

1991

Dear David,

I hope that you're doing OK. I'm not sure what I want to say to you but it feels like I might burst without you. They've told me all sorts of horrible things about you. You know I don't believe them. I promise. I have to see this doctor to talk about my feelings but it's you I want to talk to, not them. I still miss you and our daughter. One day we'll be a family. I know that with all my heart. I've been counting the days until I can see you again. Until I can be in your arms again. I hope that you've been getting these letters. I know you're not allowed to contact me in response. My social worker explained that ages ago. It's so unfair. I'm out here and you're in there. They can't keep us apart forever. Just let them try.

Anyway, I have to go for now.

Love you

Alice x

Rachel's foster mother exhaled slowly again. The fact she'd signed the letter as Alice made the discovery even worse. The girl was clearly unwilling to accept David had abused her. She was seething that she hadn't been told that her foster daughter had been trying to send letters to David since their baby was born. Every one of the letters had been intercepted, thankfully.

'How long has this been going on?' She lifted the single sheet of writing paper close to Rachel's cheek.

Rachel wanted to scream. It was none of her business. Hadn't they already stolen their baby from them? What was the harm in a few letters?

'It's none of your business!' she blasted and tried to barge past until the bedroom door was slammed shut to stop her leaving the room.

'You're going nowhere until we talk about this.'

'What is there to talk about? I'm writing letters to the man I love.'

'Rachel.' Her foster mother lowered her voice. 'We've talked about this, sweetheart.'

'No!' Rachel roared in her face. '*You've* talked about it. I was just supposed to listen and nod like a good little girl.' She stormed back past her and slumped onto her bed in a sulk. 'Well, I'm not a little girl. I haven't been for a very long time.'

Her foster mother perched on the edge of the bed. Rachel was proving to be a hard nut to crack. The information she'd been given was that she was a mixed-up teenager who had been manipulated and groomed since she was thirteen by a man who'd coerced her into committing a horrible crime. But Rachel really seemed to love this man. Her idea that he loved her was fixed and unshakeable. She was still infatuated with him. He continued to have some kind of hold over her even today; all these months later.

'I know you feel all grown up,' she tackled her gently, 'but there are things you don't understand, sweetheart. What David did to you…'

'David didn't do anything *to* me.' Rachel's frustration increased. 'I wanted to do what we did. Don't you get it? Does nobody get it?' She slammed her fist into the mattress. 'We love each other!' she roared.

Her foster mother was helpless to stop her body from falling backwards onto the floor when Rachel slammed into her. She struggled to catch her breath, winded by the force. Stunned by her outburst.

'Rachel, get back here.'

Rachel had to run. She was terrified by what she'd done, not to mention what she'd wanted to do. The rage she'd felt inside the day she'd murdered her grandparents had returned. She had to get out of there.

'David,' she whimpered and rubbed stinging hot tears from her cheeks as she ran.

CHAPTER FIFTY-TWO

Arlene Angus was sitting on one of the black plastic chairs next to Tommy's bed when Jessie and Dylan arrived. Jessie stared past her slumped figure but there was no sign of Gordon.

'He's not here,' Arlene informed her without looking up. Instead she reached for Tommy's hand and kissed it then rubbed the single tear that had dripped onto the tip of her nose.

Jessie nodded to Dylan to leave them alone.

'Sure,' he whispered and moved away from the door to the ICU. He lifted his phone from his pocket to read a text while he walked. He sighed and stuffed it away without answering.

'Where is he, Arlene?' Jessie pulled up a chair next to her and sat down, keeping her voice low out of respect for the other patients in the bay.

'He's safe,' Arlene informed her without looking at her.

'Safe from what?'

'Everything,' she whispered.

Jessie saw the pain in Arlene's face. The straight-talking approach wasn't going to work here. She opted for a subtler way to get through to her. 'You're a good mum.' Jessie spoke gently; allowing her words to filter slowly through.

This statement made Arlene look up. Jessie's hunch had been right.

'Am I?' Arlene responded.

Jessie nodded. 'You love Gordon and you want to protect him. Nobody can blame you for that.'

'I do, I really do.'

'He's very lucky to have you,' Jessie added and dropped her hand on Arlene's. 'Very lucky.'

'Thank you.'

Jessie allowed the silence to settle between them. What she'd said wasn't a lie. Gordon was damn lucky. Everything he'd ever done must have been fixed by his mum. She figured Arlene had covered up so much for him. She could tell Arlene thought her son had murdered his grandparents and that it terrified her more than anything he'd ever done before.

'Where is he?' Jessie whispered. 'I promise I'll take care of him.'

Arlene stared then snatched her hand back from her. 'You couldn't possibly understand.'

'Try me.'

'I don't think so, Detective Inspector.' Arlene's mood changed in an instant. 'I have nothing further to say to you. Now, if you don't mind, I want to spend time with my husband. Tommy needs to rest.'

Jessie looked back at the ICU doorway and waved Dylan inside. She got up to walk away to the sound of Dylan's voice. It was the only way. Arlene was trying to obstruct Jessie's investigation into Gordon's involvement at the very least – but goodness knows what else she'd done to protect her son. Dylan moved forward and took hold of Arlene's arm.

'Arlene Angus, you are under arrest for attempting to defeat the ends of justice.'

CHAPTER FIFTY-THREE

Rachel had been walking for so long she'd lost track of time. Slipping away from the officer who'd been posted outside their door – mainly for her and Kenny's protection – was easier than she'd anticipated although it had been explained she wasn't under house arrest. It just felt like it. The thought of having to explain to him where she was going and why irked her. She was on bail. They hadn't convicted her yet; Rachel was still a free woman for now. Kenny hadn't told her where he was going and she'd pleaded with him not to go. Couldn't he see she was struggling? Her whole world had been turned upside down – again. This time she'd lost everything she'd worked so hard for all these years. Her beautiful home. *What if they'd been inside? Was it an attempt to murder her? Revenge perhaps.*

The huge moon lit up the night sky as she wandered. She tightened her thick down jacket around her against the cold night air. She had no idea where she was going. So many thoughts fought for space inside her clouded mind that she struggled to focus on what to do next. There was so much work to do to fix their home but Kenny had told her the police would want to finish their investigation first. The structural engineer would have to come in to make the property safe. Would they even be able to live there again? What if they said it had to be torn down?

Noise from the pub on South Street caught her attention. She squeezed her purse in her pocket and pulled open the door. The noise of laughter smacked her in the face and it felt good; a distraction from the fear that was growing inside her. The smell of beer and floral notes from the perfume that filled the air made her smile.

'What can I get you?'

The lad behind the bar looked about twelve to Rachel as he smiled, his straight white teeth glinting in the low lighting of the bar.

'I'll take a glass of red wine, please,' she said. 'What kind of crisps have you got?'

He stood back and showed her the selection behind him then checked his watch. 'Kitchen shuts in half an hour if you're looking for something hot.'

Rachel became aware of the rumbling in her stomach. 'I'd love a burger.'

'You want fries with it?'

Rachel smiled and screwed up her nose. 'Yes, please. That would be lovely.'

'Coming right up.' The young bar man turned to place her order with the kitchen before handing her a tall glass of red wine.

'Thank you.' Rachel slipped out of her coat and laid it across the stool next to her. The bar was lovely and hot compared to the freezing temperatures outside. The red wine, slipping smoothly down her throat, filled her body with warmth. It was just what she needed.

She became aware of a television blinking at the far end of the bar, subtitles instead of sound for patrons who wanted to watch the 10 p.m. news. She was aghast to see the BBC Scotland reporter she recognised standing close to her home. Rachel was shocked to find the fire at her home newsworthy until the words *possible connection to the senseless murder of elderly couple Malcolm and Jean Angus* followed by *person of interest helping police with their enquiries. No more details at this stage* slid across the bottom of the screen.

A sudden flush of heat enveloped her followed by a quick, freezing chill that made her shiver. She glanced nervously around the bar area, terrified someone had seen her reaction and figured out that she was their 'person of interest'. Perhaps they could even see who Rachel really was? She had to really concentrate on her breathing. In. Out. In. Out. Focus your eyes on a central point. That's what she'd been taught.

One of the antique mahogany pillars at the end of the bar came into view and Rachel's eyes alighted on it while her heart thudded. In. Out. In. Out.

That's it; you can do it. Rachel could hear a familiar voice inside her head. A voice she hadn't heard for a very long time. Ella. Rachel's panic attacks began in her teenage years and it was her roommate Ella who'd been the soothing voice that could calm a storm. *Ella.* Rachel hadn't thought of her for a long time. Ella had left the foster home to go off to university and the two friends had barely kept in touch. Last Rachel heard she was a doctor living in East Kilbride with her wife and a son from a disastrous marriage to a banker in Edinburgh. Despite their close friendship, Ella had never confided in Rachel what had happened to her prior to the foster home and Rachel had respected her privacy. She had enough on her own plate anyway.

'Here you go.' The bartender startled her when he handed her a plate stacked high with a huge burger roll filled with lettuce and assorted other toppings. The bowl of fries to accompany it looked like it was there to feed a family of four and some. 'Can I get you any sauces or salt or pepper?' He smiled and held her gaze. His eyes were kind. Rachel didn't know why that thought popped into her head.

'Em, no, no, thank you – I'm fine,' she answered. 'Looks delicious.'

'Enjoy.'

Rachel nodded before realising her panic had passed. Nobody knew who she was. She was just another stranger, sitting in a bar, eating a burger. Rachel felt anonymous and she loved it.

Her ringtone played quietly in her jeans pocket and the vibration made her jump. It was Kenny.

'Hi, honey,' Rachel answered with a mouthful of hot, salty fries. She listened to his concerns and thought he was sweet but she felt freer than she had for a considerably long time. She had no intention of heading home yet.

CHAPTER FIFTY-FOUR

Arlene's solicitor had managed to persuade a reluctant Jessie that keeping Arlene locked up would do more harm than good. Having her outside where Gordon could contact his mother was a much better idea, didn't she agree? Gordon was the main suspect in the arson attack on the Ferguson property. Didn't she want to use the best chance they had of catching him before he did something worse? The solicitor's words rung in Jessie's ears as she dried her hands in the station bathroom. He was right; of course he was. Keeping Arlene locked up served no real purpose other than making Jessie feel better after being treated like a fool.

'Do you need me for anything else, boss?' Dylan appeared from around the corner from the bathroom.

'No, you get off home to those gorgeous kids.' Jessie began to walk past until she became aware that Dylan hadn't moved. 'Is everything OK?'

'Yes, sure.' He started to move off. 'See you in the morning.'

Jessie yawned as she lifted a hand to wave him off. She moved to the whiteboard and removed the lid from her marker, then drew a circle around the photo of the smiling couple. Taken on a recent anniversary, she'd been told. She drew a line from them and wrote the name Rachel Ferguson and made a list of reasons to believe her guilty of their murder. Her hair. Her boot print. Her motive. Her history. Sure, the evidence was pushing her towards Rachel's guilt, but the nagging doubt that it was a little too convenient kept creeping into the back of Jessie's mind. 'Trust your gut,' she'd been told by her first guv'nor and he was usually right.

Gordon starting fires. Interest in serial killers. His obsession with Rachel and her real identity. In her crime. Psychopath. The way he sat so coolly next to his grandfather's dead body.

She added a line on the opposite side of the smiling couple's face and wrote their grandson's name. The thought that *he*'d done it seemed worse somehow. She'd arranged a team to keep an eye on Arlene's movements to see if Gordon got in touch. Her hand lingered over the board until she drew the third line.

The couple's son, Tommy Angus. As pathetic a sight as he was now, that didn't stop the possibility of him committing an unthinkable crime in order to stop himself being disinherited. She wrote Tommy's name with the words 'alcoholic' and 'will' underneath.

Jessie's head spun with the trio of possibilities. She rubbed her eyes and switched off the lamp on her desk and yawned again. A nice cold glass of Chardonnay had her name written all over it tonight.

Jessie locked up her Fiesta and walked the short distance to the entrance to her block of flats. Out of the darkness a figure moved slowly towards her.

'Jesus, you scared the life out of me.'

'I'm sorry,' Dylan said. 'I didn't know where else to go.'

Jessie's shoulders drooped at the crestfallen look on her colleague's face. She lifted her door key from her pocket.

'Come on in. I'll put the kettle on.'

Jessie handed him a large mug of hot coffee and sat opposite Dylan on one of her black armchairs by the window. 'It's decaf, don't worry.'

Dylan blew onto the top of it and then sipped. 'Thanks.'

'You don't have to tell me anything if you don't want to. I'll get you the spare duvet once I've had this.' She held her mug up then sipped. 'It's late and I don't suppose Shelly will want the wee ones disturbed at this time of night.'

Dylan's long, slow breath concerned Jessie. The couple had always seemed solid. Happy. She didn't have to wait long for the details to come tumbling out.

'Shelly says she's had enough,' Dylan said without looking up from his mug. Instead he sniffed and drank his coffee.

'Oh,' was all she could think to answer such a sweeping statement. *Nice one, Jess; how supportive.*

'Oh indeed,' he repeated her offering.

'Enough of what exactly?'

Dylan sank the remainder of his coffee and laid the mug down onto Jessie's coffee table.

'Me not being there and when I am there, my mind being on the job.' He let out another long, slow sigh. 'I've got my sergeant's exams at the end of February. You'd think she would be pleased.' He sat back on the sofa and scratched at the back of his head. 'Don't get me wrong, I know it's tough for her being at home all day with them. Och, I'm sorry, it's not your problem I just…'

Jessie followed Dylan's line of sight to a pile of papers in the corner of the coffee table that had Haley McKenzie's photo at the top.

'Are you looking into Haley McKenzie for something?' he asked as he reached for it.

'I, erm.' Jessie frowned quickly, becoming aware of the red flush rising on her cheeks. 'You know Haley?'

Dylan tossed the photo back down. 'Yes, sure, you don't remember?'

Jessie shook her head. 'No, should I?'

'Haley McKenzie is the daughter of a judge. You must remember. She knocked someone down while she was drunk behind the wheel. The woman survived but she ended up with horrific injuries to her legs, I think. I was in uniform at the time. Me and Shelly were just going out – 2010 I think it was.'

'What happened to her?'

'Suspended sentence. Mandatory alcohol counselling, you know the kind of thing. She's working for a lab in Edinburgh I think that processes forensic evidence or something. I know because she was a friend of Shelly's.'

'Oh,' Jessie found herself repeating. Tonight was becoming quite the revelation.

'What's your interest in her?'

Dylan's question took her off guard. 'Och, she's come up in something I've been looking into.'

He seemed satisfied with her answer. Dylan's information caused more questions to burn in Jessie's mind but chiefly how the hell had Haley McKenzie met Dan?

CHAPTER FIFTY-FIVE

Rachel's eyes snapped open as the sunlight spilled through the gap in the bedroom curtains. Kenny wasn't lying beside her but she heard him in the bathroom down the hall. She hadn't wanted to come home at all last night and for a brief second considered keeping on walking away from this nightmare. She was to meet with her solicitor later that day to talk over her defence. *Her* defence. Surely her innocence was her defence she'd told him on the phone.

The knock on the front door made her jump. She grabbed her jumper from the chair at the side of the bed, which did nothing to stop the goosebumps growing on her arms. She tried to rub warmth into her freezing skin before peering into the spyhole to see who their early-morning visitor was. *Of course, who else could it be?*

'Good morning, Caroline.' Rachel painted on a smile and opened the door wide to invite her inside.

Caroline smiled back. 'The policeman checked my ID just in case you're wondering.'

'Great,' Rachel replied, unsure what Caroline meant by that. Perhaps she was trying to reassure her that the police were paying attention.

Rachel heard the toilet flushing, relieved that she wouldn't have to make much more small talk.

'I won't be a minute,' Kenny announced as he wandered from the bathroom to the bedroom wrapped in only a towel.

'Any news on the cause of the fire?' Caroline asked.

Rachel could only shake her head. 'Not so far.'

'I'm sure they're doing everything they can.'

Rachel turned to face her, painting on another smile, right before the kettle clicked off. 'I'm sure they are.'

'I don't have time for coffee,' Kenny, now dressed, said from the doorway. His face was still flushed from the hot shower. 'I've got a meeting with the hauliers' association in Dundee so we better make a move.' He snatched up his car keys from the worktop and kissed Rachel's cheek. 'I'll try not to be too long. Your solicitor is coming at half eleven, remember?'

As if I could forget.

Rachel leaned in to her husband's kiss in search of support.

'Aye, see you later,' she remarked and stirred two sugars into her mug.

Rachel watched the pair walk towards Kenny's Land Rover as she dropped her teaspoon in the sink. She frowned when Caroline glanced back up at her from the passenger seat with a smile. Rachel mouthed the word, 'Bitch,' as she smiled back.

The warmth of the water from the shower cascaded from Rachel's shoulders down onto her breasts before dripping onto the floor of the small shower cubicle. She scrubbed the smell of beer from her hair; she'd been shocked that Kenny hadn't challenged her about where she'd been last night despite the late hour she got back. She should probably enjoy these moments. If DI Blake got her way, Rachel would soon be behind bars for a double murder. She was forty-four years old. Double murder meant two life sentences. If she did ever get out, she would be an old woman.

She had to put that out of her mind. This morning she had to get over to the horses then back there for the meeting with her solicitor. Rachel slipped a thick sweater over her T-shirt and vest then pulled on her leggings and boots. She wished that all she had to think about today was riding out her horses. It was cold but the sun was out and it felt fresh on her skin. She locked up the flat and headed down the few steps into the block's car park. She knocked on the officer's car window.

'Hi, I need to get over to my horses this morning.' Rachel leaned into the police patrol car. 'I've been told I need to ask you to take me.'

'That's right; hop in.' The police constable yanked his seatbelt on and started the engine.

Rachel got in and wished she didn't ever have to come back. She wondered how much money it would take to persuade the handsome young officer in the front seat to just keep driving.

CHAPTER FIFTY-SIX

Arlene Angus was getting sick of being followed. She couldn't prove it but she had an inkling. The pretty, dark-haired girl behind her in the corridor seemed out of place as Arlene waited for the entrance to the ICU to be opened for her. She wanted to yell, 'Why can't I just visit my sick husband in peace?' but resisted. Why couldn't they see Arlene couldn't help them? She didn't know where Gordon was any more than they did. She couldn't tell that DI Blake anything.

The cheerful, ginger-haired ICU nurse opened the door for Arlene. 'Good morning, Mrs Angus.'

Arlene offered her dark-haired pursuer a smile as the door was closed behind her. The machines supporting Tommy Angus's recovery beeped and blinked to show he was still fighting on. The swelling that had appeared around the bleed in his brain had gone down considerably Arlene was told. Finally, some good news. She took hold of Tommy's hand and held it to her cheek.

'You're coming back to us soon, sweetheart; I know you are,' she whispered. 'I'm going to take care of you. You and Gordon.' Arlene kissed the palm of Tommy's hand and allowed a single tear to drip from her cheek onto the bed. Moments later Tommy's breathing changed from a steady, controlled rhythm to a sharp, gurgling cough. Arlene wiped her face with the palm of her hand and tapped the buzzer while she shouted for help.

'Somebody, please, hurry – he needs help!'

Arlene was quickly swept aside as the curtains were hastily drawn around Tommy's bed again. *No, Tommy, please! I need you. Don't leave me. We can work this thing out.*

The sound of coughing followed by a simple whimper hit Arlene's ears and she stopped, held her breath, confused by the development. A hoarse, dry voice struggled to be heard above the sounds emanating from the life-support equipment keeping the other patients alive.

'Looks like your husband wants to rejoin us faster than anticipated.' An older, bearded doctor smiled at Arlene as she peered round the curtain.

'What's happening?' Arlene sobbed. 'I don't understand.'

Tommy's eyes were barely open and he was clutching his throat. His words exited in a rough growl that Arlene could barely hear.

'Tommy has come round by himself, it seems. What did you say to him, eh? Whatever it was, it worked.' The doctor signed his name against a chart tucked in a folder hung on the bottom of Tommy's bed. 'He's still very groggy and I'd like him to rest but this is a good sign, Mrs Angus.'

'Thank you,' she whispered while the doctor and his small team filed out, leaving the couple alone again.

Tommy opened his mouth to speak, barely able to produce a rasping sound. He slipped his fingers up and down his throat and found it hard to swallow without pain catching him.

'The tube in your throat, that's what made your throat hurt. Do you want some cold water?' Arlene fussed and tidied his blanket further up his chest.

Tommy managed a nod then flopped his head back onto his pillow. Arlene held the straw close to his lips and watched him wince against the sting it caused in his throat until he moved his head away. A gentle silence fell over the couple. He'd come back to her. There was plenty of time to talk later.

Arlene held Tommy's hand and watched his eyes close and open in quick succession. He'd lost weight despite the short time since the accident. His face looked pinched and his skin grey and pallid. He was going to need a lot of care even after getting out of hospital.

Tommy's eyes snapped open and he gasped. Arlene watched him take long, slow breaths. He turned to face her.

'Where's Mum?' Tommy whispered through the pain. 'Is she with you?'

Arlene's blood ran cold. The accident meant Tommy had lost some of his short-term memory, then the bleeding on his brain had postponed breaking the inevitable bad news.

'Don't you go worrying about that just now,' was all she could manage. The last thing she wanted was for the shock of that horrific news to set his recovery back or, worse, kill him, which was more than possible given the weak state of his body, especially his heart.

'Is Gordon with her?' he added.

Arlene wished she had the answer. The truth was it was better that none of them knew. She'd given Gordon money and dropped him off where he'd asked her to. If she didn't know where her son was then that detective couldn't persuade her to tell her.

CHAPTER FIFTY-SEVEN

It had been easier to get into the house than Gordon had anticipated. Dumb police officers. They'd parked the car out on the front drive to his grandparents' house, conveniently leaving the back unguarded. A hunch had told Gordon that might be the case. He tugged his collar up against the howling, bitter early January wind and smirked at the sound of the radio booming out of the officers' car. He wondered if they were the same officers that had been assigned to spend New Year sitting there too.

'Idiots,' he muttered under his breath as he unlocked the back door that led into the utility room.

Once inside he pressed the door closed gently, giving them the benefit of the doubt. Gordon couldn't afford to be too complacent. The room smelled of wet washing left sitting in the washing machine since Boxing Day. He opened the door and removed the towels then tugged the drying screen from the cupboard. Gordon hung them in order, the way his gran had shown him. Small towels on the lower parts first.

'Shit!' He jumped at the sound of his ringing phone and quickly silenced the ringtone. That was remiss of him not to put it on silent. Her call made him angry. His mum had promised she wouldn't call. Gordon slipped the phone into the pocket of his hooded fleece and opened the door that led from the utility room into the kitchen slowly, peering carefully through a crack before opening it wider. He pressed it shut quietly ensuring it was held shut on the catch because the draught often pushed that door shut. It was then he spotted a window had been left slightly ajar. He frowned and sighed before tugging it shut. He thought that disrespectful. What if an intruder broke in and stole from his grandparents?

Gordon moved swiftly through the kitchen, bent over to ensure his silhouette didn't cast any kind of shadow in the sunlight that streamed in. He crept up the stairs and into the bedroom he used. He was angry with himself for forgetting to bring his research with him when he left but he'd been in a hurry.

Gordon lifted the pile of books from his bedside table and put the notebook into his pocket, then he opened the drawer and grabbed a couple of pens. Gordon dropped down onto the edge of his bed and lifted the top book from the pile. A book about teenage killers he'd found in a second-hand shop in Edinburgh. A whisper of a smile grew on his lips. It was in that book he'd been able to confirm it was her. Further research on the internet had cemented his theory. It *was* her. Finding her partner in crime hadn't been all that difficult either, and his greed had made arranging to talk to him even easier. He swore he'd not spoken to her since that day but Gordon wasn't convinced. He lived so close.

He flicked through the pages until he found the chapter he was looking for. He kissed the tips of two of his fingers then placed them on her pictures. It was time to let her know he'd found her, that she needn't worry that he knew who she really was.

He slammed the book shut and crept back downstairs and out the utility-room door again, smirking that those idiots in the car out front had never even known he was there.

CHAPTER FIFTY-EIGHT

Boxing Day 1991

A whole year. Rachel couldn't believe it. So much had changed in that time, becoming a mother the most significant thing. She wondered what, if anything, David thought about becoming a father. She didn't even know if he'd been told. Did he know that her new name was Rachel? Would he still come looking for Alice Connor? Her foster mother's voice drifted into Rachel's room. She tugged her duvet over her head and tried to ignore her. Tensions between the two were growing and it was getting harder for Rachel to walk away from confrontation every day.

'Rachel.' The voice outside her bedroom door followed two gentle taps. 'I've done us a cooked breakfast, sweetheart. Bacon, eggs, sausages, the works. Come on down before it gets cold.'

'I'm not hungry,' Rachel shouted from under the duvet.

Instead of further words of persuasion all Rachel heard were retreating footsteps. She should feel guilty. Her foster mother had been there for her when Rachel was at her lowest but all she felt was suffocated. Trapped inside a routine she hated. School was pointless. She couldn't concentrate. She struggled to sleep and always felt so tired. The doctor had prescribed antidepressants for her but all they did was make her sleepy and incredibly thirsty. It was embarrassing when her tongue felt so dry it seemed like it was stuck to the roof of her mouth. To make matters worse, Ella was spending more and more time with a girl from her class.

More than she spent with Rachel these days anyway. The next few months were so important, they kept telling Rachel. Studying and exams were crucial if she wanted a future. But she just couldn't get her head around it.

It was no use. She wasn't going to be able to sleep now. The smell of bacon invaded her nose, even from under the duvet. Rachel tossed it back and sat up, tugging her nightshirt over her knees, which she pulled towards her chest. It was cold in her room in the morning. Rachel thought her head would explode.

She reached into the drawer on her bedside table and pulled out the nail scissors. She lifted her nightshirt and dragged the blade across her thigh, revelling in the pain and release she felt at the sight of the small trickle of blood that appeared. She'd seen a girl in the dinner queue at school with scars on her arm one day as she stretched out to lift a yoghurt from the fridge. The girl quickly spotted Rachel's ghoulish interest and hurried to cover the ugly scars. But Rachel didn't think they were ugly. She was fascinated. She'd heard of self-harm but had never known anyone who'd done it. The girl had looked like anyone else standing waiting in line for her lunch – apart from the lines on her arm. There was nothing weird about her. She did well in class. She had friends. It wasn't until the first time Rachel did it that she understood properly. The relief was immense. Indescribable. Even if it was for just a short time. She could free herself from the pressure that was crushing her.

The euphoria that came after a cut meant Rachel hadn't heard the footsteps returning up the stairs. She didn't even see the door swing slowly open.

'What have you done?' her foster mum gasped.

Rachel was so startled she dropped the scissors and wiped her thigh with her nightshirt.

'Don't you know how to knock?' she screamed at her foster mother, who had dropped herself down onto the edge of her bed.

'Oh, Rachel, talk to me,' she pleaded. 'Tell me what's going on with you? Is it the date? Is it the anniversary?'

'No, I don't care about the damn date!' Rachel roared back. 'Leave me alone!'

As her foster mother reached out for her, Rachel fought her attempt to comfort her distress by pushing her onto the bedroom floor.

Rachel leaped from her bed. 'I said, leave me alone!' She snatched up the scissors then screamed and ran out of the bedroom, banging the door shut after her.

Rachel threw on a pair of jeans and a T-shirt from the laundry pile on a chair in the kitchen. Her heart raced and her head spun with so many different thoughts, but it was the rage in her body that was the worst. Every muscle trembled with anger. She scratched at her messy brown hair then slammed her hand on the worktop, making Ella jump as she sat eating her cooked breakfast.

'Where are you going?' Ella asked with a mouthful of food.

'Anywhere that isn't here.' Rachel slipped her feet into a pair of trainers and snatched a jacket from a hook on the wall next to the kitchen door.

'Rachel,' an anguished voice echoed from the top of the stairs.

Ella's eyes widened as Rachel fled out the back door and ran away from the house that was trapping her. Good, she thought. There was money in the pocket. The jacket she'd grabbed was her foster mother's. She always had a couple of quid on her for emergencies.

Rachel ran when she heard the bus coming around the corner and made it to the stop in time – just. She'd pushed her foster mother away from her to stop her from suffocating her with concern, but the rage that burned inside Rachel had wanted to do so much more. She had to flee before the monster inside her broke free again.

CHAPTER FIFTY-NINE

Rachel was grateful that her solicitor had agreed to see her back at their temporary home. The officer instructed to keep an eye on her had been kind when he'd agreed to take Rachel to tend to the horses. The water trough was full from the recent heavy rain and there was plenty of food in the stable to keep them going for a while. She was grateful the fire had been extinguished before it could damage her stables. The horses weren't Rachel's pets; they were her business. She couldn't afford these days out of her schedule, especially for Dexter. Perth's next race meeting was so close. Who was going to take care of them if she got sent down? Kenny? He would sell the horses in a heartbeat. He had no interest in racing despite the volume of money he'd ploughed into Rachel's small stable. But she had big dreams: increase the number of horses in her yard; draw in some big-name owners even. Perhaps it was her ambition that had caused all this. If she hadn't applied to make changes to the paddock, the police would have no motive for her to kill the Anguses. This was all such a mess.

Rachel thanked the police officer when he dropped her off at the flat. He was a nice lad. Friendly. Rachel hadn't felt like he was judging her and that was nice. Spending time with horses was good. Rachel's happy place.

Rachel scanned her reflection in the dusty mirror that hung above a worn table in the hall then answered the door.

'Come in, Craig, please. Thanks for seeing me here.'

'It's fine – it's no problem to meet here, honestly.'

Rachel closed the door and smiled at her solicitor. 'Please go through. It's not much but it's home for now.'

Craig Merchant, the couple's solicitor, walked on ahead and dropped his briefcase onto the kitchen table. Rachel could feel him judging the tiny room with his eyes as he sat down.

'Hopefully you won't be here long.' He smiled and pulled a notepad from his case.

Rachel lowered herself into the chair opposite. 'I could be living somewhere worse though soon.'

Craig looked up at her. 'Not if I have anything to do with it you won't.'

Rachel wanted to believe him. In his smart suit and designer shoes, Craig Merchant had helped Kenny countless times in the past. She did trust him – didn't she?

The figure crouched low behind the parked Ford Escort froze when they spotted the police officer glance over in that direction. They didn't breathe until the young man in the police car turned away again. That was close. The caller ID on his buzzing phone produced a wry grin but he declined the call. There was no time for that; they would be reunited in good time.

The solicitor was leaving now. That hadn't taken long. He stood up and walked across the small car park and climbed the stairs to knock on Rachel's front door. He smiled as she opened it, a little startled at first by his arrival.

'What are you doing here?' Rachel peered out to see who might have spotted him. The police officer was engrossed in his phone. 'How did you find me?' she panicked and was about to shut the door until he slid his foot into the doorway.

'Don't shut me out until you hear what I've got to say.'

Rachel's heart quickened. 'I really don't think there's anything you can say that I need to hear.'

He leaned in and whispered close to her ear, 'I know who you really are.'

'You have to leave,' Rachel demanded and reached over to push him away.

'I saw you.' His words confused her. 'I know you didn't do it.'

'I don't understand.' Her hand fell away from his chest.

'I can help you,' he offered. 'But I want something in return.'

Rachel eyed him suspiciously but given the circumstances she'd do anything right now. She was that desperate.

'You better come in then.'

She ushered Gordon inside before anyone else saw him.

CHAPTER SIXTY

A summons from Superintendent Crawford was unexpected. She'd only met James Crawford twice before. The black door with his name on it in silver writing swung open to reveal a tall man with fiery red hair and a paunch. Was he smiling? Jessie couldn't tell for sure. He certainly wasn't beaming, that was for sure.

'Come in, Detective Inspector.' He held the door wide and indicated for her to walk on ahead of him before he closed the door after them. 'Please take a seat and don't look so worried,' he said as he lowered his hefty frame into a tall-backed black leather chair that strained a little under his weight.

'Thank you, sir,' Jessie replied, feeling nervous suddenly where she hadn't before.

Superintendent Crawford tidied away a file that was open on his large mahogany desk and retrieved another one from a drawer. He sat back in his chair, making it give a little.

'You're leading up the investigation into the Angus murders. I wanted to talk to you about word that's hit my ear that says you're not one hundred per cent sure of Rachel Ferguson's guilt.' He leaned his elbows on the desk and created a steeple with his fingers on which to rest his chin. He stared at Jessie while she considered her answer.

She could lie. The evidence all pointed towards Rachel but the nagging doubt didn't leave her.

'Let me put it another way,' he said before Jessie had a chance to muddle through the thoughts that crammed inside her head.

'Your job is to secure a conviction for the murder of Malcolm and Jean Angus. There's a strong case against Rachel Ferguson.'

Wait a minute, Jessie thought. *Is he ordering me to back off any other lines of enquiry?*

'With all due respect, sir—'

Superintendent Crawford's raised hand silenced her.

'I'm going to tell you something – in confidence, you understand.'

Jessie nodded, intrigued and confused in equal measure.

'I was a DS in Portree the day Rachel – or Alice as she was known back then – and her boyfriend were arrested for the brutal attack that killed her grandparents. I interviewed her shortly afterwards.'

Was he really using the emotion of her past crime to judge her guilt today?

'I know that, sir. Rachel and I have discussed it and yes I agree her past strengthens the case against her but—'

'You saw the crime-scene photos then?' He swung his chair from side to side.

'Again, with all due respect' – this time he allowed Jessie to finish – 'all I'm doing is keeping an open mind. There are other lines of enquiry I think need exploring. The Anguses' grandson, for example. His behaviour gives me grave concerns.'

'Rachel Ferguson's DNA is at the crime scene. The size-four boot prints. The hidden gun. Her history. Her dispute with the victims.'

When it was laid out like that, of course she looked guilty.

'It's the lack of gunshot residue, sir.' Jessie left that statement hanging for him to chew over and it took him a moment to come back on it.

'Report says she washed the clothes she'd been wearing and there had been plenty of time to wash the GSR away. Rachel Ferguson is a very clever woman. Don't be fooled by the meek and mild exterior. She was able to convince the authorities David was the criminal mastermind behind the murder plot. Spent three months in a young offenders before being sent to live with a foster family, meanwhile David Law spent twenty-five years behind bars. I mean, don't get me wrong, I'm not saying he's innocent – far from it.'

'Where is David Law now?' Jessie asked.

'He lives in a homeless supported accommodation block in Dundee. The Seagate project. He has an alibi. I checked. I have his probation officer's number if you want it.'

Wow, he really is taking an interest in this case. I wonder how well he knew Malcolm or Jean Angus?

'Do you know if they've had any contact with each other recently?' Jessie asked.

He shook his head. 'Kenny Ferguson applied for an injunction to stop Law from approaching him and his wife several years ago, when he was told of his release from Perth prison.'

A phone call to the Superintendent's desk phone interrupted them and Jessie waited while he excused himself to answer it.

David Law? Would he risk being sent back to prison for revenge? Does he even care about revenge? I expect he wants to get on with his life.

'I have to take this call, so hear what I've said, Detective Inspector Blake. Rachel Ferguson.'

His wide-eyed nod for emphasis wasn't lost on Jessie but what he didn't know couldn't hurt.

After gently closing his office door after her, Jessie's first port of call was a chat with David Law.

CHAPTER SIXTY-ONE

'I'm Detective Inspector Jessie Blake. This is my colleague Detective Constable Logan. Can we come in and have a chat with one of your residents – David Law?' Jessie smiled at the pretty, middle-aged woman who opened the door to the supported accommodation project. The woman looked closely at both ID cards with her eyes narrowed.

'Come through; sorry, I left my glasses on my desk.' She smiled again while she led the two detectives through a long corridor that led to a large kitchen at the end. She nodded through the doorway at a thin, balding man making a cup of tea.

'Thanks,' Jessie said before heading into the kitchen. 'David Law?' She held up her ID as she approached.

Jessie thought he looked like he'd seen a ghost as they walked towards him. As he sat down at the long wooden table in the centre of the room, she asked, 'Do you mind if we sit?'

David shrugged before taking a sip. 'I can't stop you, I suppose.'

Jessie figured it was his years inside that had created his dislike of the police. *That and perhaps his sense of betrayal that he was left to carry the can for their crime?*

'When did you last speak to Rachel Ferguson?' Dylan asked as he sat down opposite the gaunt figure.

'Who?' David asked.

'You'll know her better as Alice Connor,' Jessie announced.

'I can't believe she can still be allowed to haunt me every day,' David remarked without looking at either of them. 'I've done my time. I'm sorry for my part in it. I wish I'd never met Alice Connor. I've said that so many times now. I just want to get on with my life.'

Jessie remembered Superintendent Crawford saying David Law had an alibi but she had to be sure.

'Where were you on Boxing Day morning, David?'

His derisory laugh wasn't unexpected. 'Oh, I don't know, Detective, in the bosom of my large, loving family, tucking into leftover turkey sandwiches over a crackling open log fire in our cabin in the country. Where were you?'

'No need for the sarcasm,' Dylan said.

'I was here. The lassies in the office and the two support workers on that day can tell you that. There's a book we have to sign in and sign oot of. Check that.'

Jessie rested her chin on her hand as she leaned her elbow on the table. Her lips were pursed while she watched him sink the remnants of his cup of tea.

'You didn't answer the question?'

'Look, I haven't spoken to Alice or Rachel or whatever she calls herself now. I haven't since that day. She wrote to me. I got told that after I got oot.' He scoffed. 'One of her letters had a picture of oor bairn in it. I was never allowed to see her either. You any idea how that feels? So no, I haven't seen her. If that's all you came for then I'm sorry to have disappointed you.'

Jessie had a hunch that she couldn't shake. She pulled the photo of Gordon Angus from the front pocket of her bag and held it up.

'You ever seen this lad before?'

'No, should I?' David answered without looking at it properly.

Jessie slid it across the table at him. 'David, I'd appreciate it if you'd take a proper look?'

David Law sighed and picked the photo up. He sniffed then handed it back. 'Never seen him before.' He glanced at his shoes before crossing his legs. 'Who is he? Has he got something to do with Alice?'

'Why do you say that?' Dylan piped up.

'Because that's what you're here to talk to me about,' he scoffed. 'But if there's nothing else, can I go? My room won't tidy itself, will it?'

Jessie produced one of her cards from her jacket pocket and slid it across the table at him.

'If you see this young man could you let me know?' Jessie requested as she and Dylan both stood and pushed their chairs in close to the table. David left them with just a nod and curt goodbye before disappearing out of sight.

'What did you make of that?' Dylan asked as the two detectives made their way back to Jessie's car.

'Mm, not sure. He's certainly pissed off with his life. I would be too if I was him,' Jessie answered, thoughts whirring through her head.

'Yes, but pissed off enough to shoot two people in cold blood?' Dylan challenged.

'Good question.' Jessie pointed at him and lifted her phone from deep inside her pocket. 'Perhaps we should keep a little eye on Mr Law, just in case.'

Jessie looked back at the figure staring at the two detectives from an upstairs window in the supported accommodation unit. She held his gaze until her call was answered.

'Yes, this is DI Blake. I have a person of interest I need you to keep an eye on.'

David allowed the curtain to drop back into place. He unplugged his phone from the charger and dialled her number.

'Come on – pick up,' he urged then sighed when it went to voicemail. 'It's me; call me back when you get this. The police have been here. What the hell did you tell them?'

CHAPTER SIXTY-TWO

Benito smelled gorgeous like he always did as he kissed Jessie's cheek when he arrived at the restaurant only a few minutes after her.

'Did you park OK?' she asked.

'Yes, not far actually. Somebody was leaving so I nabbed their space. Lucky really because there was a queue of cars behind me.' He paused as his eyes ran the length of Jessie's body. 'You look lovely.'

Jessie blushed. Benito Capello had the knack of making her feel like a teenager again. It was his brooding Latin looks. The way his big brown eyes twinkled like he was sharing a naughty secret when he smiled.

'You too,' she replied then realised she was twirling her hair when she spoke. *It's just dinner. Stop acting like it's a hot date.*

The restaurant began filling up around them and Jessie scanned the menu. In reality, she knew what she'd be having. Same thing she always did – lasagne. For a moment, she considered whether Benito would think she was ordering that to impress him because of his Italian roots. The truth was it was her favourite.

'Something from the wine menu?' The waiter's deep Highland lilt startled her when he approached their table from the bar behind them. Jessie stared up at the young lad, slim and quite feminine in appearance. She wondered where on earth that strong voice came from.

'Jessie, what do you think?' Benito suggested. 'Not that I'm hinting I could stay at yours or anything.'

There it was again – that naughty schoolboy grin. If Jessie wasn't careful she could find herself falling for Benito.

She shrugged with a grin. 'Why not? Maybe a wee Chardonnay – is that OK for you?'

'Sounds perfect,' Benito agreed.

Jessie's attention was drawn to a couple who walked in. The young woman let go of her male companion's arm to wipe rain from her hair. That face. She would recognise it anywhere. It had been etched in Jessie's mind ever since that day. Her heart almost stopped.

'Jessie, are you OK?' Benito asked. 'You look like you've seen a ghost.

Jessie coughed and turned away from staring at Dan and Haley who, much to Jessie's horror, were now making their way towards their table.

'What – erm, no, no… it's fine.' She tried to smile through the anxiety that was growing inside. It was no good. 'Excuse me – I have to use the little girls' room.'

Jessie stood to leave until her way was blocked by Dan and Haley.

'Ben, how weird to see you here of all places,' Haley chirped.

Jessie wanted to scream. She wanted to shove her shoulder into the obstruction and get the hell out of there but instead had to smile.

'Jessie, this is Haley, a colleague at the lab,' Ben introduced her.

'Lovely to meet you.' Jessie nodded to Haley then smiled at Ben. He didn't have to know this wasn't news to her. 'Will you excuse me a minute?'

Jessie slipped past, aware of her racing heart with every step away from the table. She thought she'd escaped too until Dan's fingers curled around her wrist.

'Jess – wait,' he pleaded. 'If this is going to be awkward, me and Haley will go.'

Jessie snatched her arm out of his grip.

'Get your hand off me,' she growled through gritted teeth.

Dan raised his hands in the air. 'I'm sorry, I'm sorry.'

Jessie's anxiety was morphing into anger as she headed inside the restaurant's ladies' room. Her cheeks had gained a pink hue from the stress of their sudden arrival. Haley looked like a nice woman, smiling from ear to ear when she saw Ben. She had a right to know about Dan, didn't she? Jessie wondered if he'd told her about their son. Their marriage? His abuse?

Jessie rinsed a little cold water over her hands and ran her fingers over the back of her neck to cool herself down. She didn't want this to ruin her evening with Ben. She'd been looking forward to seeing him all day.

She moved to a cubicle and locked the door, then exhaled away the stress of their unexpected arrival. She supposed she should be better prepared in future. If he was living in Perth, they were bound to encounter each other occasionally.

From inside her cubicle she heard another customer enter the bathroom and thought nothing of it until she unlocked the door.

'Haley,' she greeted her while she washed her hands.

'I hope this isn't too awkward for you,' Haley said. 'I know about you and Dan.'

Jessie could only smile while she shook her head. 'Ancient history.'

'Good; I'm glad. I would hate that, with you being with Ben. This probably won't be the only time we'll bump into each other.'

The thought of seeing them regularly horrified Jessie. For so many reasons. She couldn't stand the thought of watching Dan destroy this lovely young woman the way he had Jessie. She fought hard to stop herself grabbing Haley and shaking her. Telling her to run and never look back.

'Perhaps,' Jessie replied instead.

This wasn't the right time or place. So she simply smiled and tugged at the paper towels. After tossing the paper in the bin she headed back to her table. The sight of Ben smiling and laughing with Dan, who was still standing next to their table, made Jessie feel sick. She was a fool to think she could do this. Ben grinned as she returned to the table.

'I'm sorry, Ben, something's come up – I have to go,' she lied.

Before he could answer Jessie was already on her way out of the door. His voice echoed across the now crowded high street.

'Jessie, wait—' he repeated.

Ben caught up with her with ease and spun her to face him, his eyes filled with concern when he saw the moisture in hers.

'What's wrong?' he urged.

'Ben,' Jessie murmured. 'I can't—' She broke away from his embrace.

'Jess,' he called after her as he watched her walk away.

CHAPTER SIXTY-THREE

Jessie was so glad to be inside her flat. She locked the door and tossed the key into the bowl. Her boots were kicked under the hall table while she stared at her reflection in the mirror above it. Her face was red from crying but not because she was sad. These were tears of anger mixed with fear.

She picked Smokey up into her arms and nuzzled her cheek into his while he purred. She didn't know what she'd do without him. Poor Smokey. He'd dried many a tear in his ten years. Jessie cuddled him close and carried him into the kitchen where she poured a tall, chilled glass of wine from the bottle in the fridge and sank its contents. Her pulse had finally returned to normal. Her stomach rumbled as she placed Smokey back down. She'd been looking forward to that meal.

Jessie opened the fridge again and pulled out a large block of cheese and the butter. She was disappointed to find the pickle jar all but empty. She managed to scrape out a little to enhance the cheese sandwich she made and took it into the living room, where she sank into the corner of her sofa. Her sandwich was tasteless but she was famished.

The knock on her door made her jump. Jessie froze. The sound of knocking grew louder. Jessie tiptoed through the hall to peer through the spyhole. Her relief was immense as she opened the door to Benito.

'What the hell, Jess?' Ben's perplexed expression made Jessie feel guilty. 'Haley is just a friend from work.'

Jessie frowned, confused by why that was relevant. 'I know that.'

'Then why did you rush off like that? It's clearly not work.'

Ben's attitude was strange. He'd never challenged Jessie like this.

'It was, it was...' Jessie heard herself ramble but couldn't stop it. 'It was just— Nothing, Ben. I'm sorry. Look, come in...' She held the door wide for him, avoiding eye contact. 'I'm sorry for rushing off like that. I owe you an explanation.'

'Thanks,' Ben whispered.

Jessie watched the back of Ben disappear along the hall and into her kitchen. She drew in a long, slow breath while she closed the door. She leaned her head on it and allowed her shoulders to droop with the reality that was weighing down on her. She couldn't avoid this any longer. It wasn't fair to the people who cared about her. Even Dylan. Yes, she would arrange that dinner and tell him. He deserved to know why Jessie behaved this way. But for tonight, she had to tell Ben everything.

Jessie felt so exposed that she wanted to curl up and die right then.

'Ben, say something,' she urged, her hands trembling.

Why isn't he saying anything? Jessie thought.

Benito remained silent because he didn't have to say anything. He pulled Jessie into his arms and held her there, then kissed the top of her head. From inside his embrace Jessie felt safe.

'Thank you for trusting me,' he whispered and kissed her head again.

Jessie was wrong to think Ben would judge her. He wasn't Dan, but when someone had been hurt like Jessie had then trusting again seemed impossible. She lifted her head up from his chest. This was it. The moment she couldn't – she wouldn't – stop.

CHAPTER SIXTY-FOUR

Arlene Angus filled a cup with water for Tommy.

'Here you go.' She held the straw close to his lips until he reached out his hand.

'It's OK; I can manage.' His voice was still hoarse. 'Thank you.'

Arlene corrected herself and handed it to him. 'I know; I'm sorry.' She sat back down.

'It's fine.' Tommy smiled. 'I like that you're fussing over me.'

Tommy pressed his hand on hers. Arlene quickly wiped away a tear she felt escape. This was a happy moment. She was just being silly.

'This is so good,' Tommy told her after taking a long, slow sip. 'Nice and chilled.' He licked his lips and handed her the cup before laying his head back onto the pillow. He closed his eyes for a moment. 'Why do I feel so damn tired? I've been out for the count for so long I should be rested by now.' He tried to laugh then winced from the pain in his ribs.

'Doctor says it's normal. You'll be exhausted for a while yet. Your body has had a shock and needs time to recover,' Arlene informed him while she squeezed his hand in hers. That touch. That connection was good for both of them.

'What's Gordon doing tonight?' Tommy asked without opening his eyes.

'Shh, never mind about Gordon,' Arlene responded and leaned over to kiss Tommy's cheek. 'You get some sleep. I'll be back in the morning to see you.'

'OK, boss,' Tommy murmured as he drifted into a deep sleep.

Arlene stroked his cheek and watched his chest rise and fall. She stood up and leaned down to kiss his forehead. He had to be told about what had happened to Malcolm and Jean, but the thought that it would have to come from her scared her.

As she walked away from the ICU towards the hospital car park Arlene's phone buzzed with a number she didn't recognise. She stopped by the driver's door of her car.

'Hello,' she answered tentatively.

'Arlene Angus?' a woman's voice said.

'Y-Yes, who is this?' Arlene stuttered. 'How did you get my number?'

'That's not important. I just want you to know that you don't have to worry about Gordon. He's fine. He says you'll worry but please don't. I'll take care of him.'

Panic slammed into Arlene's chest and she had to gasp to catch her breath.

'How do you know my son?' she pleaded. 'Where is he?' A silence followed her pleas. 'Hello, are you still there?' Arlene's chest tightened. 'Please let me speak to him.'

She could hear muffled voices in the background before Gordon's voice came on the line.

'Mum, I'm fine. I've promised I'll help her so please don't worry about me. I'll be home when it's all over.'

'Gordon?' Arlene shouted out as she heard the call end. 'Gordon!'

Arlene immediately dialled the number and almost dropped her phone in shock. The voicemail message that she was connected to once the call rang out was not what she'd expected at all. What the hell was she supposed to do now? If she did nothing she feared Gordon was in danger. If she told DI Blake then Gordon would surely be arrested.

CHAPTER SIXTY-FIVE

Jessie blushed at the memory of the night before but couldn't stop smiling. She stared out of her office window at the low winter sun, only just peaking over the spire of St Ninian's cathedral. Thinking about Benito triggered the same butterfly sensation she remembered when she was a teenager. It wasn't exactly an unpleasant feeling either.

'Detective Inspector Blake.'

A woman's voice tore into Jessie's daydream, catching her off guard a little, making her spill her coffee onto the floor by the window.

'Och, now look at me – what a mess,' Jessie remarked and laid her mug on her desk before wiping drips from her shirt. 'I'm DI Blake, yes. What can I do for you?'

The pretty, brown-haired woman smiled and pulled out a chair next to Jessie's desk.

'My name is Julia Dean. I work for Kenny and Rachel Ferguson.'

'Ah yes, pleased to meet you. How can I help?'

Jessie was intrigued at this woman's reason for visiting. Why would one of Rachel's employees be there to talk to Jessie?

'I heard that you think Rachel killed that couple,' Julia announced. 'You're wrong. Rachel wouldn't do that.'

Jessie eyed the woman with interest. She sat back in her chair and considered her words. Jessie wondered how much of the evidence Julia knew about.

'How can you be so sure?'

'I know it looks bad. The evidence. The DNA. But she can't have done it.'

'If you know about all the evidence, how can you be so sure?' Jessie dug a little deeper. Did this woman know *all* the evidence? The history? She could see there was something she needed to say but was struggling to get it out.

'Do you know something about what happened to Malcolm and Jean,' Jessie asked directly, 'because right now it looks like Rachel killed them?'

'No!' Julia shouted. 'She didn't.'

Jessie was becoming increasingly confused and somewhat irritated by her lack of real information.

'What are you not telling me?'

Julia got up. 'Look, I'm only saying what I overheard him say.'

'What who said?' Jessie urged.

Julia looked terrified. 'Promise me you won't tell him I told you. I need that job.'

'I promise,' Jessie answered, worried for the girl's sanity, the state she seemed to be getting in. 'Just tell me.'

Julia looked Jessie straight in the eye. 'It was Kenny.'

'Kenny Ferguson?' Jessie repeated.

Julia nodded. 'I overheard him on the phone. I think he was arranging to have them killed.'

Neither of the two women had heard Dylan arrive until he gasped at the revelation. Jessie stared at him in disbelief.

'How do you know that's what he was doing?'

'Because I heard him mumbling something about killing and now that old couple are dead.' Julia's voice grew louder. 'He didn't know I was standing outside his office door.'

'Can you prove any of this?' Jessie asked. 'Who was he talking to?'

Julia shrugged. 'I don't know.'

Her answer exasperated Jessie. Just when she was potentially so close.

'How can you know for sure that's what he was saying?' Jessie continued. 'Could you have got the wrong end of the stick? Your boss is a well-known businessman.'

'You don't know him as well as I do, Detective,' Julia interrupted. 'He'd do anything for Rachel.'

CHAPTER SIXTY-SIX

David Law watched the back of Kenny Ferguson until he disappeared out of the park gate and round the corner. He smirked at Kenny's threat. If Kenny thought he could scare him, he was very much mistaken. David had encountered far more intimidating men than an overweight, ageing businessman. Sure, threatening to go to the police might work on some people but like David said, how badly did he want to keep his wife's secret identity?

The echo of running footsteps got closer until they stopped near to the bench he sat on. He smiled at the pretty blonde jogger when she paused to take a drink and wipe her sweat-soaked head.

'Nice day,' he commented, his eyes skimming her petite frame as he spoke, but got nothing in response. Instead the girl simply checked her watch and took off running again.

He didn't blame her for blanking him. He was a mess. Thin. Tired. Black circles crowding his eyes after years inside. He hadn't been able to afford to do anything to improve his life until recently.

That young lad reaching out to him had been a shock to begin with. Having someone ask such intimate questions wasn't anything new, but this lad wasn't asking for any reason other than pure delight. The way he'd revelled in the details had appalled David at first. He'd come close to telling his probation officer – as close as lifting his phone to call her – but something had stopped him. The money.

But David was clever. He hadn't gone right out and started splashing the cash. He didn't want to draw attention to himself.

He'd managed to put a large amount into savings for their futures. He'd been unable to help either of them when he'd been locked away but he could now and he would. He'd not really opened up to Gordon for his own personal gain at all. He'd done it for his girls. Not that he told him that. Talking about it all again after so many years exposed the feelings David had tried to push down. He'd had to. Any sign of weakness gets you preyed on in prison; there are predators in there just waiting to devour you.

David's hand slipped into his pocket. He tightened it over her last letter; something he carried with him always. Like a lucky charm, he supposed. She'd been through so much without him. If he hadn't been so stupid all those years ago none of it would have happened.

As soon as he could, David planned to rent a little flat just for the two of them. Make up for the lost years. The ones stolen from them.

Kenny's text made him grin.

Oh, old man, don't make threats you can't follow through on.

David quickly typed his answer then stuffed his phone into his jeans pocket. He leaned right back on the bench and inhaled a long, deep breath, taking in the fresh, chill winter air which was still a luxury to him. David wanted the money in cash the next time the two men met. What he was asking for was a mere drop in the ocean to Kenny. He'd explained it wasn't blackmail; it was simply reparations.

Kenny had become angry when David asked how well did he really know his wife because he hadn't been there when that hammer had connected with Peter Connor's skull. He hadn't seen the ecstasy grow on her face. He hadn't heard the whimper of pleasure escape her lips. She'd been so beautiful. The injunction was pointless, David had laughed. Her secret was too big to risk. David had all the power today and he intended to use it.

It was Gordon's voice that brought David out of his daydream.

'Hello again,' Gordon remarked and sat down next to him. He pulled an envelope from the inner pocket of his fleece then rubbed his hands against the cold. 'It's good to see you.'

David took the envelope and looked inside before flicking the notes between his fingers. That was close, he mused. Not that he really cared whether the two men met. His donors.

'How's your dad doing now?' David asked and tucked the envelope away into the pocket of his jeans, barely able to make it fit. He shifted position on the bench to stuff it as far down as he could get it.

'Fine; my dad's fine.' Gordon seemed irritated by the question. 'I've just seen her. I came straight here after.'

'What did she say?'

Gordon shrugged and blushed. That made David smile. 'I told her what I saw.'

'Mm, how did she take that?'

Gordon grinned. 'She looked relieved, happy even. Once I explained, of course.'

'You really do like her, don't you?' David teased and grinned at the redness increasing on Gordon's face. 'I don't blame you. Alice is—' He paused to correct himself. 'I mean, Rachel. She has a way of making you feel…' David couldn't explain it. He fell silent for a moment.

'I feel weird when I think about her,' Gordon admitted.

David recognised that feeling. 'You love her. That's what that weird feeling is – love.'

Gordon frowned. 'Is it?'

David didn't know whether to feel pity or to envy Gordon's reaction. Falling in love with Alice – as she would always be to David – happened so quickly. She'd hooked him with her innocent charms before he'd realised it was happening.

'Has she asked you to help her?' David asked.

Gordon shook his head. 'No, she didn't ask. I offered. I promised.'

'Oh,' David commented. 'What did you promise exactly?'

'I said I would help her with her police problem.'

CHAPTER SIXTY-SEVEN

Gordon's stomach was turning upside down standing there with his mental shopping list. There was so much choice. But he'd made his decision. He'd even chosen the name the press would call him. He picked up the hammer he'd struggled to take his eye off. It was a thing of beauty. Not too heavy. The handle felt right in his grip – non-slip too. The last thing he wanted was her blood causing his fingers to slip, and he hoped there would be lots of blood. She looked like she'd bleed, just the way David described.

Gordon slipped the hammer into his basket and moved round to the gloves. He needed something close-fitting but comfortable. He tried on a pair he liked the look of. No, they were too loose. His fingers would slide around inside them so he hung that pair back up. He pursed his lips before nibbling on his thumbnail and leaned down for a better look.

'Can I help you with anything today?'

From so deep inside his thoughts Gordon jumped with fright at the assistant's offer.

'Erm, no, no, thank you,' he answered. 'I can manage.'

The assistant smiled and walked away on seeing an elderly woman struggling to lift a pair of gardening gloves from a high hook. Gordon picked up a pair of black and red gloves that felt like rubber but were thicker. Latex gripper gloves. Multi-purpose. He squeezed the material in his hand then slipped his fingers inside. He balled his hand into a fist then stretched his fingers out. They were comfortable. Snug but not too tight.

He reached into the shopping basket and lifted the hammer out with his gloved hand. He tightened his grip around the handle. Perfect. He removed the glove and placed them, along with the hammer, back into the basket then moved to the array of trash bags on display. He'd need something thicker than a black rubbish bag. Gravel bags – yes, they'd be just right. He dropped them in. Plastic sheeting. He'd better buy a lot. It might get messy.

'That will be twenty-five pounds ninety-five,' the cashier told him without cracking a smile.

Gordon packed his kit, as he planned to call it, and took his change. The camera fitted into the top corner of the shop doorway moved slightly as he walked away. He glanced up at the source of the noise and stopped to stare at it, much to the irritation of an overweight builder dressed in an orange high-vis vest.

'Watch where you're going,' the man blasted as he guzzled down a can of juice.

Gordon didn't care. He continued to stare then smiled before moving on. It wouldn't be long before lots of cameras would want to capture his face.

CHAPTER SIXTY-EIGHT

A background check on Julia Dean showed nothing out of the ordinary. She was almost thirty and had worked for Ferguson Haulage for six months. The first female driver in the company's history. Perfect driving record, no criminal record – not even a parking ticket. She lived alone in a flat in the centre of Perth. The warrant to obtain Kenny's phone records hadn't been difficult. The brutality of the Anguses' murder meant the need to find who was responsible was a priority – especially given that the weapon of choice was a gun.

Jessie picked up the marker pen from her desk and snatched the lid off as she moved closer to the evidence board. She wrote Kenny's name next to Rachel's and circled it. She drew a single line between his name and the smiling faces of Malcolm and Jean Angus. But why kill them? Sure, they'd got in the way of Rachel's plans but that wasn't enough to kill them, was it?

Then an awful idea struck Jessie. Could Rachel have persuaded another man who loved her to do something unthinkable. Had she been more in control of the killing of her grandparents? Had she manipulated David?

'I got it.' Dylan beamed from his desk and ushered Jessie over.

'Let's see who he's been talking to then, shall we?' she remarked.

Julia had given them the exact time she'd heard Kenny on the phone. Jessie ran her finger down the list of numbers on the laptop screen, but there was nothing logged around the time she'd said she'd heard him.

'That's strange,' Jessie commented. 'She was adamant, wasn't she?'

'Hang on – there's a link here to—' Dylan paused while he hovered the mouse over the second link he'd been sent. 'This is Kenny's office number.'

Jessie narrowed her eyes and scanned the numbers on the list, which was considerably long.

'There!' Dylan pointed to a number on the screen and grabbed a pen to scribble the number down.

'That's the code for Dundee,' Jessie chirped and lifted the handset for her phone. She dialled the number Dylan had scribbled on the paper and waited.

'Hello.' A deep, gruff voice answered the call after five rings.

'Who am I talking to?' Jessie responded.

'Who are you looking for and I'll see if I can find them for you?'

Jessie frowned. She would have to wing it. 'I'm not sure exactly. Whose number is this?'

'This is the residents' phone. Is it one of the residents you're looking for?' the voice added.

'Which residents would that be?'

'Seagate project.'

Jessie had to admit she was a little taken aback and thanked the man for his help.

'Well, well, well – looks like Mr Ferguson has some explaining to do. Why would he be calling the Seagate project, I wonder?'

'Good question,' Dylan agreed. 'Considering he told us he hadn't seen or spoken to David Law.'

'You take Law and I'll talk to Kenny at the same time. Keep them separate. Don't give them a chance to talk to each other.'

'Sure.' Dylan nodded and zipped up his jacket then pulled his car keys from his pocket.

Jessie grabbed her keys and tugged her jacket from the back of her chair. She closed the laptop on Dylan's desk and followed him out.

*

Gordon tucked himself down behind the Astra parked in the furthest corner of the station car park. He checked his watch and tugged his rucksack higher over his shoulder. His heart was racing now as her car slowly drove past. The hunt was on.

CHAPTER SIXTY-NINE

Arlene wanted the ground to open up and swallow her whole. Swallow both of them. Take them away from this pain.

'I don't understand,' Tommy pleaded with hot tears stinging his eyes. 'They can't be dead. How, but…' He couldn't form the words he wanted to say.

Arlene had to be strong, for both of them.

'I know this is a lot to take in,' she began. 'Do you remember anything about Boxing Day? Your parents? The accident? Anything?'

Tommy shook his head then ripped back his blanket and tried to get out of his hospital bed. Arlene stood and placed her hands on his arm.

'What are you doing? Get back into bed. You're not well enough.'

'How can I stay here?' Tommy shouted. 'My parents have been murdered.'

A nurse moved quickly to where Tommy was struggling with the IV drip in his arm.

'Tommy, please,' Arlene begged.

'Get this thing out of my arm,' Tommy roared at the nurse who tried to calm him down.

Arlene felt helpless because she was unable to say anything to take his heartbreak away. Tommy was finding his parents dead all over again.

It took the nurse several minutes but Tommy did eventually flop down onto the edge of the bed. He stared past the nurse at Arlene, who was wiping away the mess of tears from her face. He held out his hand and she took the place of the nurse and sat next to him.

'I'm so sorry,' Arlene whispered.

Tommy took a long, slow breath and kissed the top of Arlene's head.

'I know you are,' Tommy whispered back. 'Can you take me to the station?'

'Tommy, I don't think…' Arlene suggested until she saw the heartbreak in his eyes. She nodded. 'Yes, grab your jacket. It's freezing out there.'

Tommy leaned heavily on the sticks the hospital had given him despite their reluctance to agree to his discharge. Tommy had to sign that he understood the risks he was placing himself under by leaving against medical advice, but that wasn't a problem as far as he was concerned.

'Take your time.' Arlene held the passenger door open for him and helped put his seatbelt over him.

Tommy's strength had withered with the shock of the accident and his body was taking its time to recover, but he would fight with everything he had to find out what had happened to his parents.

'Why can't I remember anything?' Tommy announced from within the silence that surrounded the couple on their journey.

'The doctor said that can happen after a serious head injury. It might come back in time.'

Arlene helped Tommy to get out of the car again at the police station.

'It's fine; I can manage,' Tommy told her as he winced while he leaned on the sticks.

'I need to speak to Detective, erm, Detective—' Tommy began but struggled to remember the name Arlene had told him. His memory remained poor. She patted Tommy's arm gently.

'You go and sit down over there.' She kissed his cheek as she pointed to the black plastic chairs a little way from the reception desk.

'I'm sorry,' Arlene began. 'We need to speak to Detective Inspector Blake.'

The overweight officer behind the desk picked up the phone and called Jessie's office phone. He frowned while it rang out before trying her mobile, which went direct to voicemail.

'I'm sorry, DI Blake is unavailable. Can I give her a message?'

Arlene turned round to face Tommy. 'He says—'

'I know; I heard. I'm not deaf. We'll come back in the morning but tell her I need to speak to her, will you? I think I know who killed my parents.'

The look of shock on Arlene's face didn't go unnoticed.

'Tommy?'

'Don't tell me you haven't considered it?'

'Tommy, don't do this,' Arlene pleaded.

'Who else could it be?' Tommy added. 'We both know he's capable of it.'

Arlene moved quickly to face her husband.

'Shut up – you don't know what you're saying.' She spoke through gritted teeth and prayed the officer couldn't understand what Tommy was saying.

'Well, where is he then?' Tommy blasted and limped past Arlene, nudging his shoulder into her.

Arlene tried to smile at the officer behind the desk before following Tommy back outside.

'Gordon, what are you doing here?' Tommy remarked on seeing his son from the back, walking quickly towards the car-park exit. 'Gordon!' he called out louder this time.

Gordon stopped then turned round to face them.

'I was looking for that detective,' Gordon admitted and gripped the rucksack tighter to his body. 'But she's not here.'

'Yes, we know,' Tommy answered.

Father and son eyed each other, neither willing to admit the real reason they were there.

'Come on, son – let's go home.' Arlene pointed towards the right. 'The car's just here.'

'No, I've got stuff to do,' Gordon insisted and started to move away then stopped. He frowned as he turned to face them. 'Why are you both here?'

'Gordon, I think you should come home with us,' Tommy urged, trying to avoid his question. 'You've been through a lot.'

'Tell me why you're here,' he insisted again. This time his tone was darker and more threatening.

'It doesn't matter why we're here, just get in the car.' Tommy was losing patience. 'Just do as you're told for once in your life.'

'Tommy,' Arlene interrupted and reached for Tommy's arm, until he snatched it back from her.

'You see what you've done? Mm, do you? Look at him. He doesn't give a shit that his grandparents are dead.' Tommy leaned heavily on his sticks and limped over to his car. 'Leave him, Arlene. I'm done trying to reason with him.'

'Gordon,' Arlene murmured. 'Please, son.'

Gordon stared blankly at his mum and walked away. 'I'll see you at home. I've got stuff to do.'

CHAPTER SEVENTY

Dylan held up his ID to show the woman who had let them into the building the last time.

'Hello, again,' she said and stepped aside, while holding the front door wide for him. 'You better come in.'

'Thanks.' Dylan nodded to the elderly, unkempt man sat on a chair in the office as he passed the door.

'It's David you're looking for again, is it?' she commented. 'He's where he always is. In the kitchen.'

'Thanks,' Dylan said again and walked through the long, thin hallway past a noticeboard with pictures of missing persons pinned to it.

He followed the strong smell of garlic to find David slumped at the kitchen table, almost exactly in the same spot he'd left him after they'd spoken last time. He held his ID up for David to examine.

'What can I do for you this time, Detective?' David dipped a digestive biscuit into his mug then bit a chunk off before washing it down with a sip of tea.

There was a cockiness to the man this time, Dylan decided. The T-shirt he had on looked new too. Dylan dropped down into the chair right next to him, pressing his arm next to his. David pulled away.

'I have a couple of questions for you,' Dylan began as he tucked his hand inside the inner pocket of his jacket. He clicked his pen while he laid the notebook flat.

'I told you and your lady friend everything the other day,' David continued to sip.

'Remind me again – when did you last see Rachel Ferguson?'

'I told you. I haven't seen her – Alice – since that night.'

'What about Kenny, her husband? When did you last talk to him?'

David's jaw clenched, just for a second, but Dylan saw it.

'I haven't spoken to the man.' David started to stand up to leave the table.

'What if I told you I have proof that you have?' Dylan suggested and watched David stop to turn round to face him.

'What proof is that exactly?'

David sank the remnants of his mug of tea and dropped it into the sink.

'A call was logged from Kenny's number to the phone' – he pointed at the door – 'in the hall.'

Dylan could see him mulling over the suggestion the two men had been in communication.

'How do you know he was talking to me?'

'Who else would he be talking to?'

David shrugged then smiled at Dylan. 'If there's nothing else, I have somewhere I have to be.'

Dylan had to think fast. It was clear that David Law thought he'd found a flaw in his argument. That was clever on his part, Dylan had to admit. Using a communal phone. But he was holding the trump card.

'How would your probation officer react if I called him to tell him you're refusing to help me with my enquiries?' Dylan pulled his phone out of his pocket and started scrolling. He hoped that Law didn't know that Dylan had no idea who his probation officer was.

'Wait.' David lifted his hand then sat back down. 'It *was* me he was talking to.'

Dylan tucked his phone away then listened in wide-eyed disgust at David's story of blackmail and greed.

'I wouldn't have given Alice – I mean, Rachel – a second thought if that young lad hadn't contacted me.'

'By young lad I'm guessing you mean Gordon Angus.' Memories of Gordon's murderous obsession returned. 'What did he want from you?'

'My story, plain and simple,' David told him. 'In return for a generous payment. I didn't ask how such a scruffy young man got hold of that amount of cash.'

'How much?'

'Does that really matter?'

'No, I'm curious, that's all,' Dylan remarked. 'More or less than you bribed out of Kenny Ferguson?'

David shifted uncomfortably in the chair.

'That was the real reason for your interaction with him. Money?' Dylan added.

David sighed. 'I'm not proud of doing it, if that's what you're getting at.'

'I never said that.'

'No? Well, he owed me,' David interrupted angrily. '*She* owed me, and that boy coming round here asking me to relive it all, it got me thinking. Thinking about it all. My life – or rather my lack of life.'

'Blackmail is also a crime,' Dylan pointed out.

'Is that right, Detective?' David spat. 'Funny that because so's murder but I didn't see Alice Connor banged up for long.' He clenched his fist and pummelled the table.

'Right, that's enough or I'll arrest you,' Dylan asserted just as Law's phone rang on the table. Dylan didn't get a chance to see what the caller ID said before it was snatched up and switched off.

'I only wanted what I was entitled to,' David added.

'I understand you're feeling hurt. It didn't seem fair that you were the only one doing serious time for your crime.'

'My crime?' David scoffed and shook his head. 'My only crime was being stupid enough to fall in love with *her*.'

Dylan eyed him carefully. 'She was just a teenage girl. Are you telling me she was the mastermind behind the murder?'

David Law laughed. 'Trust me: she was no innocent teenage girl. Have you asked yourself the question – if *I* did what I did for her, who *else* has she manipulated into helping her? Convenient, isn't it, that couple being dead now? Alice Connor never liked people that got in the way of what she wanted. What makes you think *Rachel Ferguson* is any different?'

CHAPTER SEVENTY-ONE

Jessie knocked once and waited. She glanced around at the drab grey surroundings and thought the Fergusons must be hating it. Two cherry trees and a small patch of grass was as much countryside as they had for now. A world away from their acres of land with views of rolling green hills, even if they were dotted with wind turbines.

When she got no response, she knocked again. This time a light blinked on inside the hallway, followed by footsteps that got closer. Jessie could hear voices inside before the door opened. She smiled to greet Rachel, who nodded and immediately began to walk away, leaving the door wide open.

'You better come in,' she said as she moved away.

'Thank you,' Jessie responded and closed the door behind her. 'It's Kenny I'm here to speak to – is he in?'

Rachel stopped and turned back round. 'Why do you need to speak to him?'

'I have a couple of questions I'd like to ask him, that's all. Is he here?'

Jessie turned on hearing the front door open and shut again behind her.

'Hello, Detective,' Kenny said. He removed his heavy jacket and hung it up on the hooks by the door.

'She needs to speak to you, apparently,' Rachel commented.

Kenny frowned. 'Really?'

Jessie sensed the atmosphere darken. She was clearly not welcome there but that was too bad. She went where the evidence led. She wondered if Dylan's presence was being any better received but sincerely doubted it.

'I have a few questions I'd like to ask you. Can we go and sit down?' Jessie suggested. Kenny threw a glance at Rachel, who walked away, closing the bedroom door behind her.

'Come through. We can talk in the kitchen.' Kenny brushed past Jessie in the narrow hallway and opened the kitchen door to the smell of some kind of cake baking in the oven. Jessie wasn't sure what it was but it made her hungry.

'Please sit.' Kenny lifted a jacket from the back of an empty chair and pulled it away from the table for her then flopped down opposite her.

Jessie noticed his anxiety immediately. He avoided her gaze and didn't look comfortable at all.

'Why did you lie to me about not having seen David Law?' Jessie got straight to the point and watched Kenny's wide-eyed response. His cheeks blushed pink as he shuffled forward in the chair. He leaned heavily on his elbows before closing his eyes and sighing. Then he shrugged.

'I didn't want to admit what a fool I'd been.'

Jessie hadn't anticipated that as his answer. 'How so?'

'I thought I could talk him round. Make him see the damage exposing her would cause but he insisted that if I didn't pay he would.' He stopped and shook his head before inhaling a long, slow breath. He exhaled loudly as he stared at the ceiling. 'She wouldn't be able to cope if it got out. It would destroy her. You've seen how fragile she is.'

Jessie opened the text that blinked into her phone. It was from Dylan.

Law has admitted to the blackmail. Seems adamant Rachel has convinced someone, maybe even Kenny, of killing the Anguses. See you back at the station.

She tucked her phone away. 'What did he want?'

'Ten thousand now and another ten in three months and so on. Quarterly instalments.'

Jessie whistled. 'That's no small change. He clearly thinks you can afford it.'

'Look, what does this have to do with the death of Malcolm and Jean? We've already told you everything we know. The rest is my business.' He sighed. 'I can handle it. I have to, for Rachel's sake.'

Jessie felt sorry for the pathetic sight sitting opposite her. He'd aged considerably in the past week.

'You must love your wife very much,' she suggested to him, and for the first time since she'd arrived she saw him smile. His whole face lit up and he made proper eye contact with her.

'From the minute we met. I'll give him everything if it means he keeps quiet.'

Jessie believed him when he said that. What was it about this woman that had men risking it all for her?

'I have to ask. A witness has told us they overheard you arranging to have someone killed?'

'What?'

'Who were you calling at the Seagate project?'

'David Law – you know that by now, I expect. I haven't asked someone to kill him, for God's sake.'

'Did you ask David to—'

Kenny stood up. 'Are you insane? Are you suggesting I asked him to kill the Anguses? That's the most ludicrous thing I've ever heard and I want you to leave – now.'

'Kenny, what's going on?'

Neither Jessie nor Kenny had heard Rachel arrive.

'It's nothing, sweetheart. DI Blake was just leaving.' Kenny lifted his hand to indicate the door. 'If you wish to speak to either me or Rachel again, please do so through our solicitor. We won't be answering any more questions without him being present. Goodbye, Detective.'

'Kenny?' Rachel repeated with a frown.

'I said, goodbye, Detective,' Kenny repeated.

Jessie stood. She didn't have enough evidence to arrest him and she wasn't going to get anything more out of him today.

'I'll be in touch,' she commented and smiled at Rachel. 'I'll see myself out.'

Jessie pulled out her phone and dialled Dylan's number as she crossed the car park, shivering in the cold wind that nipped at her cheeks.

The slender figure watched Jessie's car reverse out of the parking space and disappear out onto the main road back towards town. She slipped past the officer in the patrol car nearby, pulling her scarf up over her mouth and nose as she walked. He knew who she was by now. She gave him a nod when he glanced up and made her way to the front door of the flat.

CHAPTER SEVENTY-TWO

'Caroline, what's happened?' Kenny was aghast at the sight of his PA standing in his doorway, blood pouring from a split lip, her eyes blackened. 'Come in, come in!' He wrapped his arm around her shoulder. 'Rachel, grab some ice,' he called out.

'What – oh my goodness!' Rachel gasped. 'Wait, I'll get the ice – go and sit down. I'll be as quick as I can.'

Rachel jogged into the kitchen and snatched a bag of peas from the bottom drawer of the freezer. She wrapped the bag in a tea towel.

'Here, take this.' She handed it to Caroline, who held it to her swollen lip.

'What the hell happened? Who did this to you?' Kenny asked, moving Caroline's fringe out of her painful-looking black eyes. 'Rachel, call the police.'

'No, I don't want any trouble!' Caroline shouted and pulled the ice from her face. 'I didn't get a look at them anyway. They were coming out of my flat.'

'Your flat?' Rachel asked. 'Did a burglar do this to you?'

Caroline nodded slowly. 'They snatched my bag after hitting me on their way out.'

Rachel sat next to the visibly shocked young woman. She almost felt sorry for her.

'You'll need a police number for your insurance. What do you call it, a – erm, a crime reference number, that's it,' she informed her.

Caroline's head dropped.

'Don't tell me you don't have insurance?' Rachel announced.

'Let's not worry about that for now,' Kenny interrupted. 'We can replace any belongings, you know that.' He pulled her face close to his chest and stared at his wife over the top of Caroline's head.

A small pang of unexpected jealousy rose inside Rachel, which unsettled her.

'I'll go and put the kettle on,' she said. 'Strong, sweet tea. That's what you need.'

As she walked away she heard Caroline cry on Kenny's shoulder, touched by his concern. Kenny was a good man despite his carnal weakness. Who could possibly want to hurt Caroline like that? But was she just the victim of a random burglary that had turned violent when she'd arrived home unexpectedly? Or was something more sinister going on? Rachel wondered if she was being paranoid, wondering if Caroline's misfortune was connected to her situation. There was such a thing as coincidence, after all.

'Here you go. I've put three sugars in it for you. For the shock.' Rachel pressed a large mug of tea into Caroline's trembling hand. 'I'll go and find some blankets. You can stay here tonight and we'll come back with you tomorrow to assess the damage.' She smiled. It was the least she could do. She knew Caroline was estranged from her remaining family and she didn't know of any friends to speak of.

'I can't expect—'

'Nonsense. You're staying here and that's the end of it.'

Kenny's father-figure persona was beginning to show through. Despite her reservations about Caroline, Rachel liked this part of her husband. It was what she'd fallen for all those years ago. Perhaps Caroline was more like her than she allowed herself to recognise. Kenny had picked Rachel up from a very dark place. A very dark place indeed.

'Thank you. Both of you. I don't know what I'd do without you.'

'Don't be silly. It's what friends are for.' Rachel had said it before she knew it.

But perhaps taking care of Caroline in her hour of need was what she needed to take her mind off the coming week. Fixing her husband's broken little mistress would take her mind off the impending double-murder trial.

Who was she kidding? There was nothing that could do that. No – that wasn't true, Rachel reminded herself. Her horses. They could help her through even the darkest day.

CHAPTER SEVENTY-THREE

Jessie must have drifted off to sleep because the text that rang out made her jump, sending Smokey heading for the floor. She and Dylan had gone over what both men had said. From the brief intelligence she'd been able to gather from Kenny, it appeared they had the facts. A simple case of blackmail with a big secret at its heart.

Law had gone on to tell Dylan more about Gordon and how finding out who and where Rachel was had made him feel. Jessie had suggested to Dylan that David Law must hold such resentment against her. The thought that he was setting Rachel up for the murder did cross her mind but there was no proof of that at all. Jessie doubted him being a criminal mastermind capable of that anyway. She'd told Dylan to get off home because they were both tired, and he'd told her things were better on that front. They'd sought advice for Katie's sleeping problem and so far it seemed to be working, which had made Shelly feel better. The knock-on effect was less stress on her leading to a happier Dylan, Jessie was relieved to find.

'Shit!' Jessie sat bolt upright and struggled to see the buttons on her iPhone. 'No way,' she muttered when she could see another text from Haley waiting for her. She didn't bother to read what it said. Jessie had no interest in developing any kind of friendship with Haley. Watching her being destroyed by Dan was the last thing she wanted to witness first-hand.

Then a thought occurred to her. She wondered if this was Dan's doing and not Haley's at all. A horrible feeling hit her gut. Perhaps Dan was using poor Haley's phone now. Was his grip on the young, naïve girl tightening? Jessie knew that coercion crept up on you before you realised what was happening. Little by little, Dan would be chipping away at her confidence followed by her self-worth, before she lost all sense of reality altogether. Jessie had to do something, didn't she? It was the right thing to do. No matter how awkward and difficult. Over coffee maybe?

Hell, now Jessie would never get back to sleep. This case. Double murder. Dan. Haley. Her mind spun as she got up to go to the bathroom. She stared at her reflection in the bathroom mirror and jumped when Smokey leaped onto the toilet seat to nuzzle into her leg.

'You daft thing,' she said and scratched behind his ears, causing a loud purr to vibrate against her bare leg.

Jessie headed into the kitchen and filled a tall glass with cold water from the tap and took it through to her bedroom. She set her alarm and grabbed her Kindle. She flicked through the books on her digital bookshelf but nothing grabbed her attention and she yawned as she closed her eyes.

Dan laid the phone back down onto the bedside table and smiled at Haley, who was in bed beside him.

'Was that my phone?' Haley asked.

'Shh, come here, you.' Dan pulled Haley close and placed a long, lingering kiss on her lips and covered her body with his. Then he coldly got up and grabbed a sweater from the back of the chair next to the bed.

'I have to go out,' he said abruptly. 'Don't wait up.'

CHAPTER SEVENTY-FOUR

The knock on the door startled Jessie out of a deep sleep. She sat bolt upright and listened. She frowned at the time on the clock – 1.30 a.m. All she could hear now was its gentle ticking. She reached around for Smokey, who wasn't there. He must be in his own bed for once, she thought. She switched on the bedside lamp and waited. She wondered if she'd dreamed the knocking.

When only silence filled the room she switched the light off and snuggled back down. She tugged her duvet up around her shoulders against the cold night air, sighed deeply and closed her eyes – then sat straight back up. There it was again. She hadn't imagined it. Shivering, Jessie grabbed a cardigan from the chest at the bottom of her bed and zipped it right up. She crept quietly to the door and peered through the spyhole then gasped and moved away.

'Shit,' she muttered and looked again.

How did he know where she lived? Had he followed her? The thought sent shivers down her spine. He knocked again. Jessie looked again. She lifted her phone from the hall table and dialled 999 but didn't press the call button. She wanted it there just in case before she did anything. She paced back and forth and heard the handle moving. She took a deep breath and slid back the chain, dropping it down out of her fingers. Her heart raced.

'What do you want, Gordon?' she called out, her hand hovering over the lock.

'I need to talk to you.'

'Can't it wait until morning?' she suggested. 'Come to the station first thing. We can talk then.'

'I have something I need to tell you. I—' She heard him hesitate. 'I know who killed my granny and grandad.'

Jessie looked at her phone then picked it up, fingers poised over the call button, then she slowly unlocked the front door and pulled it open. Smokey hissed and ran out past Gordon and into the garden. She really was completely alone with him now. *What the hell are you thinking?*

'Can I come in?' Gordon asked and brushed past before Jessie had a chance to respond. Her heart raced and a pounding headache burst forward between her temples. Jessie pushed the door shut and exhaled the large breath that crippled her chest. She followed Gordon deeper into her flat and found him sat on her sofa with a rucksack she hadn't noticed earlier on the cushion next to him.

'You said you know who killed your grandparents.'

Gordon nodded.

Jessie swallowed hard. 'Was it you?'

Gordon's head snapped up, a look of disgust on his face. 'No,' he blasted. 'Why would I kill them?' he scoffed.

'Why set fire to Rachel Ferguson's place?' she added.

Gordon's jaw tightened but he ignored Jessie's question.

A strange sense of relief enveloped Jessie in that moment. Confusion, too, but certainly relief. Perhaps he wasn't a murderer.

That relief quickly evaporated once Jessie spotted the blade glimmering inside the bag.

'W-Why are you really here, Gordon?' she stuttered, her mouth suddenly feeling very dry.

'When I found David Law I couldn't believe my luck – until I realised maybe it wasn't luck. Maybe finding him was the first step in fulfilling my purpose.'

Jessie couldn't speak. Fear gripped her. She'd been so stupid. What had she been thinking letting him in? She watched him pull a hammer out of the bag and place it gently onto her coffee table.

'Give me your phone,' he instructed her.

Nausea gripped Jessie's stomach. She had to fight the urge to be sick as she lifted her phone from her cardigan pocket then handed it to him in her trembling hand.

'I'm disappointed.' He held up the phone and deleted the 999 as he shook his head. 'I only came here to talk.'

'You know, you won't get away with whatever you've planned tonight.'

Gordon smiled. 'Sit down, Detective.'

Jessie lowered her trembling legs onto the chair behind her. Gordon lifted a pair of gloves from his bag and slid his hands into them. *Keep it together, Jessie.* She fixed her mind on getting out of this no matter what. *Think, Jessie, think.* She scanned the immediate vicinity for something to defend herself with. One thump on his temple with something heavy and hard should do it.

'Don't be scared,' Gordon whispered. 'This will be beautiful. You will never be forgotten.'

'Gordon.' Jessie's voice sounded more confident than she felt but she couldn't let him see that. 'I don't know what you think you're going to achieve by doing this. Do you want to be like your heroes, is that it?'

'Get on your knees and turn and face the wall.'

'No,' Jessie murmured.

'I said, turn round!' Gordon screamed.

Jessie got down onto her knees and did as she was told. Benito's face slammed into her mind as she shook. She couldn't feel her legs. They'd gone numb with absolute terror. She had pins and needles through her feet. She felt the breeze created by Gordon's arm as it lifted above her head. Then nothing until a familiar voice filled the space.

'Dan!' Jessie called out and watched him punch Gordon into submission, over and over, until he no longer resisted.

Jessie couldn't stop the tears that tumbled out unchecked until she vomited on the floor next to her. She struggled to regain control of her breathing and gasped for air.

'It's OK now.' Dan held out his hand.

Jessie stared at him without saying a word. She grabbed for her phone, which Gordon had tossed onto the sofa. She had to step over Gordon's still body to get away. Jessie ran and locked herself in the bathroom to dial 999.

CHAPTER SEVENTY-FIVE

'Jessie, it's OK – Gordon's gone,' Dylan said softly through the bathroom door. He glanced back at Dan, who was giving a statement to one of the uniformed officers who had attended the scene within ten minutes of Jessie's 999 call. He listened for movement inside then tapped his knuckles on the door. 'Jess, it's me,' he added gently.

The lock clicked and Dylan stood up straight to see the door move slowly open. He held out his arms to her. Jessie slammed her body into Dylan's and allowed him to wrap his arms around her. Through the open door she could see Gordon sitting in the back of a police car, staring back at her and grinning, his face covered in blood. She pulled out of Dylan's arms and ran to slam the front door shut, then stood for a moment, her eyes fixed on the closed door. She turned round and leaned her back against it. She caught sight of Dan watching her and nodded to him. Dan nodded back. Neither of them had to say anything.

'Here – drink this.' Dylan handed her a cup of sweet tea once everyone else had left. 'There's three sugars in it.'

Jessie took the cup from him and took a sip before screwing up her nose. It was far too sweet. She'd declined the paramedic's offer to take her to get checked out at the hospital. There was no need. Thanks to Dan, that was. Jessie shivered at the thought of what would have happened if he hadn't turned up. It felt like a bad dream.

'I don't mean to pry but who was that guy?' Dylan probed.

'Dan is someone from another lifetime ago,' Jessie said without looking at him. She glanced into her living room through the open kitchen door. There was nothing out of place. Nothing to suggest a maniac had been here less than an hour earlier trying to kill her with a hammer.

'You don't have to talk about it,' Dylan commented. 'I'm just glad he was here when you needed him.'

Jessie took another sip of the sickly-sweet tea and had to put it down. She pondered the irony of Dylan's remark. She'd been trying to shake Dan out of her life for so many years. The phone calls. The flowers. His relationship with Haley. Jessie thought that was part of his sick game too. Where did she think Dan was at that time of night? Why was he even *there* at that time of night? Had he been stalking her all this time? She shuddered at the idea he'd just saved her life.

CHAPTER SEVENTY-SIX

The sun was just starting to rise when Rachel crept past a sleeping Caroline on her way into her kitchen. The walls in this tiny flat were beginning to close in on her. She intended to spend the day with the horses. Being with them was the only place she knew could keep her calm. Another local trainer had agreed to step in and take over starting tomorrow. He was going over to take the horses back to his yard, which was just a few miles along the road. Rachel was lucky to have him.

'Good morning,' a small voice spoke from the darkness.

'I'm putting the kettle on. Would you like a cup of tea?' Rachel asked.

Caroline yawned and winced from the pain in her lip. 'That would be lovely.'

The women heard Kenny move through to the bathroom. Caroline got up to join Rachel in the kitchen.

'Kenny will take you over to your flat this morning,' Rachel promised. 'See what needs doing and what needs replacing.'

Caroline tried to smile. 'You've both been so kind. I don't know what I would have done without the two of you last night.'

Last night. Rachel recalled the enlightening chat she'd had with Caroline over a nip of whisky. Caroline's childhood sounded tragic. Her mother had died when she was just five and because there was nobody else to take care of her, Caroline had been shuffled between foster homes until she was adopted by the Peters when she was eight. She'd hinted that some unpleasant experiences had taken place in that home but neither Rachel nor Kenny had pressed her on it. Now even they were gone, Rachel recalled from an earlier conversation. Tragic. It had seemed Caroline was just grateful to have someone to talk to. Rachel could relate to that. She'd felt alone once upon a time. She was glad to hear that Caroline had struck up such a friendship with Julia too. The two women were around the same age, and both had been adopted at a young age too.

'There you go.' Rachel placed a mug on the kitchen table in front of Caroline. She seemed fragile sitting there. Thin, even bird-like.

'Thank you.'

'Did you manage to get much sleep? I'm not sure that sofa is particularly comfortable.'

Caroline sipped from her mug then smiled. 'It was perfect.' Her smile quickly fell into a frown, followed by tears. Rachel moved to put her arm around her shoulder.

'Hey, you're safe now. I know you've been through an awful ordeal. It must have been very scary for you, but you're safe now.'

'I know and I'm sorry. I think it's still just the shock,' Caroline admitted. 'You never think something so terrible will ever happen to you.'

Rachel heard Kenny coming out of the bathroom and moved over to pour him a cup of tea. Caroline's words echoed in her ears. How she wished all she had to worry about was a petty burglar. She kissed Kenny's cheek when he joined them in the kitchen.

'I'm off,' she told them both. 'I'll try not to be too late back.'

'Would you like me to come with you?'

Rachel was pleasantly surprised by Kenny's offer. Perhaps he wanted a day out in the country. He must be feeling the strain of the situation too. That and not having his dogs with him. They were lucky the kennels they often used had space for all three Labradors. Especially at that time of year.

'No, you stay with Caroline. Help her get things straightened out. I'll be fine.'

She kissed Kenny's cheek one last time before grabbing her jacket and keys. She stepped into a pair of boots by the front door and pulled it shut behind her. Outside, she inhaled a huge breath of the biting winter chill – the cold didn't bother Rachel. It was the suffocating heat in the small one-bedroom flat that made her uncomfortable. She was terrified at the prospect of the prison cell she might soon have to endure. But the plan she'd put in place would hopefully help her avoid that. It wasn't exactly a lie – more a welcome secret that she'd discovered. Her solicitor had been excited to hear of the development. It had come as a shock to discover he felt that way about a woman he hardly knew and wondered if she was being cruel to use that to her advantage now. But what choice did she have?

CHAPTER SEVENTY-SEVEN

'Wow,' Jessie exclaimed when Dylan told her what Gordon had said the previous night. 'An alibi?'

Dylan nodded. 'That's what he said.'

'Did he tell you why he—' Jessie had to stop for a moment to collect her thoughts. Her chest tightened at the memory of last night. 'Why he came to my flat?' She couldn't bring herself to say what had really happened. *Why he came to kill her.*

'He said he was ready to know how it felt to kill someone.'

Jessie shuddered at the simplicity of his reason. 'But why me?' she asked.

Dylan shook his head. 'No, sorry, he didn't say.'

Jessie didn't know if she was disappointed or not. She wasn't sure if knowing why made any difference.

'What do you make of the alibi?' she asked.

Dylan shrugged. 'It gets Rachel off the hook, that's for sure. Says he saw her that morning his grandparents were killed. It couldn't have been her that killed them. She was in the stable with the horses.'

'And he knows that because he was watching her.' Jessie balked at the suggestion.

Jessie realised she and Rachel had more in common than either of them knew. Gordon had been stalking Rachel in the same way Dan had been watching her. Neither woman had known they were there, observing their everyday lives, yet in an obscene kind of way both men had saved them from their respective fates.

'At least he's being remanded in custody. The thought of him being out there doesn't bear thinking about,' Dylan remarked.

Jessie couldn't agree more. There was no way she'd have felt able to stay at her flat with Gordon on the loose even if she could rely on Dan to be her saviour. *Dan*. Jessie knew she'd have to talk to him about what had happened. This wasn't something that could easily be forgotten by either of them.

CHAPTER SEVENTY-EIGHT

'You better come in,' Rachel told Jessie and walked away, leaving the door open for her.

Jessie stepped inside and followed, closing the door behind her.

'I'm making tea. Would you like a cup?' Rachel asked and as she filled the kettle.

'No, I'm fine, thank you.' Jessie sat down and unzipped her jacket in the small, stuffy kitchen space.

Rachel leaned behind Jessie to open the window – just enough to allow air to penetrate the stale atmosphere. She wiped a little of the condensation and peered out onto the frost covered ground, shivering at the thought of the freezing temperatures this afternoon.

'I don't think there's a lot more I can tell you, Detective,' Rachel remarked.

Jessie smiled. 'I'm here to tell you some good news.'

Rachel tossed the tea towel onto the draining board and sat down with her cup of tea. 'Good news?'

Jessie nodded, unsure exactly how good it was. 'A witness has come forward to say that he saw you—'

'Gordon Angus,' Rachel interrupted.

'You already knew?' Jessie said.

Rachel sipped from her cup then licked her lips and laid the cup down. 'I've known for a little while. He was going to give evidence at my trial for my defence.' She smiled. 'He said he wanted to help me.' Rachel stood up and tipped water from the kettle into her cup. 'Can I be honest with you?'

A little taken aback, Jessie nodded but before Rachel could continue, the front door opened, distracting her from her story. Both women were surprised to see Caroline walk into the kitchen.

'Caroline, what are you doing here? I thought you and Kenny were sorting things out at your place?' Rachel declared; then her eyes narrowed.

Caroline lifted a mug from the tree on the worktop and switched the kettle on again.

'He's gone to get some bits and pieces for me. A new lock for a start.' She smiled awkwardly at Jessie.

'That looks nasty.' Jessie pointed to Caroline's painful-looking lip and black eye.

'Caroline was burgled yesterday. They attacked her when she disturbed them,' Rachel told her. 'Kenny is helping her sort through her things.'

'That's awful. I'm sorry to hear that,' Jessie said.

Caroline took the milk from the fridge then stirred sugar into her tea before flopping down in the empty chair next to Jessie.

'Has there been any news on the fire?' she asked, then sipped her tea without taking her eyes off Jessie.

'That's not why she's here,' Rachel announced. 'A witness has come forward that proves I didn't murder Malcolm and Jean Angus.'

Caroline swallowed a gulp of tea. 'Oh, that is good news. You must be so pleased. After all you've been through that must be such a relief.' She moved her attention to Jessie. 'What happens now then?'

'Investigation remains ongoing,' Jessie informed her. 'There are further lines of enquiry that I intend to follow up.'

'You think it was Gordon, don't you?' Rachel's suggestion made Jessie turn.

The sound of his name sent shivers through her. Last night's visit was still raw in her mind. She had to quickly snatch her breath back from the mounting panic. She'd managed to persuade Crawford that she was fit to return to work immediately on the agreement that she saw the force's counsellor.

'Among other possibilities,' Jessie told her as she stood up to leave.

Caroline smiled. 'At least you can relax now, though, can't you, Rachel?'

Jessie headed back to her car with an odd sensation she couldn't shake. Caroline seemed rather overly familiar with her boss, in her opinion.

Her phone buzzing in her pocket distracted her.

Just checking in to make sure you're OK after last night. D x

Jessie pushed her phone deep into her pocket without answering. She unlocked her car, got in and slammed the door shut. She felt the tears trickle over her cheek before dripping off her chin onto her shirt and clenched her hand into a fist until the skin turned white. She focused on her breathing. *In and out. In and out.*

Jessie was angry with herself for breaking down but had to acknowledge that it had been cathartic. It had helped her focus on what was important: finding out who had killed an innocent elderly couple in their own homes. Gordon Angus became her target. She'd seen first-hand what this young man could be capable of and now she was on the hunt for proof that would put him away for a long time.

She nodded to the officers parked out front of the Anguses' farmhouse and unlocked the front door. There was something in that house that would lead to the killer. She knew it. She might have to look a little harder but it was there, she was sure. Jessie handed Dylan a pair of gloves and overshoes.

'You start upstairs and I'll take the kitchen,' she instructed him.

'What are we looking for exactly?'

'Anything and everything. The answer is in here somewhere. Rachel's alibi means there has to be something in here that we missed. Our killer is still on the loose.'

CHAPTER SEVENTY-NINE

Kenny drove the six miles from their flat in the centre of Perth towards Stanley. The fire service had finished their examination of the house and given him the go-ahead to visit the property: the only good news in the past twenty-four hours. He thought about the way Caroline had responded to his suggestion that they cool things for a bit, because Rachel needed him to be there for her more. She'd seemed upset at first, then the tears seemed to evaporate just as quickly as they had started. He figured the assault had taken more of a toll than she'd admitted. He'd given her some cash and told her to take a couple of weeks holiday. He wouldn't be needing her for much in the coming days anyway.

The sun that split over the hills that surrounded the village might have lifted his spirits on another day but not today. The wind turbines whirred gently, blowing the soothing sound in the air towards the shell of his home. The acrid smell of smoke lingered and the eerie silence unnerved him. He knew the horses had been collected so there was no neighing against the sound of wind. Kenny would have loved to hear the sound of his three dogs barking to greet his Land Rover; he couldn't wait to collect them.

He stepped out of his car and locked it up before walking across the driveway. He unlocked the front door and gently leaned a finger on the wood until it swung slowly open. The smell was much stronger inside. Kenny coughed then covered his nose with the palm of his hand. He stood in the hallway and just stared. It was overwhelming. The damage would run into the tens of thousands, if not more. There hadn't been any update on the arson investigation for several days. Kenny would give DI Blake a call later – see if she had any news.

He moved into what had once been a beautiful galley kitchen. A place he and Rachel had shared many delicious meals and talked about everything and nothing. It was all gone and would have to be rebuilt from scratch. Whoever did this had been intent on destroying their home. The realisation they wouldn't be able to return here for months – perhaps even a year – broke his heart. He'd worked hard to make this place a home for him and Rachel. He wanted to give her everything she'd ever dreamed of. He'd promised to take care of her.

A noise behind Kenny startled him into spinning round. Nothing. He turned back, wondering if he'd imagined it until he heard it again. Footsteps – he was sure of it.

'Hello, who's there?' he called out and retraced his steps to the front door. Nothing. 'Hello.'

This time he raised his voice. 'Is someone there?'

The eerie silence was broken by the sound of running behind him, which made him turn quickly and almost lose his footing. He was briefly aware of a heavy thud on the side of his head then it all went black.

CHAPTER EIGHTY

Jessie and Dylan searched Gordon's room at his grandparents' farmhouse. They found nothing to link him to their murder, but they did find Gordon's diary, which gave the two detectives further insight into the sickness that was inside him. His plan to make Jessie his victim was laid out in black and white. When he planned to do it. How he planned to do it. What he would need was written in the form of a shopping list.

Jessie lifted a laptop out of his bedside drawer. She tried the first password that came to her mind and the screen opened immediately. Alice Connor. His wallpaper was a photo of Rachel. It was obvious Rachel had no idea someone was watching her. Taking her picture. He was obsessed.

'Have you found anything on there?' Dylan asked as he rummaged in the bottom of Gordon's wardrobe. He closed the door and joined Jessie on the edge of Gordon's bed.

'Not yet – nothing to connect him to the murder.'

'Is he getting a psych evaluation?' Dylan asked.

'His defence hasn't asked for one,' Jessie replied. 'He probably will at some point, though.'

'Look, tell me to shut up if you think I'm prying but—' Dylan began clumsily.

'I'm fine,' Jessie chirped.

'Sorry, I'm just concerned.'

'Concerned about what, Dylan? Spill it.'

It was clear that Dylan was searching for the most diplomatic way to say it. 'There's nothing here to suggest Gordon killed them. This house has been torn apart by forensics. There's *nothing*.' He paused. 'He's a weird kid but he didn't shoot his grandparents.'

Jessie could see the anxious look on Dylan's face but he'd been right to speak up. She knew there was nothing in that house or on the bodies to prove his guilt, but Jessie was so desperate to find something: a single fibre, a fingerprint, a bullet, anything. He'd given Rachel an alibi. The reality of finding nothing meant she was back to square one – a dead couple and no suspects. She had considered the possibility of using a polygraph on Gordon but evidence based on lie detectors could easily be ruled inadmissible by a good defence solicitor. It wouldn't surprise her if Gordon knew how to beat the test anyway.

The sound of sirens drew the two detectives' attention and they both got up to see an ambulance hurtling towards the burnt-out ruin of the Fergusons' property.

CHAPTER EIGHTY-ONE

David paid for his two cups of tea and thanked the cashier. He even dropped a small tip on the plate by the till. He was disappointed that she hadn't shown up because he'd looked forward to seeing her ever since her phone call. He knew – after all those years apart – that it might take time for them to get to know each other, but he was excited about the prospect of doing just that. They'd lost so many years they could have had if things had been different.

There was no point dwelling on the past, she'd told him. Moving forward was the only thing that they could do now. She was right, but that didn't stop the lingering feeling of bitterness that remained. The money, though, would go a long way to sweetening that for them both. He was going to tell her about a flat he'd seen. He hoped she'd be happy that he'd put a deposit down and paid the first month's rent. It wasn't a huge place but more than big enough for them. He wanted her to live with him so he could start taking care of her the way he should have been doing all these years.

David held the door open for the young woman pushing a pram with an irate toddler screaming and offered a smile as she passed. He tugged his collar up against the cold breeze that swept along the street then jogged on to wave down the oncoming bus. He paid the driver and took a seat at the back as the driver indicated into Kinnoull Street, then rested his head against the window and closed his eyes. He tapped the envelope in the pocket of his jeans.

If she wouldn't come to him then he would go to her. He wanted her to know he planned to take care of her.

A while later, David pressed the bell and made his way to the front of the bus. He thanked the driver and waited for the bus to move off so he could cross the road to her flat. It wasn't right that she lived in a place like this. He walked up the stairs and knocked on her front door then waited. He knocked again but still got no response, so he pulled the envelope from his pocket and stuffed it through the letterbox.

CHAPTER EIGHTY-TWO

The caller who had contacted the emergency services hadn't left their name. Jessie wondered if they knew more about the attack on Kenny than they let on. Whoever had made the call, whether involved or not, had saved his life, though. He was unconscious when paramedics arrived but breathing, however he'd regained consciousness in the back of the ambulance and was lucid and talking by the time they arrived at the hospital. Jessie smiled as she approached him, her gaze skimming the huge bandage wrapped round his head.

'Hello, Kenny. How are you feeling?' she asked. 'That's a nasty knock you've taken.'

'DI Blake.' Kenny was curt in response as he sat up in the hospital bed.

Jessie didn't get a chance to say much more as Rachel swept past her and pulled Kenny into her arms. That call had sent shivers right through her whole body. For all his faults – and there were plenty – Rachel was struck by the fear of losing him.

'I'm all right, don't worry,' Kenny reassured her and tried to smile. 'Takes more than a bump on the head to knock me off my perch.'

Rachel took his face in her hands and kissed his cheek. 'I was so worried about you.'

Kenny waved away her words before she could finish. 'Enough of that. I'm fine.'

'Did you recognise the person who attacked you, Mr Ferguson?' Jessie piped up. 'Did you manage to get a look at them?'

Kenny shook his head. 'It all happened so fast. I remember hearing what sounded like footsteps so I turned to see who was there and the next thing I remember was a crushing pain in my head.'

'My colleague DC Logan is at your house with a forensics team to see if they can identify who was present at the time you were attacked. You have my word we're doing everything we can to find who did this to you.'

Kenny shook his head then looked away with a sigh.

'We'll be in touch when we get any new information, and in the meantime, if you remember something more, please don't hesitate to give me a call.'

It was when Jessie was about to close the side-room door behind her that Kenny called her back. She ignored the text that buzzed on her phone and rejoined the couple.

'You remember seeing someone?' Jessie asked as she watched the confusion grow on Rachel's face too.

Kenny sat up in the bed. 'No, no, it can't be.' He scratched at his bandage and winced.

'What is it? You're scaring me,' Rachel announced.

'I didn't see anyone but I smelled them,' Kenny remarked.

Jessie frowned and her eyes met Rachel's.

'You smelled them. What does that mean?' Jessie chirped.

'I smelled her perfume.'

CHAPTER EIGHTY-THREE

Jessie's gaze met Rachel's. Their interaction at the flat earlier had seemed odd. Jessie remembered sensing something off in Caroline's demeanour. She could see Kenny's mind whirring at a million miles an hour.

'She wasn't very happy with me the last time I spoke to her,' he informed Jessie.

'Don't be so ridiculous. You're not suggesting it was Caroline that did that to you?' Rachel pointed to the bandage on Kenny's head. 'Why would she?'

Kenny looked anxiously at Jessie then back at Rachel. 'Look, can I talk to DI Blake alone for a minute.'

'Erm, sure but—' Rachel tried to say.

'Please,' Kenny whispered and reached for her hand.

Rachel pulled her hand back far enough to avoid contact with his before turning and walking out of the side room.

'What's on your mind?' Jessie asked. 'Clearly something you don't want your wife to know.'

'You must understand I love my wife.'

'What's that got to do with you getting hit on the head, Mr Ferguson?' Jessie was losing patience with him. 'Just tell me what you know.'

Kenny sighed. 'Caroline and I – we've been having an affair. I told her I thought we should cool things a bit. Gave her money to take a holiday. She got upset then took the money and left.'

'Rachel doesn't know, I assume.'

Kenny shook his head. 'I don't think so. I'd appreciate it if she didn't need to.'

'I can't promise she won't ever find out,' Jessie told him. 'Especially if this case comes to court.'

Jessie watched the horror spread across his face.

'God, this is such a mess.'

Jessie spotted Rachel's face appear in the window of the room door and opened it for her. Rachel came in and placed a plastic cup of coffee on the table next to her husband.

'Is everything OK?' she asked.

Jessie looked at Kenny, who nodded. 'I'll be in touch. Hope you feel better soon.'

She pulled the door closed behind her and headed for the lift, irritated not to get signal on her phone. She pressed the button for the ground floor and watched the doors close then considered Kenny's news carefully. It certainly warranted checking out even if it seemed doubtful that a woman as small as Caroline would be able to floor a large man like Kenny with such ease.

She stepped out of the lift and turned the corner towards the exit. She pressed Dylan's number on her phone and waited for him to answer.

'Hi, it's me, meet me at—' Jessie stopped dead. Her heart raced at the sight of him standing in front of her. 'Sorry, Dylan, I'll have to call you back.' Jessie slid her phone away from her face and stared, unable to speak.

'Hello, Jessie. It's good to see you again.'

CHAPTER EIGHTY-FOUR

'I have to be somewhere.' Jessie started to move past Dan until he reached out and touched her arm.

'I'm sorry,' he responded and pulled his hand away. 'How are you?'

Jessie stared at him. 'If you're waiting for me to thank you for saving me then you'll be waiting a very long time.'

'That kid was going to kill you.' Dan pushed Jessie aside as a trolley moved past them quickly.

Jessie scoffed and shoved him aside. 'And that excuses you being there in the first place, does it?'

'What's that supposed to mean? If I hadn't been there—' he started to say.

'Yes, he would have killed me. I know – you've already pointed that out.'

The door to the ladies' bathroom along the hall opened to reveal a tired, pale-looking Haley.

'Does she know, hmm? Does Haley know about your act of heroism?'

'No, she doesn't,' Dan spat.

There it was in his eyes. The venom Jessie knew well.

'Goodbye, Dan.'

Jessie started to walk away until Haley's voice called her name. She stopped and turned to say hello.

'It's good to see you, Haley. How have you been?' Jessie painted on a smile.

'Has he told you?' Haley chirped. 'I know it's a bit sudden and unexpected but sometimes if it's right you just know, don't you?'

Jessie frowned as she shook her head. Dan wrapped his arm tightly around Haley's shoulder and kissed her cheek. His hand drifted down to her stomach.

'Didn't I mention that we're having a baby, Jess?'

Jessie's blood ran cold. She didn't know what to say. Jessie wanted to scream. She felt sick.

'Congratulations,' she murmured and turned and walked away to the sound of her phone ringing. Her stomach was in knots.

'Hi, Dylan. Kenny has given me some information I think is worth checking out. I'm going to send you an address. I need you to meet me there.'

Jessie said goodbye to him and jogged back towards her car, trying to put Haley's baby out of her mind.

CHAPTER EIGHTY-FIVE

Jessie instructed that two officers be stationed outside Kenny's hospital room until further notice and called Dylan back from the Fergusons' house to join her at the address Kenny had given her. She waited outside the old stone block in Perth's Chaffey Street – a street with not the best reputation in town and a postcode often visited by both police and ambulance services due to the high population of drug users in residence. From her car, it wasn't hard to spot discarded needles amongst the array of rubbish scattered up the narrow street. Black plastic rubbish bags lined the entrance to the alleyway into the block and a single light blinked on and off sporadically. The text Jessie had initially ignored was from an unknown number – again. Dan must have acquired another phone. The message was simple: all he wanted was to talk. For them both to be able to talk without their past coming between them. Jessie had scoffed loudly at that.

Jessie hadn't noticed Dylan's car pull in further back up the street and she jumped when he tapped on her window. She got out to join him and the smell struck her first. The whole street stank of rubbish, old, decaying trash, even soiled nappies, on all sides.

'So he says it's his PA that cracked him over the head?' Dylan remarked. 'Ouch.'

'Well, he says he didn't see her. He smelled her. He recognised her perfume before he passed out.'

Dylan glanced around at the mess around them. 'What a tip. I didn't realise it was this bad down here still. I've not been here for years. Last time would have been when I was still in uniform.'

'I think uniform are here most days, Dylan. Come on, let's see what she has to say.'

Jessie and Dylan wound their way up the circular staircase to the first floor, being careful not to lean on the ramshackle handrail that barely clung to the wall, held in place by two screws. Jessie tried not to breathe in too hard and covered her nose with the cuff of her jacket. A strong stench of urine penetrated the air.

'It's this one – 5A.' Jessie stopped outside what seemed to be the cleanest front door in the block and glanced down at the ironic welcome mat. She rang the bell and waited. When she got no response, she hammered the door hard with the palm of her hand, causing it to move and swing slowly open. Jessie gave Dylan a wide-eyed stare. She hadn't expected that. She listened for movement.

'Hello, Caroline, it's Detective Inspector Blake. Are you in?'

'What do you want to do?' Dylan reflected as he looked along the hallway at the chaos of clothes and broken furniture. 'Something's not right, Jess.'

'Shh, listen,' Jessie announced and leaned her cheek inside the hall. 'Caroline, it's the police. We're coming in.'

Jessie and Dylan stepped carefully over the doorway.

'You go that way. Check the bedroom,' Jessie whispered. 'I'll go through here.'

'Sure.' Dylan put on a pair of plastic gloves while he acknowledged her instruction and split off to the right of the hall.

'Caroline, are you here?' Jessie repeated as she entered the kitchen, aghast at the state of the room. The air in the kitchen was stale, flavoured with something rotten that clawed at Jessie's nose and throat. There were dishes piled high, encrusted with food at varying stages of decay. Stagnant water with a film of gunge across the top filled the bottom of the sink.

Jessie covered her nose and tried to stop the retching that threatened. She put her gloves on and began to open the cupboards to find little in the way of food. A few tins, a jar of tomato pasta sauce and some cheap, dried spaghetti. The cooker wore a layer of dust on the stove top. Clearly Caroline didn't cook much. The microwave on the other hand was sprayed with the remnants of several ready meals. A pile of laundry lay in a heap on the small pine fold-away kitchen table under the window. There were two chairs, one either side.

Jessie opened the drawer closest to the fridge. Inside she found a collection of letters wrapped in a pink elastic band. Jessie undid the band and noticed the letters were addressed to a Miss Caroline Law and several of the letters had different addresses.

Wow, I did not see that coming, Jessie thought as she opened the letter on the top, which was dated November last year. Jessie's eyes scanned the pages then stuffed it back into its envelope before devouring another then another. She gasped at the enormity of her discovery. She really hadn't seen this coming.

'Wow,' she murmured and placed the letters into an evidence bag.

Jessie heard her name being yelled and jogged quickly to where Dylan was standing in Caroline's chaotic bedroom. He held up both hands, each holding an item of interest.

'Where were they?' Jessie asked as she rushed over and took them from his grip.

'Boots in the wardrobe. Hairbrush stuffed inside.'

'Caroline Peters is not who we think she is, it seems,' Jessie told him.

She handed him one of the letters and watched the realisation grow on his face.

'Does this mean she wants some kind of revenge? Some of this stuff in here is pretty explosive.' Dylan tutted. 'Do you think they're Rachel's boots and hairbrush?' he suggested.

Jessie was about to answer when a man's voice called out Caroline's name. Jessie slammed the boots and brush back at Dylan and spun on her heels to intercept the arrival, but Caroline's visitor had heard the detectives and was making his way at speed out of the block. Jessie gave chase, trying not to touch the filthy walls as she made her way outside. She could see the figure moving quickly away.

'David, stop! I know everything,' Jessie yelled as she pursued him. 'Where is she? Where is your sister?'

CHAPTER EIGHTY-SIX

The man she was chasing stopped after Jessie called out his name. He turned slowly and pulled down the hood of his jacket. Jessie walked towards him.

'Why didn't you tell us Caroline was your younger sister?' Jessie asked. 'When we came to talk to you about Rachel, you should have mentioned it then.'

David Law shrugged. 'What's that got to do with anything?'

'I think the fact that your sister works for Rachel is very important. I mean, does Rachel know?'

Jessie doubted she had any idea, nor Kenny. Kenny would never have hired her if he'd known there was any connection between Caroline Peters and David Law, Jessie was sure of that. That couple had lived with and tried to keep that secret buried for thirty years. There was no way they would risk that getting out.

'Caroline works for Ferguson Haulage, not Rachel.'

'Stop being pedantic, David. You knew what I meant.'

David shrugged. 'I don't know where my sister is if that's what you're about to ask. She hasn't been in contact for a couple of days. She was supposed to meet me. I've been getting worried.'

'What did she say when you last spoke to her?'

'Nothing much. She just mentioned that Rachel had been arrested.'

'How did that make you feel?'

David shook his head slowly. 'No, you don't get to ask me that. You don't get to insinuate I'd be happy to see Rachel behind bars or – worse – that I put Caroline up to it. Is that what you think now?'

'Why does your sister have Rachel's hairbrush?' Jessie's question seemed to startle David. 'And her riding boots?'

He frowned while he tried to regain some composure.

'How should I know?' he retorted.

'What connection did Caroline have to Malcolm and Jean Angus?'

'Why are you asking me that?' David remarked and lifted a hand to wave away her question. 'I'm not answering any more of your questions. I'm here to see my sister and she's clearly not here.'

David started to walk away.

'I can arrest you,' Jessie pointed out. 'Withholding this information constitutes attempting to defeat the ends of justice.'

David stopped dead and spun round to glare at Jessie and Dylan, who had joined them.

'Cuff him, Dylan,' Jessie instructed.

'Wait, wait, no, hang on a minute,' David protested. 'Look, I'll tell you everything I know – just please, no charges. I've done enough time to last me a lifetime.'

Dylan's eyes searched Jessie's for further orders. She pursed her lips.

'Go with DC Logan. I'll see you at the station, where we can continue this conversation.'

Jessie watched Dylan put David into the back of his car and drive off. Before heading back to her car Jessie called in a forensics team to go over Caroline's flat – this time for evidence that she was involved in a double murder.

CHAPTER EIGHTY-SEVEN

The forensic sweep of the flat found photos of Caroline and David: smiling, sitting picnicking on the Isle of Skye; Caroline as a toddler grinning up at her big brother, who was reading a book to her as they sat on a rug under a tree. David was a lot older than Caroline but they looked close in the photos. Dozens more letters had been stuffed into shoeboxes under Caroline's bed dating back several years, the details of her life often harrowing in places. The frustration in David's words at all the lost years was obvious. Not long after his conviction for murdering Peter and Mary Connor, his mother had suffered a stroke and with nobody else to take care of her, Caroline had gone into foster care for some years, eventually going on to be adopted by the Peters family after her mother passed away. It was clear the siblings had remained close and grown closer still on David's release.

'Where is your sister?' Jessie asked David again. 'Please don't make this harder for her or yourself. We know what's happened.'

'Yes, what?' David shrugged, keen to maintain the front.

'Your sister tried to frame Rachel for the murder of her neighbours.'

'Don't be daft,' he responded. 'Why would she do that? And don't say to get revenge. Caroline isn't like that. She's been through stuff you could never imagine in your worst nightmares and I wasn't able to be there to stop any of it.'

Jessie was sure she saw his eyes moisten a little before he sniffed and turned away.

'I know what your sister's been through – well, some of it.'

Jessie had to admit she didn't know everything but it was obvious to her that Caroline's teenage years had been traumatic. Letters from social work and mental-health services were also amongst the items found at her flat; appointments with psychiatrists, psychologists, community nurses as well as other voluntary-sector organisations. Details of support groups for victims of child abuse too. Newspaper clippings – there were lots of them. Stories from the time of David's arrest and conviction. It was clear Caroline's mind was troubled, disturbed even.

'My sister is a vulnerable young woman.' David sighed. 'Look, you have to find her. I'm getting worried about her. It's not like her not to contact me.'

A real look of concern crossed David's face. Jessie got that. He was scared for his sister's well-being.

'Can you think of any place Caroline would go to feel better or somewhere that makes her happy?'

'That's me. She always says I'm where she feels happy. Safe,' he ended in a whisper. 'You've got to find her.'

There was no reason to keep David at the station. Nothing concrete. What Jessie really needed was for Caroline to get in touch with him. Jessie told him in no uncertain terms that she would come for him if she got so much as a whiff he was sheltering his sister, who was now a murder suspect. With Gordon's alibi for Rachel and the evidence – the overwhelming evidence – at Caroline's flat, it *had* to be her. Her motive was revenge, Jessie decided. Revenge for the loss of her family, which had led to the abuse she'd suffered through her teenage years. Abuse that had screwed up her mind, making even double murder acceptable. Malcolm and Jean Angus had merely become pawns in Caroline's plan. Convenient victims who had to die like Rachel's grandparents.

Jessie knew she had to find Caroline before she took her final revenge on the woman she thought had ruined her brother's life.

CHAPTER EIGHTY-EIGHT

Caroline stopped dead. She was relieved she'd spotted the police officer stationed outside her block of flats before he'd seen her approaching round the corner. She retreated as fast as she could. It would have been better of course if she'd managed to sneak in and pack a few things, but that wasn't going to be possible now. She had to think on her feet. *They must know*, she thought. That was the only sensible explanation for that officer's presence. But how could they know it was her? Kenny hadn't seen her – she was sure about that. He'd been easier to bring down than she'd imagined. One carefully placed thud had done the trick. Caroline had been pleasantly surprised by that – though it was a pity it had come to that. Kenny was a good guy. He'd even believed her story that she'd been mugged. The stupid man shouldn't have tried to send her away like that. How could she enjoy Rachel's downfall if she wasn't right there in the middle of events? She had rather hoped that detective would blame Gordon.

Caroline had wanted to get closer to the couple – keep an eye on the investigation – and knew kind-hearted Rachel would insist she stayed with them. What Kenny saw in Rachel was a mystery. There had been so many times she'd wanted to call her out for the monster she was. Alice Connor. Caroline had never forgotten the agony her mother had gone through because of her – the pain on her face when she'd had to watch her son being taken down after the jury delivered their devastating verdict. Caroline might have been young but she remembered the crying and the drinking.

It hadn't taken long for the woman's heart to break completely, leaving Caroline alone in the world. Alone and vulnerable to the predators who'd preyed on her for all those years. The world wouldn't show such compassion to Alice this time.

Caroline's pace quickened but she wasn't fast enough to catch up to the bus that pulled away just as she reached the stop on the Dunkeld Road. She wasn't sure where it was headed but she was cross at herself for missing it all the same. She tugged up the collar on her duffle coat against the biting wind, despite the sun that glowed above the row of Victorian-era stone-built flats that lined the road, not far from the group of bed and breakfasts nearby. Caroline pulled out her purse and looked to see how much cash she had on her. Using her credit or debit card would be a mistake – she knew that much.

Caroline spotted a vacancy sign in one of the windows, which was lucky given it was still the festive season. She pressed the button and waited for the green man to cross the busy Dunkeld Road. Caroline jogged across the road and headed straight into the hotel. That detective wouldn't possibly think to look for her there.

Caroline's phone buzzed in her jeans pocket, making her jump with fright. She smiled, desperate to answer his call. She'd done it all for him but that Detective Blake must have figured it out by now, she thought. It wouldn't have taken her and that good-looking partner of hers long to find the boots and the hairbrush. Hell, they probably even had all of her letters. The thought of them rummaging through all her personal possessions made her feel dirty. Violated. The way her adoptive father had all those years.

Caroline couldn't risk any contact with him until she knew for sure. She let his call go to voicemail then turned her phone to silent.

David hung up without leaving a message. The fact she'd ignored his call meant she knew he'd discovered the truth. She would be hiding and probably scared, he feared. But if his sister did contact him, David would have no choice but to inform Detective Blake. He couldn't risk being sent back to prison, and defeating the ends of justice would do just that to him.

Before heading back to Dundee he had someone else he had to see. He doubted he'd be welcomed with open arms but he *had* to see her – to explain what Caroline had done but more importantly why.

CHAPTER EIGHTY-NINE

Jessie locked up her car and jogged over to where Rachel Ferguson was shouting loudly in David Law's face.

'What's going on?' Jessie called out. 'David, you know you shouldn't be here.'

David turned but not fast enough to escape Rachel's heavy shove, which sent him off balance into the thick purple berberis bush outside the front of the property.

'You heard Detective Blake – you shouldn't be here!' Rachel yelled at him.

'I know, but I need you to hear it from me. I need you to understand why.' David regained his footing and stood up in front of Rachel. 'Just give me five minutes, please,' he pleaded.

David looked at Jessie, in the hope she agreed with him, she figured. Jessie eyed him carefully. She decided having him there might help add some context.

'I think it would be a good idea if the three of us went inside and talked, Rachel,' Jessie informed her.

'What the hell could you possibly have to say that I would have any desire to waste my time listening to?' Rachel blasted.

'Rachel, please,' David murmured. 'It's important.'

Rachel glanced at Jessie then back at David's solemn expression and sighed.

'This better be good,' she remarked then stepped back inside the flat, leaving the front door hanging open for them to follow her inside.

David indicated for Jessie to go on ahead of him. Jessie smiled at him in response; she appreciated the gesture. The pair joined Rachel in the kitchen.

'You've got five minutes. I have to get back to Kenny. I'm only home to collect a few bits for him,' she said after glancing at her watch.

'I think you should sit down,' Jessie suggested.

Rachel frowned. 'Why do I need to sit down, for goodness' sake? Just spit it out.'

'Caroline was trying to frame you for the murder of the Anguses.' David blurted it out before Jessie had a chance to give Rachel the news. 'She stole your hairbrush to plant DNA at the scene and used your riding boots to lead the trail to you.'

'What?' Rachel answered. 'Don't be ridiculous. Why the hell would Caroline do that? That means she must have killed them.' Rachel shook her head. 'That's ridiculous. Why would you say something like that about her?'

'Because it's true,' Jessie interrupted. 'After Kenny told us he smelled Caroline's perfume before being struck on the head, we went to her flat, where we found compelling evidence to positively implicate her in the double murder.'

Rachel lowered herself into the dining chair closest to her and ran her hand through her hair. 'What evidence? Surely we would have spotted something.'

'I asked forensics to go through some of the clothes in the laundry hamper for gunshot residue and—'

Rachel covered her mouth with her fingers and gasped.

'But why would she do that? I'm well aware of her affair with Kenny – I've known for a long time – but that's no reason to kill a couple in cold blood. I'm sorry; I can't believe this.'

David shot a look at Jessie she read as seeking her permission to tell Rachel the truth. Jessie nodded gently, offering him the slightest of smiles of encouragement. David sat down opposite Rachel and Rachel focused her attention solely on him. David inhaled a huge breath then slowly breathed it all the way out until he felt his lungs empty. He tried to ignore his racing heart before starting.

'Caroline is my little sister,' he said.

CHAPTER NINETY

A week had passed since Rachel had been told about Caroline. The shock had slammed nausea into her stomach at speed. So much so she thought she might be sick. DI Blake had been kind and David had looked genuinely sorry that his sister had done something so awful. Rachel had tried to think back to things Caroline might have said or done. She had questioned whether Caroline even looked like her brother, but she just couldn't see it. They didn't look alike but it had been so many years since Rachel had seen David. She considered that if she'd spotted the clues perhaps the Anguses would still be alive.

DI Blake explained that Rachel needed to be vigilant because they hadn't managed to locate Caroline yet, despite a countrywide manhunt for the dangerous, vulnerable woman. But Rachel wanted nothing to spoil her moment today. Not *her* moment, exactly, but Dexter's. Today was the day they'd been building up to for months. The day she'd feared she wouldn't see.

The sun was shining on the racecourse but the harsh winter chill still lingered. Dexter dug the ground in the saddling box. He was nervous and excited, sweating up a little, but that was normal for him. Rachel could tell he was ready to do the job he was bred for. Being a stallion meant Dexter got revved up easily, but today he'd be on his toes as soon as he was led out. He'd been a tricky ride in his two-year-old season because of his tendency to get overexcited but Rachel hoped the earplugs she opted to use on him would help. Dexter was a big stallion too, almost seventeen hands high. Kenny had tried to persuade her to postpone, and no matter how much she explained that was impossible Kenny just didn't get it. He'd asked, what if Caroline showed up? But this was too important to Rachel and besides, she told him, Caroline wouldn't dare do anything in such a crowded arena.

Kenny paid the cheerful young barman for the drinks and slipped his change into his pocket, eager to get back to the saddling box. Rachel had told him she'd meet him in the owners' enclosure but he didn't want her to be alone that long. His wife could be stubborn but he understood her need to be here today. She thought he didn't, but he did. He'd known of her passion for horses from the moment they met, at the races. Rachel's exuberant reaction to a horse's win had endeared her to Kenny immediately, though Kenny had had to admit soon after that he'd been at the races that day courtesy of a business associate and his hospitality invitation. More of a business arrangement than a day at the races. Best deal he ever closed, he joked.

A slender woman cut swiftly through the crowd and caught Kenny's eye, but when he looked for her she was gone. It was his imagination, he tried to tell himself. It couldn't be Caroline. Like Rachel said, she wouldn't approach them in such a public place. She must be long gone by now. Besides, the police were looking for Caroline with every resource they had. There was no way she'd get past security.

'Hello, who is this?' Jessie repeated for the third time and heard breathing on the line. 'Caroline, is that you?' She waited.

Dylan was about to speak until Jessie raised a hand to silence him.

'Who is it?' he whispered more loudly than Jessie would have liked.

She shot him a disgruntled glance and held her finger to her lips.

'Caroline, sweetheart, I know it's you,' Jessie tried again, this time with better results.

'I hear you've all been looking for me.'

'Where are you?' Jessie spoke softly, so as not to spook her.

'I've decided to have a day at the races, Detective. Come and join me if you like. You can even bring that dishy partner of yours, but first I have to catch up with an old friend.'

The line went dead. Jessie tossed her phone into the bottom of her bag and grabbed her car keys. Dylan's eyes widened and he stood quickly from the edge of her desk he'd perched his bottom on while he waited for permission to talk again.

'Come on. Caroline is at the racecourse!' Jessie shouted. 'And so is Rachel.'

CHAPTER NINETY-ONE

Rachel checked Dexter's saddle for the last time and blew out a rapid sharp breath. Her heart raced. She'd done her bit. It was all down to the jockey now. She gave the short, thin man a leg up onto Dexter's back, who jinked a little sideways as he always did.

'Whoa, lad, whoa there.' Rachel took firm grip of his lead rein and patted him down the neck. 'Whoa, baby, whoa.' She gave the jockey his final instruction and disconnected the rein that connected her to her horse. Rachel allowed her hand to slip down by her side and watched him trot away from her. 'Bring him back safe,' she whispered as part of her pre-race ritual. A little prayer she always said.

Rachel nodded to some of the other owners and moved away from the crowds to watch the race in greater privacy. She wondered what was keeping Kenny, but if she was honest having him chatting in her ear during the race was the last thing she wanted. Things between the couple were improving – slowly.

She returned to the saddling box to collect some things she'd left lying around. She was scooping her notebook from the floor at the back when the voice hit her ears. Her blood ran cold and she turned to see Caroline standing in the doorway, blocking her exit. Neither woman spoke. Rachel's eyes were drawn to a shimmering silver blade in Caroline's left hand. Rachel's phone rang out in her pocket before going to voicemail.

*

'Where's Rachel?' Jessie quizzed Kenny when they'd caught up with him.

'I don't know. Dexter is at the start. She should be here by now. They won't let me back into the saddling area. Trainers only.'

'Wait here.' Jessie patted Dylan's arm and pulled her ID from her pocket to show to whoever needed to allow her access to the area.

'You can't come through here,' the stocky blonde man started to say then stepped aside at the sight of Jessie's badge. She heard him muttering into his radio as they disappeared around the corner towards the saddling boxes.

Jessie quickly spotted Caroline standing in the entrance to the box at the far end of the row of five. Thankfully the other four were deserted. She gasped at the sight of the knife dangling at her side. Rachel had to be in there. She must be trapped.

'What do you want?' Rachel's words struggled to exit her mouth, almost sticking in her dry, terrified throat.

'What. Do. I. Want?' Caroline tapped the long blade against her cheek in time with the words.

Caroline's slow, deliberate answer sent shivers through Rachel's whole body. The laughter that followed matched her maniacal demeanour. The saddling boxes were designed to make the horses feel secure but were open enough to prevent them from feeling trapped. But the horses didn't have a deranged, knife-wielding lunatic standing in their way.

Jessie and Dylan edged closer, slowly and carefully, trying not to spook Caroline into doing something stupid. Not quietly enough, it would seem, as her head snapped round to face them. She grinned at the sight of the two detectives creeping closer.

'Well, well, well, how appropriate – the cavalry has arrived.'

Jessie's instinct for self-preservation in the face of a suspect with a knife should have kicked in and stopped her moving closer to

Caroline but Rachel's life was in danger. Jessie heard Dylan say something about calling for backup and to be careful. Jessie's attention was too focused on Caroline. The best outcome here was to take her in without injury to anyone, including Caroline herself. Jessie's hand automatically rose up in front of her chest.

'I only want to talk; please, put the knife down.'

Caroline laughed. 'That won't be happening any time soon.'

'What is it you need? Maybe I can help you. Let me help you,' Jessie pleaded as she shuffled forward – more slowly now, but she didn't want to stop if she didn't have to.

'I imagine by now you know what she did,' Caroline retorted.

'I know about David and your mum if that's what you're asking, yes.'

Caroline pointed in Rachel's direction with the blade of the knife.

'So you agree she ruined my life. Good, that's a start.'

Jessie had to dig deep. Empathy – she needed to show Caroline she was trying to understand.

'I know it feels like that to you.'

'I beg your pardon?' Caroline retorted.

Shit! Jessie thought.

'I mean…' Jessie began until Rachel intervened.

'I know you must hate me, Caroline, but I never meant for you to get hurt. I was just a fourteen-year-old kid!' Rachel shouted. 'There's not a day has gone by that I haven't been so sorry for what happened. You have to believe that.'

'Very good, give that girl an Oscar. What a performance. Go on, let's see the tears now,' Caroline mocked then frowned at the sight of Dylan joining Jessie. 'Backup has arrived, Detective. Hardly seems fair. Two against one.'

Dylan edged closer with his hand up. Being several inches taller than her, Caroline stared up at him.

'Come on,' he whispered. 'You and I can sort this out.'

'Don't come any closer – I'm warning you,' Caroline yelled.

'Dylan!' Jessie called out.

'Come on, Caroline. I get it, I really do.' Dylan smiled and stopped just within touching distance. 'Come on,' he whispered.

Jessie saw the confusion grow on Caroline's face at Dylan's approach. Caroline glanced past him then returned her focus to his raised hand, which was edging closer to the knife.

'Sure, I'll come,' Caroline said slowly then reached forward and stabbed Dylan once in the stomach. She pulled the knife back out and looked him in his wide eyes. 'You won't be such a smart-arse in future.' She nudged past him, causing him to slam his back into the saddling-box wall before sliding to the ground.

'Argh, God,' Dylan cried out and held his hand over the wound, which dribbled blood, his eyes wide and staring. 'What have you done?' he murmured.

'Dylan.' Jessie collapsed to her knees at his side. 'Rachel, pass me a towel or something!' she screamed in panic. 'And call an ambulance.'

'Go after her,' Dylan moaned and screwed up his face against the searing pain in his abdomen.

CHAPTER NINETY-TWO

Jessie was torn. She would be devastated if anything happened to Dylan. He was like her best friend – hell, her brother – as well as the best partner she'd ever had. What the hell would she tell Shelly and his kids? She called for backup.

'Hold that towel!' Jessie shouted to Rachel.

'It's OK – I know what to do. The ambulance is coming.' Rachel replied before Jessie could finish. 'Go!' she shouted. 'You have to stop her before she hurts someone else.'

'Hang in there, Dylan,' Jessie called out before racing out the saddling box.

She didn't have to look very hard for Caroline's location. She just had to follow the screams. People carrying a knife dripping with blood tend to stand out, causing alarm amongst everyone who sees them.

Jessie ran after her through the parting of the terrified crowd. Caroline weaved a path towards the entrance to one of the main stands and Jessie traced her every bloodstained step until the two women were together on the deserted top floor, most punters having been eager to get trackside for the start of racing. Jessie was sickened by the sight of the blood covering Caroline's hands, dripping down her arm and off the tip of the knife. She panicked that Dylan had lost so much blood. The sound of sirens offered little consolation. Jessie hoped the paramedics would make it to him in time.

'Caroline, stop,' Jessie called out breathlessly. 'There's nowhere left for you to go.'

Caroline halted and turned to face her.

'I didn't mean for your colleague to get hurt. You have to know that. He just got in the way.' Caroline pointed towards her with the dripping blade of the knife. 'He shouldn't have done that. He should've stayed back.'

'I know,' Jessie replied.

'You don't know anything,' Caroline remarked and tapped her head with one of her blood-soaked fingers in time with her words. 'How could you? You've never been in *here*.'

'You're right, I haven't,' Jessie agreed. 'Help me try to understand, then I'll be able to help you.'

'You don't think I've asked for help!' Caroline scoffed. 'I've been passed from one doctor to another. Nothing worked.' She tapped her head again. 'The thoughts never left.'

'I'm sorry,' Jessie said without thinking it through.

'Sorry for what? Why do people say that?' Caroline asked.

'I'm sorry that people did those bad things to you.' Jessie recalled a suggestion in some of the paperwork that Caroline had been the victim of serious sexual abuse as a teenager.

'You're sorry, so that makes it all OK, does it?' Caroline blasted.

'Malcolm and Jean Angus didn't hurt you. They didn't deserve to die,' Jessie said and watched Caroline give that statement some thought. Perhaps she wasn't as unreachable after all. 'I know you're angry with Rachel but she was just a kid. She didn't know what she was doing. Did you really think you would get away with framing her for murders that you committed?'

'Oh, and David did know what he was doing, I suppose.'

'I'm not saying that, no. They were both mixed-up kids who did an awful thing that has had terrible consequences for a lot of people, you included.'

Jessie's phone buzzed in her pocket, which startled Caroline into stepping backwards away from her.

'It's OK, Caroline – it's just my phone.' Jessie pulled it from her pocket and held it in the air then laid it onto a seat next to her. Jessie was relieved to see that it was a text from one of the officers who must be using Dylan's phone. He must be OK. 'It's from my partner. He's all right.'

'That's good. I liked him. He looks like a gentle man. Caring.'

'He is,' Jessie replied. 'And he's a good father.'

'Not like the men my adoptive dad let do those horrible things to me. They weren't gentle.'

'I'm sorry that happened to you.'

'But it wouldn't have happened if David was around, would it? If Mum hadn't died when he went inside. We could have stayed a normal, happy family but *she* stole all that, didn't she?' Caroline glanced down at the blade then lifted it higher.

Time seemed to move in slow motion as the knife slid across the front of Caroline's throat, causing blood to pour onto her clothes.

'No!' Jessie screamed and surged forward. She grabbed hold of Caroline's falling body and dropped to her own knees. 'I need some help in here,' she roared into the air and forced both of her hands onto the four-inch-long slit in Caroline's throat that was now leaking her life out onto the floor.

CHAPTER NINETY-THREE

Caroline was pronounced dead as soon as she arrived at the hospital, but Jessie knew she'd been lost long before that. Jessie had cradled the young woman while the ground around them filled with a river of Caroline's blood. Keeping her hand on the wound to stem the flow became futile. She wasn't sure how long the ambulance had taken to arrive. It was still such a blur. The paramedic had insisted that Jessie should be checked out too and she'd been powerless to stop herself being swept up on the wave of concern. She couldn't remember calling Benito but here he was jogging towards her before scooping her up in his arms.

'Jessie, I was so worried about you.' Benito kissed her cheek and held her close to his chest. His touch seemed to bring Jessie round from the fog of her shock. She pulled out of his embrace. 'I have to see Dylan.' Jessie tossed aside the blanket the nurse had given her.

'Hey, hey, Dylan is fine. It wasn't nearly as bad as doctors first thought. He's going to be fine. Sure, he'll be sore and bruised but he's OK. His wife is with him,' Benito said and kissed her lips gently. 'You'll be fine too,' he whispered.

'Will I?' Jessie asked.

Benito nodded. 'I'll take care of you.'

The doctor gave Jessie a clean bill of health and discharged her. She and Benito were walking hand in hand towards his car when Jessie felt in her pocket for her phone.

'Damn, I've left my phone. I'll catch you up,' she told him and turned back towards the ward.

The sound of crying could be heard as she passed one of the rooms that had its door slightly ajar. Jessie's curiosity drew her closer and she gasped when she spotted Haley slumped on the bed, holding her wrist. She was clearly in pain. Jessie felt sick. She wanted to go in and tell her to run and never look back, but before she could move Dan snuck up behind her.

'Jessie, what's happened to you?' He looked concerned by the blood on her clothes.

Jessie recoiled from his touch and stepped back.

'What have you done?' she asked, her voice trembling a little under the pressure of the fear she felt.

Dan put his arm round Haley's shoulder. 'Haley tripped, didn't you, you silly thing?'

Jessie's eyes met hers, pleading with her to cry out for Jessie's help. Jessie's heart pounded. *Come on, just say it!*

'Yes.' Haley's voice shook. 'I tripped.'

Jessie knew her smile wasn't real.

'Take care then,' Jessie told her and pulled the sideroom door shut quietly behind her.

Jessie walked away and clamped her hand over her mouth to stifle the tears that tumbled out. There was nothing she could do for Haley, for now.

When Jessie spotted Benito waiting for her by his car, her pace quickened until she found herself running and slamming her body into his warm, safe arms.

EPILOGUE

Six months later

Jessie waited in line to buy the coffees. It was her treat. Passing his sergeant's exam was a big thing for Dylan – something he'd wanted to do for a long time. Jessie was happy for him even if it meant he might move away from her. It wouldn't be quite the same without him, but she'd just have to wait and see what happened. She owed him so much for the support he'd shown her following Gordon's attempt on her life. Gordon's defence of not guilty by means of diminished responsibility was accurate as far as Jessie was concerned. The lad clearly had problems, and she hoped he would get the support he needed. His admission to starting the fire on Rachel's property didn't surprise Jessie. He'd said he wanted to ensure her secret remained hidden. Gordon would have done anything for Rachel.

Jessie had to admit it was uncomfortable seeing him flanked by prison officers at Malcolm and Jean's funeral. Tommy Angus had looked like a broken man who was barely holding it together as he leaned on Arlene. Jessie's heart had broken for the man. It had looked like his battle with the booze was still ongoing.

'Detective Inspector Blake.'

Jessie turned at the sound of her name being called, surprised by the familiar face standing behind her.

'Hello, Rachel,' she answered. 'It's good to see you. You look well.'

'I am – I mean, we are.' Rachel pointed to the woman with the short brown hair sitting at the table in a far corner of the coffee shop, sipping from a tall glass.

Jessie followed the direction she was pointing and wondered what Rachel meant because she was indicating towards Julia Dean, one of Kenny's drivers. It was clear Rachel had noticed Jessie's confusion.

'Caroline wasn't the only one of Kenny's staff who was keeping a big secret.'

'Sorry, you've lost me,' Jessie admitted.

Rachel leaned in closer to avoid being overheard by the other people in the queue.

'Julia is my daughter,' she whispered. 'The baby I had to give away.'

'Oh,' Jessie remarked with her eyes wide, remembering the photo she'd found in Rachel's drawer. *She must be the baby in the photo. David's daughter too.* 'I'm happy for you both. Finding each other after all that time must be wonderful.'

'She knows everything too,' Rachel whispered this time from behind her hand. 'She already knew before we met. How she found out I don't know. I don't care. She hasn't judged me, not once. I have her back in my life and that's what matters.'

'I'm really happy for you,' Jessie repeated as Dylan returned from the men's bathroom.

Rachel nodded to acknowledge him then said her goodbyes before rejoining Julia at their table.

'Wow,' Jessie exclaimed.

'What?' Dylan asked and took his cup from the counter before moving across to tip three sugars in it.

Jessie's phone rang before she could fill him in on the news. She narrowed her eyes as she listened then gave Dylan's arm a tap.

'Come on – grab your coffee. You'll need to drink it on the go. We've had a shout.'

Jessie walked on ahead and unlocked the new car that she'd bought only two weeks previously. She'd gone for a Fiesta again because it was simple and easy to drive and that's all she needed.

Jessie smiled at Dylan, who was wiping coffee from his tie as he walked towards her. A woman pushing a pram across the road caught her eye. Jessie smiled and waved at Haley before turning away and getting into her car.

A LETTER FROM KERRY

Hello, readers,

Thank you for downloading the next instalment in the Jessie Blake series. Please do sign up below if you'd like to be kept in the loop with news and information on other books in the series. Your email address won't be shared and you can unsubscribe at any time.

www.bookouture.com/kerry-watts

For those of you that have read the earlier books I hope you have enjoyed this one as much as the others and that you are growing to love Jessie the way I do. If you have enjoyed this next part of the Jessie Blake series I would be very grateful if you would leave a review for me on Amazon and Goodreads, not to mention tell your friends and family about her.

Hearing from readers is something I enjoy and I'm always keen to connect on social media, where I can be found most days chatting and talking nonsense.

Thanks
Kerry xx

 KerryWattsAuthor

@Denmanisfab

ACKNOWLEDGEMENTS

Thanks go first of all to my wonderful editor, Helen Jenner, who continues to believe in me. I will be forever grateful for her support and enthusiasm, not to mention her honesty and calmness in the face of my many wobbles. Thank you to everyone at Bookouture for allowing me the opportunity to share Jessie Blake with the world. For Noelle and Kim, I owe both of you more than I can ever pay back for your unwavering support. Your constant words of encouragement on my darkest days are appreciated beyond words.

Thank you to Mark, Hannah and Flynn for their massive encouragement of my efforts. Your enthusiasm for my writing is truly humbling. Especially during times I've struggled to find inspiration.

Dad, for your continued excitement for my writing and Denise, for your words of wisdom and support.

I think it's important to mention the avid crime-fiction readers who use social media to share and discuss my books every day, recommending them to new audiences. Norma Ormond, Susan Hunter, Andi Miller, Louise Mullins and all the other members of Crime Fiction Addict and UK Crime Book Club. Caroline Maston and David Gilchrist – thank you for everything you do.

Thank you to a whole host of author friends on Facebook who have encouraged and shared advice with me on every topic imaginable – Billy McLaughlin, Jacqueline Evans, Kevin McManus, to name a few.

To those who make me laugh every day – you know who you are.

Thank you to the members of the Bookouture Authors' Lounge for your words of advice and encouragement when panic and crushing self-doubt struck.

And thank you, Tetley and Mr Kipling, for sustaining me through all those first drafts, edits, rewrites and proofreading. I owe you both more than I can ever repay.